Mad Beautiful Love

Alan —
To our fearless
leader! You're the
best —
Love you! XO
Kim Carson

Mad Beautiful Love

A Novel

Kim Carson

ISBN: 1546312730
ISBN 13: 9781546312734
Library of Congress Control Number: 2017906994
CreateSpace Independent Publishing Platform
North Charleston, South Carolina

For Cat, Stella, Jagger, and Louis

You pierce my soul. I am half agony, half hope. Tell me not that I am too late, that such precious feelings are gone forever.

—JANE AUSTEN, *PERSUASION*

Chapter 1

"Open the door!" yelled Penny, pounding on the front door again. "I want my things! You can't keep them like prisoners! Open the freaking door!" She put her ear to the door, trying to hear a sound. He had to be inside, avoiding her.

The evening started well. She met a group of friends for wine at a bar in Soho. On her way home, it occurred to her that she didn't have to sit back and cater to his schedule; she could actively charge forward and make him uncomfortable. After all, it was his fault. When she boarded the one train to Brooklyn Heights, it never occurred to her it was two in the morning, nor did she consider the other residents in the building. Her bravery was fueled by rage. She was able to pry open the front door of the brownstone with her credit card. Beckett's apartment, their apartment, was on the third floor. She scolded herself for returning her key to him so quickly. It felt wrong to stand on the outside of the locked door.

"Beckett, I know you're in there; I'm not leaving without my stuff! I'll be here all night if that's what it takes." She was wearing a black minidress and black knee boots. The mascara that she carefully applied hours earlier was smudged under her eyes, and her long red hair was damp and frizzy from the shower of rain she encountered on her walk from the subway. She didn't care.

The front door of the building opened. She could hear it from the third floor. Was it the sound of walkie-talkies? There were multiple people entering the building at once. It took her five seconds to figure it out. The police! She ran up the stairs to the sixth floor of the building, hid in a corner, and then laughed at herself. There would be no hiding or running. It would be impossible to get out of the building without being caught. "I'll explain it to them," thought Penny. "It's my only option."

Slowly, she meandered down the stairwell, meeting the cops on the third floor. "Good evening, Officers," Penny chimed.

"Evening? It's the middle of the night. Are you the one making all the noise in the hallway?"

"I can explain." Penny offered them a smile and wiped her eyes, making the mascara even worse. The reality of the situation was sobering her up.

"We'd love to hear it," said the young male officer.

"I shared this apartment with my boyfriend for the past year. We broke up recently. I was out with some friends in the city, but on my way home, I wound up here. I need to get my personal belongings back from him…it seemed like the perfect time."

"The middle of the night seemed like the perfect time?" asked the other cop, a female.

"You two have this handled," said another officer from the group. "The rest of us are going to head back to the station."

"Yep, we've got it."

"Do they always send eight cops to a building with a noise complaint? I must say, I'm flattered," said Penny with a chuckle.

"You won't be laughing when you're spending the night in jail."

"I'm sorry." Penny lowered her head. "We were in love. He cheated on me. Surely, you know a broken heart can make you do stupid things."

"He'll cheat on her too," said the female cop. "Where do you live now?"

"I have my own place in the West Village."

"Hey, Burns, wanna give her a ride back to the city?"

"Yep, we can do it." He looked at his partner and offered her a wink.

Penny smiled. "I'd really appreciate it."

"You have to promise us you'll stay away from here. If you need your belongings, have a friend arrange it with him. Sounds like the two of you need to stay away from each other for a while. Passion can make people do stupid things. We see it all the time."

"I promise," said Penny. "Honestly, he doesn't deserve the extra effort." A sigh of relief washed over her. "I'm not a kid; I'm a thirty-one-year-old professional," thought Penny, scolding herself for the situation and silently thanking her lucky stars that a pair of young cops pardoned her.

Fifteen minutes later, the officers dropped her off in front of her building. Penny thanked them for their kindness, climbed the stairs to her apartment, and went to bed. Before she drifted off to sleep, she thought, "I'll deal with you later, Beckett Martin."

Three months later

It was a magnificent New York City late afternoon. Penny peered out the window of Think Coffee, wondering where her best friend was. "Kate is never late. This isn't like her." She pulled her iPhone out of her handbag and checked it again— no text message.

Moments later, the front door swung open, and a huge blast of wind blew through the room, followed by a disheveled Kate. "I'm sorry, Penny; stuck on the 'A' train…can you believe it? It was horrific! I'm in the subway car at a standstill for ten minutes. Ugh! It totally freaked me out."

"It's OK, sit; you sound like you're hyperventilating," said Penny, getting up from her chair and offering it to Kate.

"When I finally got off the train, I ran here instead of stopping to text you," huffed Kate. "You know how dangerous text walking is." She was bewildered with how many people walked around the city with their face in their phones, distracted. It was dangerous and annoying. People bumping into each other on the sidewalk like robots. Seeing the stupidity,

Kate promised herself she'd never do it. She could always stop walking, take a moment away from foot traffic, and send a text. Putting her and others at risk wasn't worth the message. Plus, she didn't want to look like an android.

The befuddled Kate made Penny smile. Kate was a successful real-estate agent and a control freak and rarely showed signs of frustration. This was a rare moment, and Penny wanted to enjoy it.

"No worries. Let me get you some water." Penny scoured to the coffee-shop counter. "Could I grab a glass of tap water for my friend?"

Coffee barista guy reached for a tall glass mug. "Sure, no problem." The tattoo on the barista's arm was mesmerizing; dark ribbons of red, bursts of orange, and an angel drew Penny in, rendering her momentarily speechless.

"Is it a goddess or a fire angel?" pondered Penny without saying a word.

Barista guy noticed her gaze. "She's the goddess of fire," he said as he slid the mug of water toward her.

A butterfly tattoo adorned Penny's left butt cheek, but few people ever saw it. She was impressed with the beautiful work of art on his arm. "Wow, it's, uh, nice; I mean, intense…cool." Penny stumbled over her words, turned away quickly, and bumped into the man behind her. Her glass of water bounced off his chest, drenching the front of his shirt. "I'm so sorry, so sorry," screeched Penny, fumbling with the small square paper napkin she held in her hand. "Gosh, you must be furious; so very sorry," she said again and, without thinking, spontaneously began to dab the napkin over his wet shirt.

"Let me get you a towel," yelled the barista, witnessing the awkward event. The clumsy chick was making it worse with the paper napkin.

"It's OK, really; just a tall caffè latte to go," said the wet shirt. He turned his attention back to Penny, whose face was a pale shade of red. "No need to worry; it's not a big deal."

"He is gorgeous, this water-shirt man," thought Penny. She felt a flash of adrenaline when his bright-blue, almost turquoise, eyes bore into her. "I was rushing this water to my friend; she's in a bit of a tizzy. Guess I was distracted, not paying attention. Let me pay you for the dry cleaning; it's the least I could do," huffed Penny. She backed away and stumbled, almost tripping over her own feet. "Give me another moment to stand here looking at you, looking into your eyes," thought Penny. She was surprised at her inner dialogue but he was tremendous.

"Nope, it's fine. I'm not crazy about this shirt anyway. It's a brown-shirt day, and I'm wearing a navy one. The shirt's all wrong; you did me a favor." He flashed a warm smile. The woman was clearly unhinged, a bit of a nutcase, but her embarrassment was charming, and he had to admit she was stunning.

"I typically pay attention when I have a beverage in my hand. Thank you for being so kind." Penny glanced at Kate, who was busy tracking down a chair for their table. She missed the entire water event. Penny smiled once more at *the gorgeous* before she scurried back to Kate.

"I mean, you know I'm not a claustrophobic, but sitting in a subway car packed with people at rush hour is not exactly a lot of fun," panted Kate.

"I know; it's very unnerving. Did they give you updates?"

"Yeah; I mean, they mumbled about traffic and something about a police investigation at Thirty-Fourth Street. Everyone trying to look cool, face in phone, eyes on book, paper in hand; you know the drill but silently screaming inside, wondering if someone will break out in a tirade or, even worse, if they will."

"Yes, of course, we've all been there. Fortunately, it hasn't happened to me in a while." Penny knocked on the table for good luck.

"Me either until today. Ugh! OK, let me gather myself together," said Kate, getting up and taking off her coat, smoothing down her sweater, and doing a full head-turn stretch to each side.

"Might as well do a sun salutation; it'll make you feel better. Go ahead; reach your hands up to the sky, exhale, fold forward and down."

"Penny, I don't need a sun salutation; I could use a drink. I thought you were getting me a glass of water."

"I did get you a glass of water and then poured it all over *the gorgeous* at the counter." Penny nodded her head in his direction, and Kate's mouth dropped open.

"Wow, is he for real?" questioned Kate.

"You should see his eyes. They could melt ice."

"Yep, there it is," said Kate as *the gorgeous* turned around to leave and glanced their way. "His shirt is soaking wet; way to go, Penny!" Kate looked back at Penny, who was pretending she wasn't talking about him. "That's a good one!" Kate squealed with delight. Penny was a klutz. It was a joke among their circle of friends. She was continually bumping into something, tripping over a chair leg, or dropping objects. Fortunately, she never seriously injured herself or anyone else, but it was a source of amusement, seeing where Penny's clumsiness would take her next. Kate recognized it was her height and thin frame, although Kate was a little taller than her. Penny was short as a child, and at the age of thirteen, she shot up, growing five inches in two years. Now, she stood at five foot six, but her skinny frame made her look taller.

"I know. It's totally embarrassing. Sorry, I'll try again for your water once he leaves. I'm too humiliated to go back to the counter again now." Penny glanced down at the table, hoping to avoid any eye contact with the water-shirt guy.

"Oh, forget about the water. Let's get out of here and catch a happy hour. Aren't we celebrating our three-month hiatus from men?" Kate remembered her mission: get Penny out of her head and into a bar.

"Be careful out there, ladies," said the wet shirt, with a wink on his way out the door.

"I think I just peed in my pants," said Kate.

"Really, Kate, don't be gross. Ugh, I'm sure he's another Beckett looking for a woman to destroy."

"Not everyone is like Beckett," said Kate.

Penny met Beckett Martin when she was working on Wall Street. The firm's very important client threw a Halloween ball at the Grand Room on the upper west side of Manhattan every year. The client took Halloween very seriously; in fact, no attendee was allowed into the club unless dressed in full costume. Beckett showed up as a pirate, and Penny a mermaid. They were instantly drawn to each other. The Halloween ball was like no other in New York; anyone in the finance loop lusted for an invite. It was mysterious and playful but with a hint of danger. No expense was spared in the execution in order to make it a magical experience. An invitation to the Halloween ball was treasured; it was the year's most important event. Penny's entire body was painted, and sequins were glued to her skin in order to make the mermaid costume come to life. It worked. She was a hit, with her boss giving her a raise the following Monday, which delighted and annoyed her. Clearly, the client was pleased.

Beckett was beautiful; she could barely see him through his costume, but she knew he was special. His energy was electric. Eventually it was the cool, calm, velvet voice of Beckett that wooed her into a back room and out the side door. They ran across the street to Lincoln Center with their hands clasped together. She felt like Cinderella running away from the ball, her mermaid tail dragging down the sidewalk. In the open courtyard, Beckett got down on his knees, pretending to be a pirate enticing a mermaid onto his ship. She laughed so hard tears ran down her cheeks.

Later the same night, back at her place, Beckett contemplated the best way to get the sequins off without hurting her. "Didn't you think about removal before you let someone put these things on your body?" He was lying next to her in bed.

"Epsom salt," Penny said with a giggle, slightly intoxicated. "They said to use a bath salt." She leapt from the bed, suddenly remembering the directions. Fortunately it worked; the sequins and glue were released from her skin.

They lay in bed the entire next day nursing their hangovers, laughing at each other and replaying scenes from the outlandish event the previous evening. It was the most wonderful ball she'd ever attended. The Beckett Martin adventure had begun.

"You can't think every man is out to break your heart," said Kate.

"You're too optimistic."

Kate Wesson was vivacious, and although she looked like a model, everything about her was comfortable. She was always impeccably dressed, pants pressed, heels polished; nothing about Kate was casual, and yet people relaxed around her. Her warm smile and easygoing attitude drew people in like a magnet. It was the secret to her success in business and relationships.

"Ugh, I'm so tired of being sad," said Penny.

Kate laughed. It wasn't what Penny said; it was the pathetic way she said it.

"I'm glad you find it funny. I need help; I truly do." This wasn't her first breakup, but it felt like her first real adult heartache. She tried to be patient with herself, but the constant reminders of Beckett seemed to be everywhere.

"Everything is going to be all right," said Kate, feeling a twinge of desperation. Penny was her best friend. They'd been through a lot together over the years but nothing compared to the loss Penny felt from the Beckett betrayal. Kate walked a fine line between sympathy and tough love, whatever it took to get her friend back on track. She was a problem solver but had to dig deep into her tool bag to figure this one out.

"I know, it's only temporary, but it feels like forever," said Penny with a pout.

"How are the dogs you're tending to?" asked Kate, getting her mind back on business. Penny could go on for hours about how Lulu and Poochie communicated with each other. She was completely caught up in the secret language of dogs. Kate was perplexed; she couldn't understand what happened to her financial-whiz best friend. Out of the blue, Penny proclaimed she was done with her career on Wall Street. Kate was baffled but begrudgingly encouraged Penny to follow her heart. She didn't agree with it or completely understand it. Penny worked hard to achieve success and then she was done. She claimed she needed to create a more meaningful existence. One of her neighbors asked if she had time to walk his dog, and Penny accepted. After a while, a few other people asked her to sit or walk their pets. Now she was busy with little time to think about what she planned to do with her life. Kate was waiting for Penny to figure out her career plan, but Beckett happened, and well, now, nothing was being figured out.

"Oh, they're good; happy homes, happy dogs. Rachel took the puppies to their country house this morning. They're going to run like little wolves."

"Nice, sounds fun. Hey, let's run like wolves in the city. Penny and Kate out on the town; it's been a long time." Kate reminded herself to take baby steps. Penny was a free spirit, but she was bogged down with dread and regret. Kate intended to offer emotional encouragement until Beckett was a faint memory or they were reunited and his debauchery was forgiven.

"It has been a while. Remember when we used to dance the night away on the lower east?"

"Oh yeah, I remember," said Kate. "Then we became obsessed with our careers. Which reminds me, have you thought about when you're going to reenter the professional world again?" Kate loved her job; she couldn't imagine doing anything else. Her personality coupled with her ambition sent her soaring to top-agent status three years in a row, and her wallet was proof of it. Whether she was walking into a brownstone or walk-up apartment, her mind danced with ideas. Real estate was her calling, and no dog or cat would ever take her away from it.

"No, I haven't decided yet. I'm working, Kate; I'm not just lying around doing nothing."

Kate mumbled, "Well, I think it's time you start looking." Kate pulled an *Entertainment Weekly* magazine out of her bag. On the front cover was a very confident Beckett Martin, Penny's ex. "By the way, I picked this up at the newsstand before I got on the subway."

"What? How is he on the cover of *Entertainment Weekly*? Ugh!" Penny picked up the magazine and pounded her head with it.

He stepped down, trying not to look long at her, as if she were the sun, yet he saw her, like the sun, even without looking.

—LEO TOLSTOY, *ANNA KARENINA*

Chapter 2

"*U*bersexy, huh? His new indie film is so good; he's been named one of the top ten hottest young directors in Hollywood." Kate picked up the magazine and stared at the picture.

"Hello? Whose side are you on?" Penny gave Kate a hard look. Three months had passed since she called off her engagement to Beckett. She glanced at her finger, hoping to see the ring, but it was hidden away in the back of her jewelry drawer.

"Earth to Penny," said Kate, jolting her back to the present. "I'm not on any side, but he loves you." Kate reached over and gave Penny's hand a tight squeeze. She was desperate, if Penny would accept his apology, things could go back to the way they used to be. Beckett was madly in love with her, but she refused to discuss their relationship. He crossed a line, and Penny wouldn't exonerate him.

"I don't want to hear nonsense. I can't believe you're so delusional. C'mon, let's get out of here," said Penny, taking a final swallow of her cold coffee.

"OK, where should we go?" Kate slipped her coat back on and followed Penny out the door.

"I'm not sure." Penny felt the cold wind hit her face. She stood on the sidewalk watching an empty soda can bounce along the edge of the street. She paused to watch it, caught up in the action. The wind picked it up, tumbled it on its side, and then tossed it again. "It's dancing," thought Penny. "Even the garbage in New York City is artistic."

"Hello? Where would you like to go?" Kate joined her on the corner.

"Oh, right. What about the Blind Tiger for an IPA?" Penny reached down and picked up the can, saving it from the dance down the sidewalk. "I've got to feed Wasabi soon. He was incredibly quiet today. I'm kind of worried about him." She tossed the empty can in the trash receptacle.

"The ancient Wasabi, how old is he now?" questioned Kate. She was worried about Penny emotionally and financially. She seemed distant and distracted, and it would be tragic if she were forced to sell her coop. Kate could never stand by and let that happen.

"He's almost seventeen. I wonder if he's going to set a record for the longest-living pug in history. Would be awesome, Wasabi making history…he deserves it."

"Wasabi," Kate pondered. "Maybe it's his name bringing him a lot of long-life luck. That's a tongue twister; say it… long-life luck." Kate elbowed Penny in the side.

"Long-life luck," said Penny. They both laughed out loud together.

"OK, let's stop for a beer and then I'll go with you to see Wasabi," Kate interlaced her arm through Penny's as they walked south on West Fourth Street.

"Hey, let's skip," said Kate, grabbing Penny's arm and pulling her forward. "Did you skip in elementary school?"

"No, I'm not going to skip," muttered Penny, crossing her arms across her chest. "Yes, I skipped in elementary school when I was seven years old."

"It's guaranteed to make you smile and forget director ex-boyfriends with hot girls throwing themselves at him."

Penny stopped abruptly. "It's guaranteed to make me forget my worries and problems? Listen up, everyone…you only need to skip. I didn't know skipping would heal my heart, or I'd be bouncing all over the city like Tigger from *Winnie the Pooh*."

"Stop with the pessimism and skip with me. C'mon, it'll be fun."

"Three blocks. I'll give you three blocks." They interlaced fingers, skipping down West Fourth Street, and their laughter rolled through the air.

"Sorry," yelled Penny over her shoulder as Kate and Penny narrowly dodged a couple walking out of St. Ambrose. "We almost took them down."

"I know. Didn't I tell you this would be fun? Let's move it to the street, too many people on the sidewalk."

They skipped their way to Seventh Avenue, weaving in and out of crowds before finally halting on the corner of Bleecker Street, stopping to catch their breath.

"You're a crazy person," said Penny, laughing and gasping for air at the same time. "I can't breathe. Stop making me laugh!"

"See, you're only worried about catching your breath; nothing else is in your mind, like magic." She was certain if they'd gone to the same elementary school, they would have shared patty-cake and hours' worth of skipping.

"Brilliant. I'll remember the assignment, but I can't skip all day." Penny smirked and opened the bar door for Kate. "Another reason to drink beer."

The Blind Tiger was packed, as the after-work crowd drifted in. A mix of young and old, business and casual, yuppies and artists having a great time downing pints of beloved ale.

"It smells like beer in here."

"They serve beer, Kate." Penny wiped her hand across her forehead. Even in the cool winter air, she'd worked up a sweat.

"I know…I'm making an observation."

"You haven't gotten too sophisticated for beer, have you?"

"I'm not sure that could ever happen. Which beer shall I try tonight?" Kate eyed the chalkboard for choices.

Penny watched Kate carefully examining the chalkboard for the perfect beer. It was typical Kate behavior, completely opposite from Penny. Whether Kate was picking out a new sweater, a handbag, or a condo, it was done with complete control, with the desire for flawlessness. Penny was more the fly-by-the-seat-of-your-pants type. "Twenty One for me."

Penny spotted two stools at the bar. "Hurry, two guys are leaving; let's grab their seats."

Penny and Kate rattled off their orders to the bartender. "Looks like somebody works out." Kate nodded her head toward the bartender as he turned around.

"Either that or he's got an amazing gene pool."

"Cheers to us," said Kate when their ales arrived. "It's been a long, tedious, man-less three months. But we've made it to the halfway mark. Another three months to go until we reach our goal." Kate made the bet with Penny with an objective: keep Penny away from predators who might sense the heartbreak she wore on her sleeve. It was time for her to be alone for a while. She needed this phase of emptiness to heal. Kate wasn't a pushy helicopter friend, but she looked after her when a crisis occurred. She felt confident; Penny could come through this time of sadness stronger and fiercer than before. Kate knew Beckett loved her with all of his egotistical heart, but she needed Penny to find the answer on her own. She'd give her a gentle push now and then. It was all in the name of love.

"A very long three months," Penny mouthed the words to Kate, but her thoughts drifted to Beckett. They enjoyed popping into a questionable bar for a beer when they were walking around in the city. Beckett always ordered for her, which she found irritating. He'd gloat when she was pleased with the selection. "He was so arrogant. I never saw it. How could I have been so stupid?"

"Did the magazine cover get to you? I shouldn't have showed it to you. I'm sorry. You know, the only reason he's seeing the tall blonde is because his redhead ditched him. Are you sure you don't want to get together with him and hear what he has to say?"

"Kate, stop taking up for him. He lied; he cheated on me. It's over. Get it through your head, and no, I'm not upset with you. I'm OK, really. I'm going to be OK." Penny sounded harsh, but she wasn't angry with Kate. Her intentions were good, but it was obvious that she needed to let go of Beckett as well.

"We are strong, fearless, independent women," said Kate, sitting up a little taller. "Aww, Penny, I'm sorry. How about a hug from your best friend?" Kate put her arm around Penny and gave her a squeeze. "Besides, he wasn't a huge director when you met him. I think you inspired him to greatness, and the ride went to his head. He did some stupid things, that's all."

"That's all? He's been calling you, hasn't he? You're like his little cheerleader…come clean, Kate." Penny glared at her.

"No, he hasn't been calling me to talk about you," mumbled Kate.

"I knew it! I can't believe you're talking to him. Stop talking to him, Kate. He'll have you believing anything. He's that good." It was typical behavior for Beckett. He was always confident he could get his way; he'd try every angle to achieve success. Penny realized she was just another goal to attain. Whether he was trying to get financing for a new film or seats to the hottest new play, he was relentless, convincing people he was doing them a favor. His gift was negotiation; she'd watched him maneuver with admiration. This time, however, she was the prize and Kate would have to cut the cord.

"He's very charming." It was clear to Kate; she wasn't going to win Penny over. Kate believed their love was genuine. Beckett messed up, but she wanted Penny to forgive him. He was devastated and called or texted Kate every day for updates on her. The pity card was a hard one for Kate to turn her back on. Plus, she loved how happy Penny was during their engagement.

"Right, exactly." Penny sipped her beer in silence. "I thought I knew a lot about psychology before I moved to New York City where, as we both know, everyone is completely off the chart when it comes to being 'normal.' Did I use air quotes?"

"You did!"

"Seriously, I'm getting a buzz off a few sips of beer." Penny giggled. "I think New Yorkers are the happiest people in the world, though, don't you?"

"Yes, I do—the happiest and the most miserable at the same time. How is it possible? Yet, it is! Gosh, this beer is strong. IPA is so good."

"It's a trend, you know. We'll be back to drinking crappy beer before you know it."

"Hey, look who walked in!" Penny spotted Kate's brother Luke and his friend Billy.

"Yay, it's Luke and Billy. I'll go get them." Kate scampered across the crowded bar, grabbed Luke by the arm, and pointed in Penny's direction. They grabbed an empty barstool nearby and joined her at the bar.

Luke was Kate's older brother. He moved to New York City three years before her and was an established fashion designer with a tall reputation in the business. Luke began his career at Calvin Klein and quickly grew in the ranks. Later, he joined the Donna Karan team and most recently moved to Dior. From what Kate gathered, he was able to name his price. Luke was a pillar of stability in her life. Billy, a fashion photographer, met Luke early in his career, and they quickly formed a friendship. Penny admired both of them. They'd rescued her and Kate on numerous occasions.

"What brings you to the Blind Tiger?" asked Penny jokingly. "Wait; don't tell me Kate texted you to meet us here!"

"Nope, nobody told us you were going to be here. You know, we like to get out and mingle like the rest of you," said Billy. "So good to see you, Penny." Billy gave her a hug and kiss on the cheek. "I hope it's not rude of me to bring it up; I was sorry to hear about your breakup. Now he probably has some idea about the huge mistake he made. Cheers to you, sweetie; don't let it get you down. There's lots of fish in the sea, and you, my dear, can have your pick of them."

"Thanks, Billy." Penny appreciated the expression of love but didn't want to bore them with her sorrow. It was too exhausting. They were always the life of the party. Whenever Penny hosted a dinner party, Billy and Luke were on the top of her list. They were beacons of light and happiness, and if anyone could make Penny laugh, it was Luke. She could lay her troubles on them, and they'd listen and comfort her. They'd offer advice, but she was simply tired of bringing people down with her tale of woe. After all, she had Kate to babble to, and Kate was known to give her a kick in the hinny if she became obsessed.

Luke gave Penny a bear hug and whispered "ditto" in her ear. "We were at an art opening in Chelsea and decided to drop in for a beer before heading home." Luke recently purchased a brownstone on Ninth Street, and they were planning to throw a big shindig before or after the holidays. "It's too crazy right now with the decorator. We were thinking we'd have some friends over to toast the new home and the New Year at the same time. You two will be the first to know when we set the date."

"We'll be looking forward to it," said Penny enthusiastically.

Luke constantly had a new fashion story to tell them. Penny could hardly wait for their next party. "Congratulations on your new position and your home purchase. We can't wait to see it! I know Kate was thrilled when she sold it to you." Penny elbowed Luke in the side playfully. "Nothing wrong with sibling love and commission."

"Hey, we're going to be doing a shoot in St. Bart's late February. You girls should join us," said Billy.

"Wow, a perfect time to leave the city for an island, right in the heart of winter," said Penny, wondering if she'd feel like traveling.

"Maybe we could swing it," said Kate, thinking she could never leave work for more than a week.

"Yesterday, Mindy Sans was in the studio," said Luke. He proceeded to mimic the supermodel. "What kind of designer would make a dress out of cotton? In this day and age when we're supposed to be earth conscious! They went out and cut down trees to make this dress. I could never put it on my body!"

Penny and Kate howled with laughter.

Luke was standing up and acting out the scene, thrashing his arms around and panting. "'I'm going to call my agent. You can all take a break. I don't think this shoot is going to happen today. Not on my watch!' Then she stormed out. She thought trees were destroyed in the making of cotton!" Luke always had a good story about models. It was forever hysterical.

The accidental meeting made Penny's heart soar. Her soul needed this wonderful and unexpected gathering.

"By the way, Billy has branched out from fashion, and he'll be showcasing his black and whites at an art gallery in Chelsea in a few months. The dates haven't been pinned down yet, but we'll keep you posted."

"Wow, that's amazing news. We'll definitely come," said Kate.

Luke leaned into the group with a whisper. "Don't look now, but a guy in the corner has been gawking at the two of you for a while now. He's a six, any interest? Maybe we should invite him over?"

"Bite your tongue, Luke," said Kate. "Penny and I are off the market."

Penny got up to stretch and glanced toward the corner. She sat back down. "No interest, but he looks familiar." Penny looked at Kate. "Do you know him?"

"I'll go in for a hug so I can get a glance." Kate stood up and hugged Billy and quickly caught a glimpse of the gawker. "Nope, never seen him before." Kate looked at her watch. "Penny, the time is flying. Don't we need to leave?"

"Oh yeah, we've got to be going; a senior pug is ready for his dinner." Penny dug in her purse, pulled out some cash, and started to leave it for the bartender.

"We've got this," said Luke. "It's the most fun Billy and I've had for months. We've been all work and no play. I'll check in with you in a few days to see what the holiday plans are."

"At least let me give you advice on fabrics," said Kate, changing the subject. She wanted to help decorate Luke's new pad, but he hired a professional. She was a real-estate agent with a passion for interior design.

"It's all being taken care of, Kit-Kat. You don't have to worry about it. But I promise if you don't love it, we'll have another look at it."

That was enough to please her. Luke was always considerate of Kate and her ideas. He was protective of her self-esteem. "You have impeccable taste, and I respect your ideas. I told you before, you'd be great in fashion."

Kate laughed. "The fashion world only has room for one Wesson." She gathered her coat and bag. "Can't wait for the party. We'll see you both soon. Love you."

Penny and Kate walked out of the bar and, once on the sidewalk, realized a winter storm was upon them.

"Did I miss the weather forecast?" questioned Penny, grabbing a lamppost.

"Don't worry; it's only a little wind." A street sign flew off its hinge and tumbled down Bleecker Street. "OK, a lot of wind!" shouted Kate.

"Let's crawl over to my building and check on Wasabi." Penny was being sarcastic, but she was scared. The wind was ridiculous. "This is bad."

"Should we let go of the lamppost and continue on our journey?" yelled Kate.

"Stay low and walk close to the wall so we can grab a door handle, a pipe, or something solid if the gust picks us off our feet," screamed Penny over her shoulder.

"Is this insane or what? I think we've got fifty-mile-an-hour winds. I should have put a few bricks in my purse." They'd both grown up on the West Coast. It took time to get used to the cold, frigid New York City winters. A good pair of snow boots and a hefty down water-resistant coat helped them navigate like natives, but the wind was an entirely different layer of problems.

"You know I don't like you talking to Beckett!" Penny yelled over her shoulder. She turned onto Bedford Street, with Kate trailing behind her. "We're almost there, Kate; stay low."

"I know, Penny. I'm sorry; I'll respect your decision."

Minutes later, they grabbed the railing of her apartment building and pulled themselves up the stairs to safety. The wind could really kick up in Manhattan. It was an island, which was easy to forget when surrounded with stunning views of skyscrapers and quaint neighborhoods lined with brownstones.

"I've never been so happy to be inside your building!" exclaimed Kate. The front door slammed shut with a bang. Kate took off her coat and shook it out, turned her head upside down, and rustled her hair.

Penny laughed. "You look like a dog doing a shake. Did you know they do it to relieve tension?"

"Interesting…nothing like a winter storm to get your anxiety flowing, huh?"

"Ugh, I really don't like strong wind!" Penny dug in her purse for the key to Wasabi's apartment. Minutes later, she unlocked her neighbor's door and headed inside, finding Wasabi asleep on his bed. "He looks so sweet, lying there. When he wakes up, he'll yell at us about something. It's the dementia. He's deaf, but he'll feel our presence in a minute."

Wasabi opened his big pug eyes and gave the girls a long stare.

"I think he's smiling at us," said Kate.

"Of course, he is." Penny gave him a pat on the head. "Hi, Wasabi! I've got some delicious food for you." She took care of Wasabi on a regular basis and found it challenging due to his age. Her friends called her "the dog communicator," but Wasabi was hard to read.

"Ooo, woooo, awww, oooolll," started Wasabi.

"What is that?" Kate stood perfectly motionless, glaring at the pug. "I've never heard those sounds coming from a dog."

"Oh, he's just getting started." Penny snapped open the can of dog food.

"Really?" Kate was startled by the noise. "It's kind of daunting."

"Yep," said Penny as she hurried to get Wasabi's food in his dish. "The faster he got his meal, the sooner the wailing would stop."

"Ooohhhh, waaalll, ooo, awwww," yelled Wasabi.

"Make him stop and fast. It sounds like he's in pain or really, really pissed off."

"No, he's not in pain; he's moody." Penny lost her balance, and Wasabi's food dish teetered on the tip of her fingers. "That was close," said Penny, catching the dish and sliding it quickly under Wasabi's nose.

He immediately stopped whopping, took a few long sniffs in the air, and then stuck his entire pug face in the bowl.

Kate watched with amusement. "I've never seen anything like it. He's so happy."

"He's very dramatic." Penny watched Wasabi digging into his food, tossing it around with his head high and then diving back in the bowl for more. "He's passionate about his meals. It's adorable and messy." Penny grabbed some of Wasabi's towels out of the washing machine and threw them in the dryer. Beckett flashed into her mind. She wondered if he was in the city or on the West Coast.

Kate shouted from the kitchen, "Penny, come here. I think Wasabi passed out!"

"Oh, he's just messing with you. Pick him up and show him his food again. He can't see it," yelled Penny from the laundry room.

"Penny. I think he's dead. I'm not picking him up." Kate liked dogs but had no desire to own one. She was more into cats. Cats were regal and self-supportive. Dogs were needy, and she didn't have a lot of patience for needy.

"Wasabi, don't you die on me, silly *puglet*." She picked him up and placed him on his feet, but he fell over. "Shoot, I've never seen him do this before. We've got to get him to the vet."

"Gosh, back on the street in the wind? Are you sure? Stand him up again," said Kate desperately. She didn't want to go back out in the storm. It was vicious and cold, and they were in a warm building, with wine and food steps away. "I'm so hungry. Can't we take him upstairs to your place?"

"It's like he's passed out or something. I've got to get him to the vet. Here's my key; go upstairs and watch TV or something until I get back," said Penny. "There's some sushi in the fridge. I bought it today."

"I'm hardly going to let you deal with the windstorm and Wasabi alone." Kate wanted nothing more than to go upstairs and relax, but Penny was on a mission. Maybe the pug was tired and wanted to sleep. Whatever the issue, Penny was going to the vet, and she'd tag along. Moral support.

"Thank you." Penny grabbed a towel and wrapped Wasabi in it. "Get the door for me. Let's grab a cab as fast as we can."

"You really need to rethink this pet-care thing," said Kate, opening the door for Penny.

"Really? This is not the time for a career lecture. Help me get a cab!"

The madness of love is the greatest
of heaven's blessings.
—PLATO

*P*enny clutched the rail of the stoop with one hand while holding Wasabi tightly with her other arm. The wind tossed her thick hair across her face. "I can't see a thing, Kate; get a cab on the corner."

"Penny, I've got one—run," said Kate. "Run!"

Minutes later, they walked into the vet hospital. The door slammed behind them with a thump. Most of Penny's neighbors used the same vet, and she was in and out of the clinic often. Most of the time, it was for checkups, vaccinations, food orders, and pharmacy pickups. Tonight, it was an emergency.

"Hi, Penny," said Ellie, the receptionist, a Brooklyn hipster studying medicine at NYU. "It's crazy out there."

"Completely crazy. I've got Wasabi. I think he passed out, but I'm not sure what's going on. You know he's almost eighteen. Is Dr. Green in?" Penny was fond of Dr. Green, an attractive, upbeat young woman with a passion for animals. Penny thought it must be hard to see animals in pain on a daily basis, but if the journey of pet medicine had worn on Dr. Green, it was difficult to see.

"No, Dr. Green is off today, but Dr. Lane is here. He's new to our practice but a renowned vet guru from our up-town location. Let's get you into an exam room, and I'll let him know it's a rush."

"Thanks, Ellie," said Penny, quickly rushing down the hall with Wasabi in her arms. Kate followed closely behind. Penny opened the door to the exam room and ran body to body into a fireman.

"I'm sorry, I…" said Penny, a little disoriented, backing away.

"I'm sorry," said the fireman.

Penny glanced up, and his eyes burned into her. "I know you," said Penny with a jolt. "You're coffee guy!"

"You're crazy water-glass girl," said the fireman.

"Crazy is a little harsh. No way; I'm literally bumping into you the second time in one day," said Penny. "This is so weird."

"Odd," said the fireman. His steel-blue eyes drilled into hers with curiosity. "I'm Wes." He reached out his hand.

"Hi, Wes, I'd love to chat, but I've got a pug emergency," said Penny, placing Wasabi on the large silver table. "He's very old, and we love him so much, I don't know…" Her voice cracked. Penny turned her head to one side so Wes couldn't see the tears brewing in her eyes.

"I'm sure the doc will help you out; don't forget to breathe." He glanced at Wasabi on the table. "Good luck, big guy."

"Thanks, hope so, good to see you again," babbled Penny, not looking in his direction.

Wes tipped his hat and closed the door behind him.

"Wow, what are the chances," said Kate. "You pour water on a fireman and then you bump into him with a dog emergency. You should definitely break the hiatus and go out with him."

"Geez, Kate, it's only a coincidence. Besides, he hasn't asked me out. We don't even know if he's single, and it's bad luck to break a hiatus."

"He feels single," said Kate dreamily. There was something about this fireman Kate found interesting. Not only was he gorgeous; he seemed oddly magical. "Weird," she thought. Normally, she didn't welcome strangers so immediately.

"Let's focus on Wasabi. He's the reason we're here. I need him to be OK." Penny leaned on the silver table and sighed. If something bad happened to Wasabi, she would surely collapse. "Please, Wasabi, don't be sick. I need you to be all right."

"Don't worry; I'm sure Dr. Lane will know what to do." Kate joined Penny at the table, both of them stroking Wasabi gently.

Seconds later, the doctor walked into the exam room. "Hi, I'm Dr. Lane, and who do we have here?" he asked, picking up Wasabi's chart.

"He passed out," said Penny. "I, we, I mean, I'm his caregiver. I look after him when my neighbor is away," said Penny, stumbling over her words. "He's moody and dramatic, but this is a new one. I've never seen…" Penny took a deep breath. "He was eating and fell over with his eyes closed and no movement. He's elderly, and his back legs are weak, so I picked him up to steady him, but it didn't work."

"Wasabi," said Dr. Lane, checking Wasabi's heartbeat. "His heart is fine. He seems to be breathing normally."

"Did he have a stroke? I was afraid he was having a stroke. We jumped in a cab and got here as fast as possible." Penny knew she was rambling. Wasabi was a treasured part of his family. It would be a huge loss if something happened to him.

"It's OK, Penny." Kate grabbed Penny's hand. This wasn't really Kate's area of expertise or even in her comfort zone. All she could do was watch and try to offer support.

Dr. Lane looked into Wasabi's eyes, opened his mouth, and looked in his ears. "Penny, could you tell me a little more about Wasabi, his daily activities and personality?"

"Wasabi is passionate about his food. I think it's a good sign for an old fellow." Penny paused, thinking about Wasabi and his daily life. "He gets four short walks a day, and I feed him often because when he isn't eating, drinking, walking, or sleeping, he's typically yelling about something. I've talked to Dr. Green about it. We believe he has a touch of dementia. I give him two pills a day for his arthritis and extra liquid iron with his meals and eye drops several times a day. Actually, Doctor, he's a bit of a pill, but I figure it's due to his age."

"Would you say he's a trickster?" Dr. Lane glanced at Penny.

"I would say, I do say, but no one believes me." Penny continued, "Once I thought he was having a seizure on the sidewalk and he only wanted a biscuit."

"I believe you." Dr. Lane's assistant walked into the exam room and handed the doctor a package.

Wasabi's legs were starting to give out, which was common in older pugs, so he didn't get the pleasure he once did from a walk. His father raised him from the age of six weeks, and they shared a special bond. His work as a business operations manager was demanding, and Penny was hired to share the workload of caring for an elderly, yet beloved, pet.

"This should let us know what's up with Mr. Wasabi. "We'll give him a tiny bit under his nose and see…" Wasabi's eyes flew up. "Hi, Wasabi, sir, I think you're going to be just fine."

"Are you kidding me?" questioned Penny. "That's it?"

"I'm not one hundred percent sure he was toying with you. It could be a number of things. I'd like to run his blood work, and if it's OK with you, we'll keep him here tonight for observation."

"Yes, it's perfect," she said, leaning over to look Wasabi in the face. "You better have a good excuse for this one, mister." The fact that Dr. Lane got Wasabi's personality within minutes caused Penny to think that maybe he was an animal guru. She'd tried to tell others about Wasabi's tricks and devious ploys, but they'd stare back at her with a blank face. Dr. Lane seemed to understand her. He seemed to get Wasabi. It was music to her ears.

"Is the number listed here in his chart the best number to reach you?" Dr. Lane scribbled some notes on Wasabi's chart.

"Yes. Call me anytime even if it's in the middle of the night, anytime." Penny knew she'd have to call Wasabi's dad and explain the situation. There was no need to worry him until she got the final diagnosis.

Dr. Lane's assistant picked Wasabi up and carried him out the door to the back of the clinic where all the tests were done.

Penny blew him a kiss and spotted his long pink tongue pop out of his mouth and dangle. "Maybe it's your way of waving," thought Penny.

"We'll be in touch; try not to worry." The doctor wrote something else on the chart and then tucked it under his arm. "Nice to meet you; get home safely. The wind is really whipping tonight."

"Thank you, Doctor." After he left the room, Penny turned her attention to Kate. "Shall we continue back to my place and regroup? It's been a crazy few hours, and I'm feeling tired and drained."

"Same here. I think he's going to be OK, got a good feeling about it." Kate was feeling optimistic.

"Me too; thanks for coming with me. Don't forget your purse," said Penny, pointing to Kate's bag sitting in the chair. Kate could laugh all she wanted about Penny's clumsiness, but she was known to lose sunglasses, gloves, and even purses.

"Gosh, losing this thing would've been painful." Kate grabbed it off the chair and threw it over her shoulder.

Kate and Penny stopped to glance at the bulletin board on the wall, grabbing a flyer for a doggie-donation drive in the village. When they entered the lobby of the clinic, Penny stopped in her tracks. *The gorgeous* was still there, chatting with the clinic's administrator.

Penny turned her back to him and mouthed "so hot" to Kate.

Kate licked her lips.

Penny had to hold her breath to keep from laughing out loud.

Wes noticed Penny and Kate and excused himself from his conversation. "How is he?" questioned Wes. He walked toward them with confidence.

Penny felt passion in his voice, and a tingle ran up her spine. "Who is this guy?" she wondered. She'd been void of any positive male emotion for three months. Wandering around, doing her duties completely wrapped up in the drama of Beckett…the endless drama of Beckett. This spark felt odd but refreshingly good. "Wasabi is going to spend the night here, but I think he's going to be fine," she said confidently. Unfortunately, her voice cracked again, and she coughed to regain normal tone.

"Penny," said Wes, "how are you?" She felt his hand in her palm and held on to it. When he looked in her eyes, she felt her stomach rumble. "This is my best friend, Kate," she said, gathering her thoughts.

"Kate, I'm sorry I didn't get to speak with you this afternoon, but we get a second chance to meet," he said with a bright smile.

"Pleased to meet you, Fireman Wes," said Kate. "I'm a huge fan of your work, saving people and stuff." She stood back and gave him a salute. Kate couldn't help but stare at him. He was beautiful, and she didn't throw the word around carelessly. In real-estate-agent terms, he was location, location, location.

"Proud to serve," he said. "Ladies, where are you heading off to in this storm? It's been a crazy weather night in the city. I hope you don't have far to go." Most people had respected the weather warnings and stayed off the street, but he feared if the weather continued, they might be swamped from wind-damage issues.

"Well, I'm in Chelsea, but I think I'll be spending the night with Penny in the West Village, if we can manage to make our way back there," said Kate.

"I thought I could give you both a lift," he said, gesturing his hand toward the fire truck parked directly outside the clinic.

"Wow, are you telling me you're offering to give us a ride to Bedford Street in the fire truck?"

"Yep." Wes nodded self-assuredly.

"Penny, can you believe he's saving us from the wind-storm and we get to ride in a New York City fire truck?" Kate had always wanted to ride in a fire truck but never thought she'd get the chance. It was completely awesome.

Penny couldn't believe Kate was acting like a child. "We could grab a cab or Uber," said Penny. She turned her attention back to Wes. "I mean, can't you get into trouble for taking girls for a ride?" She wanted any excuse to avoid this beautiful man. He was dangerous; she could feel it in her bones.

Wes flashed his award-winning smile. "I suppose I could get into trouble if I were taking you on a joyride. It's a dangerous night to be out on the street," he said, with a serious tone in his voice. "Just doing my job." There was something about Penny he couldn't figure out. She was attractive but with an innocent face. Not the kind of face you'd see in a fashion magazine but maybe a 1950s movie. The kind of girl you'd like to look at day after day. Her pale skin and bright-green eyes were imprinted in his mind. The water incident at the coffee shop replayed in his head all day. Now, here she was again. This time, he wasn't going to let her get away so fast.

"There it is, the kind of smile that turns a *no* into a *yes*. I bet he gets a lot of *yes* and very little *no*," thought Penny.

"C'mon, Penny, he's saving us from danger," said Kate, pleadingly. She wasn't sure why she liked Wes so much. Anyway, she wanted to ride in the massive red truck.

Penny didn't want to cause a scene in the lobby of the vet hospital arguing with Kate. "OK, you're right. Fireman Wes, we'd love to accept your offer, and we thank you for saving us."

"Well, I have to get you home safely first before you can thank me," said Wes, opening the door and stepping aside for Penny and Kate to exit. "I'm up for the challenge." Wes winked at Kate.

Kate felt her knees go weak, and a giggle escaped from her mouth. This guy was exactly what Penny needed. He could make her forget Beckett and every guy she'd ever known.

Wes stepped up to the fire truck and opened the door. "Hi, crew, we've got two ladies who need to go to Bedford Street." Wes climbed into the truck and reached down to help Penny and Kate up the steps.

"No problem, boss," replied the fireman in the driver's seat.

"Boss?" questioned Penny. "Well, I guess that explains why you won't get into trouble for saving damsels in distress."

His blue eyes sparkled like flashlights in the darkness of the truck. "If it were always this easy to save a damsel," replied Wes. He felt pretty confident that getting them to Bedford Street wasn't going to be difficult. On the other hand, his intuition told him, getting Penny to loosen up might be a real task. "By the way, what are the coordinates?"

"Bedford, southwest corner of Carmine Street," yelled Kate over the load roar of the engine. "This is so exciting." She clapped her hands together. "This is great. It's so cool to see the city through the windows of a fire truck."

Wes turned his eyes to Penny. She glanced the other way and ignored both of them. "Ridiculous," thought Penny. "Kate has completely lost her mind. Sure the storm was bad, but they made it to the vet in a cab, and they could've taken Uber home."

Ten minutes later, as they neared Penny's address, an emergency call posted on the radio. The entire vigor in the truck changed. Wes no longer showed any interest in the two women. "I'd advise you both to stay in for the rest of the evening," he said and practically threw them out of the truck.

"Take care." He closed the door quickly, and the fire truck screeched off with horns and lights blaring.

Once inside her building, Penny turned to Kate with a sigh. "I expected him to come in for a cup of tea."

"You're so predictable. You wanted to be coy and reject him. I know you so well, Penny Robinson. I know how you spin it. I wouldn't play games with this guy. He's the real deal."

"A few hours ago, you were polishing Beckett's crown," huffed Penny. She threw her handbag on the kitchen counter.

"OMG, now you're about to piss me off. You know what I mean, P," said Kate, exasperated. "Maybe Penny was right," thought Kate. Perhaps it was wrong of her to plead for Beckett's forgiveness. Nothing had made her change her mind faster than the arrival of Fireman Wes. "I wonder if Wes is short for Wesley. Sizzling."

"OK, I know he's superhot. I'm not sure I want sizzling, and besides I don't know if I'll ever see him again." Penny dropped down on her sofa with a sigh.

"I have a feeling you'll hear from him. He's really into you, I could tell; it was so obvious."

"Let's think about this. I recently had a relationship end because my superhot fiancé cheated on me. The drama was off the charts. I almost got arrested, remember?"

"You were lucky for sure; those cops were cool," said Kate.

"I'm not sure I can stand another guy who has women swooning over him. This is New York City, where it's five women to every man. Why are we living here, Kate? We're already thirty-one and thirty-two." Penny was always reminding

Kate she was a year older. "Don't we want to get married and have kids? I don't want a hot guy to be the father of my kids. I want a man who will be a good dad."

"We're living here because it's the greatest city in the world. Let's not get too wrapped up in the negativity of numbers and statistics. You're talking gibberish, you know. You can't say what you want, because the second you do, the total opposite walks in the door. Love happens. I see it in real estate all the time. They want a brownstone and they buy a penthouse. They will only consider downtown lofts and they buy a sweet two-bedroom on Central Park West." Kate walked to the fridge and pulled out a bottle of white wine. "Mind if I have a glass of wine?"

"You don't have to ask, silly; of course, I'll join you." Penny walked to the cabinet in her kitchen and pulled out two wineglasses. "Really, they go from a Soho loft to Central Park West. That's kind of extreme, isn't it? I could never leave downtown Manhattan."

"Take it back; don't even say it. If you say it, next year I'm going to need a cab or subway to visit you on the Upper East Side." Kate laughed out loud. "All right, perhaps I'm speaking extremes, but seriously don't set strict guidelines, or the universe will make your head spin."

Penny heard her iPhone sound, text message. "Hmm, I wonder who is texting me. What time is it?" Penny grabbed her purse and dug for her phone.

"It's only nine thirty. Weird. The whole night has been a blur of drama," said Kate, sipping her glass of wine. "It feels like midnight. I'd suggest going to a club, but who wants to deal with that wind again."

"It's a text from Wes." Penny giggled. Her eyes lit up, and she felt a pang in her stomach.

"No way," said Kate. "What does it say?" Kate ran from the kitchen to join Penny in the living room.

"How did he get my number?"

"Forget about that; what does it say?"

"It says, *Great meeting you again tonight. Sorry for the sudden departure, had an emergency. Are you both all right and safe?*"

"Wow, he's superdreamy."

"How did he get my number?"

"Ask him," said Kate, taking another sip of her wine.

Penny inhaled deeply and then put her thumbs to her iPhone: *Kate and I are OK. Thank you for getting us to Bedford Street safely. How did you get my number?* "I don't understand this. I mean it's kind of sweet, he's checking on us, but weird too, I think."

"Uh, yeah," agreed Kate.

Penny's phone chimed again, text message: *I hope you don't mind. I got your number from my brother, Dr. Lane from the vet hospital. Glad to know you are both OK. My apologies again for the sudden departure.* Penny and Kate read the text together.

"Wow, they're brothers," yelped Kate. "That's amazing; we should have seen it in the eyes." Kate had noticed a resemblance but didn't put the two together.

"You're right; the doc has the same amazing eyes." Penny laughed but then quickly reverted to negativity. "I don't know if I like this. Really, should Dr. Lane give out my personal information?"

"You're too much," said Kate. "You should go and give Dr. Lane a hug. Two minutes ago you were secretly pouting because you didn't know if you'd see him again." Kate sat down on the sofa with her wine.

"I guess you're right. What should I say? I'm not good at texting guys. I've been out of the dating game for two years now, and everything changes so quickly."

"It's not hard," said Kate. "Pretend you're texting me."

Penny's phone chimed again: *I'm working all night but would love to have breakfast with you in the morning.*

"He wants to have breakfast in the morning, Kate. I can't break the hiatus. It would be bad luck, and besides I don't think I'm up for a date."

"Breakfast doesn't count as a date," Kate said flatly. "Say yes; it's always good to make a new friend. Give me your phone." Kate jumped up for the sofa and snatched Penny's phone out of her hand. The good-looking fireman was on hot pursuit, and she didn't want Penny to be stupid and reject him. She had to save Penny from herself, and the hiatus was senseless.

"Don't you dare; give me my phone, Kate, give me my phone." Penny lunged for it, but Kate darted behind the lounge and ran into the bathroom.

"Texting now, 'I want your hot body, sexy fireman Wes,'" screamed Kate from behind the door. She had to play dirty; this was important.

"OK, I'll go with him to breakfast; now give me the phone. Don't text something bold and embarrassing, or I'll never be able to look at him again."

"You're such a drama queen." Kate cracked the bathroom door open. "I know you're not easily embarrassed, so don't lay the innocent-girl stuff on me."

"My phone please," said Penny, holding out her hand.

"Yes to breakfast, heart sister swear." Kate clutched the phone to her heart.

"Yes, I swear, like you said, it's not really a date," said Penny. "Now give it to me."

Kate walked out of the bathroom, bowed slightly, and placed Penny's phone in her hand.

Penny smiled. "Thank you, crazy nutcase friend."

"You're so welcome, overly dramatic bestie. Go ahead; tell him you can't wait to see if he takes his eggs scrambled or fried." Before Beckett, Penny was adventurous. Kate knew it was still in her, lingering somewhere in her being. She'd bounce back; maybe Wes would be a transitional guy or maybe he'd be a friend. Whatever the destiny, Kate felt Penny should dive in and have a good time. Sometimes, she just needed a little push forward.

Penny contemplated the right location for the breakfast meet-up. "I'll suggest the Grey Dog coffee on Carmine Street. I like that place."

"Perfect! It's only steps from your apartment. You can bring him over here afterward for some dessert."

"You're delusional." Penny focused on her phone and texted Wes back quickly.

Kate grabbed a big red spatula from Penny's kitchen counter and waved it around in the air. "You are destined for great things, Penny Robinson. I grant you three wishes."

"Kate, that's my 'stay calm and bake on' spatula!"

It was a euphoric feeling seeing Penny happy about something. She had a spark in her eyes, and it pleased Kate to see it again. Maybe she'd get out of the kitchen and stop baking all those silly dog biscuits. It was hard to watch. She'd love to dig Penny's business suits out of the closet, put her in a good pair of high heels, and see if she didn't automatically wander downtown to her office. Yet, each day she appeared in sneakers and those dreadful Lululemon yoga pants on a mission to save a dog from peeing inside his or her home.

Penny's phone chimed again: *See you there at 9 a.m.— can't wait to see you again. I'll handle all glasses, both water and coffee—only have one shirt with me tonight.*

Kate and Penny huddled around her phone and giggled like tweens.

⊱✿⊰

The next morning, Kate left before Penny got up. She found the folded blanket Kate used the night before on the sofa. Penny had a second bedroom, but Kate preferred the couch.

It puzzled Penny. Why in the world would she sleep in the living room when a perfectly good bed was waiting in the other room? Maybe it was the television. Kate liked to go to sleep watching the news, but she'd never admit she had a television addiction. She left a handwritten note on top of the blanket: "Have a great time with Wes. Can't wait to hear all about it. Text me later. I'm taking a 'greet the dawn' yoga class. xox Kate."

Penny smiled. "You could have picked out my outfit before you left." She knew Kate left early to avoid making a big deal of the breakfast meet-up. "You're sneaky," Penny said out loud as if Kate could hear her. They'd been known to have telepathic conversations from opposite parts of the city.

Penny called the West Village Veterinary Hospital to check on Wasabi. "He's doing great," said Ellie, the receptionist. "Dr. Lane will probably clear him to be picked up later in the day. He left a note saying he'd call you soon with test results and prognosis."

The news sounded good. Penny was hopeful and happy. She wouldn't have to call Wasabi's dad with a horrible update. Her day was off to a good start. She stuck her head out the window of her second-floor walk-up to get a feel for the weather. The extreme wind gusts were over, and the air felt crisp. The steam heat in her building was incredibly hot. It felt like summer in her apartment 365 days a year. The only way to cool the place down was by opening windows or turning on the air conditioning. The screen on her television showed twenty-five degrees outside. "Brrr," said Penny.

"Guess I'll go with my goose jacket." She grabbed a pair of dark Levi denim jeans and a comfy black Prada T-shirt. Penny loved the feel of the soft cotton. When Kate cleaned out her closet monthly, Penny usually scored a few items of clothing. Since she left her finance career behind, she had to be frugal with money. Although, she'd been day-trading and was good at it. She was surprised at how easy it was to make a substantial profit. It was a secret; not even Kate knew about it. Penny figured she might as well use the years she spent in the business to her advantage. She stared at the black T-shirt, trying to remember when Kate had given it to her. Her iPhone buzzed.

Getting off work, see you in thirty minutes. Grey Dog.

Penny smiled to herself but then quickly regretted her promise to Kate. "What am I doing? I don't want to get involved with anyone right now. It's wrong to bring someone new into my pathetic life."

Her phone buzzed again.

It's only breakfast, drama queen, a text from Kate. Penny couldn't help but laugh.

Penny dressed quickly and then heated her hair curlers and popped them in for five minutes. A swift brush to her locks, a little eyeliner, a clear lip-gloss and she was ready to go. She opened her front door, grabbed her purse, and took a deep breath. "Here we go; no biggie, not a date, only breakfast."

Wes stood patiently outside the coffee shop.

Penny spotted him from across the street. She pulled out her phone to check the time. She hated being late; it was one of her quirks. "I'm right on time." Penny smiled to herself and took a moment to watch Wes.

He was standing with his hands in his jean pockets, relaxed, confident, and gorgeous. His sandy blond hair was tousled from a full night's work, keeping the residents of the city safe. His face was kind, yet chiseled, and a little sandy blond hair covered his chin and jawline. He was lean and fit, and she guessed his height was about five eleven. "The same height as Beckett," she thought and then pushed him from her mind. Wes didn't see her staring at him from across the street. "I don't need this right now. I'm going home. I'll text him with an excuse. My heart is still with Beckett." Penny turned to leave but then stopped to look back at him. Suddenly, she realized it wasn't his appearance but his persona she found attractive. She observed his posture and how he looked at others as they passed by. He was kind and pure. "He's a hero," she thought. It wasn't exactly the declaration she was looking for. It sounded slightly immature, perhaps overused, but yet it seemed to describe him perfectly. She was intrigued. "Wes," Penny yelled from across the street. He glanced her way, and she waved, stepping off the curb and cutting across the street.

"Penny," said Wes, rushing to her. "You can't *jaywalk*. Don't you know how dangerous it is in New York City?"

Penny burst into laughter. "Stop it; you're not on duty."

"On duty or not, you shouldn't *jaywalk* in New York City." Wes had seen his fair share of incidents in the city. He often overreacted with his friends and family. He didn't deny it. Everyone needs to be hypersensitive about safety was his motto. "Sorry, but you need to be safe so you don't have to be sorry."

"I look both ways. I'm very careful, Wes, really," said Penny, sensing the sincerity in his voice.

He grabbed her passionately in his arms and held her. She stood on the sidewalk, arms down by her side, while Wes wrapped his strong arms around her and held her tight. The touching display of affection took Penny by surprise, and she started to weep.

I am nothing special; just a common man with common thoughts, and I've led a common life. There are no monuments dedicated to me and my name will soon be forgotten. But in one respect I have succeeded as gloriously as anyone who's ever lived: I've loved another with all my heart and soul; and to me, this has always been enough.

—Nicholas Sparks, *The Notebook*

Chapter 4

"Are you OK? I'm sorry. Did I make you cry? I didn't mean to yell at you," said Wes. He grabbed hold of her shoulders and held her at arm's length so he could look at her. He silently scolded himself. She barely knew him, and he was giving her safety protocol.

"It's not you, Wes. I cry on a dime lately; I'm not sure why. It's so annoying." Penny wiped away the tear that ran down her cheek.

Of course, Penny was well aware of the reasons she cried all the time. She was a complete unraveled ball of emotions. No way was she going to unload her baggage on this man. She wanted to run away, back to her cozy apartment, back to her down comforter, and lay there all day and night until her personality returned.

"It's fine to let your emotions out. You can cry on my shoulder anytime," said Wes. He slapped his arm around her and gave her a pat on the back as if they were teammates on a football team. "Let's get some coffee; it'll make you feel better."

"I do love coffee," said Penny. "I think it's on the top ten of life's greatest gifts."

"I do too! Let's both get a cup of nature's genius. No offense, but I'll carry both cups. You already drenched me with water; don't need you to burn me." Wes elbowed Penny in the ribs and opened the door for her.

Penny was trying to keep up with the emotions he was drawing from her. In a matter of minutes, she'd been embraced like a lover, and now, suddenly, she'd become a pal. "Was it the tears?" thought Penny.

Wes grabbed a small table for two in the corner. "Stay here and cover the table. I'll fetch our coffee." He was able to draw Penny out of her home to have breakfast with him. Last night, she was aloof in the fire truck. He could tell by her vibe she wasn't interested in the fireman or the man. The fact she agreed to meet him for breakfast gave him hope. Something was troubling her, and he believed it was far more than a sick pug.

"OK, boss," said Penny. He was comfortable. How was it possible to feel at ease with a guy you just met? Penny pondered the thought. He's probably a professional ladies' man, that's how. She reverted to negativity, which was something she hated to do. Yet, negative was her go-to mode lately.

"How about something to eat? You need to eat. Maybe you're crying so much because your body is angry at you for not feeding it." Wes took his jacket off and hung it on the back of his chair.

"Highly unlikely, but sure, I'll have some food; surprise me."

"Really, you're going to let me pick your food. Awesome; now I'm not sure if you're a real girl."

"Oh, I'm real and not picky about food. I love everything as long as cilantro isn't involved."

"You have an issue with cilantro?" Now, he knew she was special. Wes couldn't understand why people loved cilantro. They had something in common. It wasn't much, but it was something, and he would go with it.

"I simply can't stand it. I don't understand how people enjoy it. But every other food or food accessory I like. You have a great chance of picking something I will find delightful." Penny gave him a bright smile.

"I can't tell you how happy I am to find a fellow cilantro hater. I mean why are they putting the stuff in a perfectly good salsa or guacamole?"

"What a pity, ruining a lovely avocado."

"We're a rare group, anticilantro foodies…by the way, how do you take your coffee?"

"Black, please."

"You got it," said Wes with a wink.

"Wow," said Penny out loud as she watched Wes walk to the counter. "What a pretty man." She thought a man probably wouldn't want to hear the word "pretty," but pretty he was. His energy was so warm and inviting she couldn't help but smile. She wanted to text Kate. Penny pulled out her phone to check her messages. There was one new text from Kate:

How sexy is Fireman Wes? Have fun!

Wes showed up with two glasses of water. "Hold on, I'll be right back with our coffee." He quickly returned with two steaming cups of black coffee.

Penny noticed the tattoo on the inside of his right arm and wondered if he had more on other parts of his body. "Yum, it smells so good," said Penny, leaning over the cup to take a whiff.

"Be right back with food," said Wes.

"You'd make a great waiter if the fireman thing doesn't work out." Penny winked at Wes.

"No need to worry about that. I'll be a fireman forever," said Wes, turning back to the counter for their food.

A few minutes later, he showed up with a variety of food, enough for three people. "I hope you don't mind, but I wanted you to have lots of anticrying food. We've got a breakfast quesadilla, an old-fashioned omelet with home fries, toast, pancakes, and, in my honor, some Irish oatmeal," said Wes with a big goofy smile.

Penny couldn't help but laugh as he hand-delivered each dish and slid it in front of her as if he was the waiter. "Gosh, I hope you're hungry; I can't eat all of this myself."

"Oh, I'm hungry, but I expect you to dig in. Don't be shy, water girl; feed your body and mind."

"You don't have to ask me twice," said Penny, grabbing a fork. "I'll try the breakfast quesadilla first." Penny was suffering from crying bouts throughout the Beckett healing process, but her appetite had remained intact. Sometimes, she would stop eating and wonder if she could taste the food. Her taste buds had been dulled by the mild depression she was suffering, but she continued to eat, and Kate declared it was a sign of her warrior spirit. She felt her jeans hang loosely from her hips and knew she was down from her usual steady weight by a few pounds. "Can I see your tattoo?" asked Penny.

"Sure," said Wes, holding out his arm. "It's in honor of a buddy of mine."

Penny touched the tattoo with her fingers. "It's beautiful." Within the flames, she could see a skull and a fireman kneeling beside it.

"Yeah, the artist did a good job. I've got more. I'll show you sometime." Wes winked, and Penny ignored it.

Several minutes of silence followed while Wes and Penny sliced their way through the abundant breakfast.

"Yum, it's all so good," said Penny, stopping to catch a breath. "Wes Lane, I'm guessing you're of Irish descent since you emphasized Irish when you presented me with this delicious bowl of oatmeal."

"Do you like it with honey or plain?"

"Honey," said Penny.

"Yes?" questioned Wes.

"Honey," said Penny.

"Yes," said Wes.

"Ha-ha, I see what you're doing. Cute," said Penny.

"I don't mind if you call me honey, sweetie," said Wes.

Penny laughed out loud. "You're hysterical." He was charming, a little unsophisticated but charming all the same.

Wes didn't laugh. He looked at Penny with his sparkling blue eyes and smiled. He seemed proud of himself for making her laugh. "I'll make you laugh every day; no tears, Penny. I want to see you smile," thought Wes. He knew better than to say it out-loud. "But to answer your question, yes, I'm Irish. My mom is Greek, and my father is Irish. He must be English as well, but he'd never admit it. My brother and I are Irish, and our oldest brother is Greek. It's pretty funny; he took after our mom, like a boy version of her. By the way, I hear Wasabi is doing well," said Wes, changing the subject. "'Excellent' is the word on the street."

"I think so; thank God. I'm waiting to hear back from your brother," said Penny. "Oh gosh, I should check my phone." Penny pulled out her phone and saw a missed call and a voice mail. She quickly felt guilty for having breakfast with Wes and missing a call from the animal clinic. "I've got a voice mail."

"Go ahead, check it; maybe it's from the doc," said Wes.

Penny clicked on the message and heard Dr. Lane's voice assuring her Wasabi was doing great, his blood work was normal, and she could pick him up whenever she had time.

"It was your brother. He said Wasabi is doing well and I can pick him up. I can't tell you what a relief I feel," said Penny. "I mean I know Wasabi is elderly, but I don't think he's ready to leave us yet, and he's so happy when he's eating and…"

"You love him; I know you do. It's always hard to let go of a pet. Fortunately, it sounds like Wasabi is healthy as a horse, or at least a dog," said Wes with a chuckle. "He's just old."

"Wasabi will be so happy to get back home and settled into his comfy bed," said Penny. She felt her heart soar from the good news. "I'm so grateful to your brother for his attention and help."

"He's a good guy. It's his job, of course, but he has a real gift with animals. He's had it all his life, even before med school. I think he was a veterinarian at the age of five."

"Wow, really? He was great with pets when he was five?" She was impressed with how Dr. Lane had picked up on Wasabi's personality. He had a gift with animals, she was certain of it.

"Not only pets, cows, pigs, you name it. Our grandfather had a farm upstate, and we used to spend summers there. Once, we found him with pop's ace bandages out in the field wrapping a cow's hoof."

"Incredibly sweet."

"Yeah, it is sweet. I could tell you some great stories about Wyatt."

"Wyatt?"

"My brother, Dr. Lane; his name is Wyatt."

"Oh, of course, I didn't actually ask for his first name or look at the vet card. Wyatt and Wes—I guess your mom and dad were into *W*s," said Lucy with a chuckle.

"Well, yes and no. There are three of us—Wes, Wyatt, and Nick. Nick is the Greek one. Are you going to finish your pancake?" said Wes.

"No, I'm totally full; go ahead. Where does Nick live, and what does he do?"

"Nick is the oldest of us three; he's a dentist on the Upper East Side. He does good work." Wes grinned big so Penny could get a good look at his teeth.

"Nice smile; it looks like he does. Does Nick live in the city as well?"

"Yep, we're all here. One group of three brothers, living and working in Manhattan."

"Sweet. It sounds so nice, having family close. I'd love it if my parents or my brother lived here. Kate is like a sister, though; we're family. Hey, do you mind if we get going soon? I can hardly wait to see Wasabi, and I have a few dogs to walk at noon. Sorry to rush you, but I know Wasabi is probably anxious to get home."

"No apology needed. How about I give you a ride over to the clinic?"

"You have a car in the city?" Penny took the subway or cabs when she needed wheels. Her circle of friends thought a car in the city was a heavy burden or a glamorous luxury item, rarely needed.

"Yeah, sure; I mean I don't always drive it since I live in Soho, but occasionally I drive to work. Got the FDNY parking decal; makes it a little easier to park," said Wes.

"Perks, yeah, I bet it comes in handy, for sure. I would love a ride to the clinic; thanks, Wes."

"The pleasure is all mine. Let's get out of here, senior pug on deck," said Wes, checking to make sure his car keys were still in his jacket. "Wyatt is working this morning. I'll grab a cup of coffee for him to go, if you don't mind?"

"No, of course not. I'll wait for you outside." Penny suddenly felt the urge to break out a cigarette even though she quit smoking months ago. Once on the sidewalk, she pulled a cigarette out of the tattered pack in her purse and tried to light it quickly. She cupped her hand around the cigarette, but the lighter flickered. Penny darted into a doorway, hoping the wall would provide a barrier. "Just a couple of drags," thought Penny, clicking the lighter again and finally getting it lit. She inhaled deeply and felt her head spin. "Wow, that's intense." A man sitting in a car across the street caught her eye. There was nothing odd about it, but she had a weird feeling she was being watched. "Now, I'm losing it," thought Penny.

Wes came out of the café looking for her.

Penny quickly clipped the cigarette out with her fingers and slid it back into the pack.

"Are you sneaking a smoke?" said Wes, walking toward her with authority.

"Ugh, no…I mean I feel like I should say no, but yes, I felt like having a puff. I mean, I quit, but sometimes I cheat. Are you going to yell at me?" Penny was cowering in the doorway.

Wes laughed out loud.

"Why are you laughing? You scolded me for jaywalking. I figure you'd take me over your knee for a cigarette."

"I'd love to take you over my knee," said Wes. His blue eyes sparkled with laughter, but there was a spark of unpredictability.

"Right here?" said Penny, obviously flirting with danger. Wes was exciting; she could tell he had a good sense of humor. She thought she'd mess with him a little.

"Right anywhere, you gorgeous, sexy, jaywalking, ciga-rette-smoking female," said Wes. He put the large cup of hot coffee on the hood of a parked car and walked toward her with a mission.

"No, seriously, I'm only kidding; you wouldn't dare," said Penny, backing up against the building.

In a swift move, he picked her up and swung her over his shoulder. He stopped to grab the coffee off the hood and started running down Bedford Street.

"Wes!" Penny shrieked as she bounced upside down on his back. It wasn't comfortable, but it was exhilarating. "Wes, stop it. Put me down," yelled Penny. "Wes, seriously, this has been fun, but I'd like to walk now."

He stopped abruptly and lowered Penny gently to the side-walk. "Here we are," said Wes cheerfully, as if running down the street with a woman on his back was part of a normal day.

"Terribly fancy for a fireman, don't you think?" said Penny, eyeing Wes's vehicle as he struggled to find the key in his jacket pocket. "I thought you'd have a pickup truck, not a BMW."

"Hmmm, are you making generalizations? I do have a pickup truck, but I took the SUV today."

"Ha, I was right; you have a pickup," said Penny teasingly.

"And let me guess, you do yoga, burn incense on a daily basis, and feel guilty if you don't meditate. Got a problem with a pickup truck, water girl?"

"Not at all. Did I offend you? I'm sorry. How do you know I burn incense, do yoga, and meditate?"

"The girl, the body, the address, and the slight smell of patchouli on your clothes, mixed with a hint of cigarette smoke, of course," said Wes.

"I enjoy both pickups and BMWs," said Penny enthusiastically.

"Now, let's get you to the clinic so you can make Wasabi happy," said Wes, opening the car door. He jogged quickly around the back of the car, sliding into the driver's seat. "Seat belt on, please; it's a rule of the car."

"Of course," said Penny, feeling a little light-headed. "I can't believe you didn't spill a drop of this coffee." Penny lifted the coffee cup from the holder. "Is this a real cup of coffee?"

"Whoa, put it down," said Wes, snatching it gently from her hand and placing it back in the cup holder.

Penny couldn't help but laugh.

"I'll drive you and Wasabi back to your place, and then I've got to go home and get some sleep," said Wes.

"Oh gosh, I forgot you've been up all night. You must be exhausted. Thank you for being so thoughtful. I'm kind of glad I poured water on you after all." Penny reached over and gave his hand a squeeze.

The gesture took Wes by surprise. Penny was emotionally distant. He didn't know why, but he assumed she'd been hurt, perhaps recently. He intended to get the full story, but their breakfast meeting was not the time or place.

"Penny," said Wes, taking her hand in his. "I'd continue our breakfast all day if I could. It's fun getting to know you." He leaned over and kissed her on the cheek. The romantic moment lasted only a few seconds. Wes cranked the car and turned back into business.

Penny felt the tingle of his lips on her cheek. The electricity ran down her body and into her feet. She felt the tips of her toes warm. He was a walking, talking heating blanket. Everything about him was cozy, like a log on a fireplace or a goose down blanket. She wanted to wrap herself inside the blanket and stay there for days. "Wrap me in your arms, Wes. Keep me warm forever," she thought.

She heard her phone chime, text message. She glanced at her phone. It was from Kate:

OMG, call me as soon as you can. Regina is coming to town.

"Something important?" questioned Wes.

"Something important and delightful. Regina is coming to town!"

"Regina?" Wes noticed a change in Penny's disposition. She was glowing; maybe this was the answer to Penny's emotional fear. She wasn't into guys. "Who's Regina?"

"Regina is the other half of Kate and me," said Penny, smiling from ear to ear. "She's a stand-up comedian and spends her life on the circuit. Sometimes, she makes it back to New York, and our threesome is whole again."

"I only heard 'threesome,'" said Wes, concentrating on the traffic and taking the side streets to the clinic. "You can't say 'threesome' to a guy driving in New York City traffic!"

"You're bad, Wes Lane," said Penny. "We're straight; we're friends, sisters."

Wes stopped at a red light and turned to Penny. "You said my name, and my heart skipped a beat." His checks were rosy from the brisk air.

"Are you blushing, Fireman Lane?" questioned Penny.

"I could be. I only heard 'threesome.' After that, it was blah, blah, blah." Minutes later, he pulled into a parking space and put the SUV in park. "Penny, repeat after me please," said Wes.

"What, uh, OK," said Penny reluctantly.

"Wes Lane."

"Wes Lane," said Penny.

"Aww, my name has never sounded so good," said Wes, placing both his hands over his heart.

"Stop it," said Penny. "You're being silly."

"I'm a lot of things, but silly I'm not," said Wes in a tough-guy voice. "Can I take you to dinner tonight?"

"Gosh, I don't know…I mean I need to check in with Kate and see what's up with Regina. I'd love to see you again, maybe tonight. Honestly, Kate and I are on a six-month sabbatical from men. She let me have breakfast with you because breakfast is not really a date, but I think I owe it to her to keep my honor."

"How far into this sabbatical are you?" Wes had a tortured look on his face. "I can't wait six months to see you, Penny Robinson. I need to see you tonight," thought Wes.

"We celebrated three months last night so three more to go," said Penny.

"Well, that's absolutely ridiculous. I mean what happens if you lose the bet?"

"Oh, nothing. I don't think we set any real ground rules as to what happens. Basically, we're both stubborn, and we always finish out bets with a draw. We figure it's bad luck to break the bet."

"Excellent. I think I can talk Kate into letting you out of this pointless game with an honorable withdrawal."

"Hmm, an honorable withdrawal…sounds interesting. You think Kate is going to cave to you, don't you? Maybe she's a lot tougher than you think." Penny needed Kate to be tough; she needed her to refuse the offer. Wes intrigued her, but she needed three more months to get her head clear. The last thing she needed or wanted was a dating schedule.

"I'll take those chances. Text me her number now, and I'll give her a ring in a few."

"OK, but don't be surprised if she turns you down flat," said Penny. "She's a lot tougher than she looks. Her real-estate success didn't come from giving in." Penny felt the need to warn him. She was counting on Kate to be solid and strong.

"I'm pretty good at negotiations." His phone chimed. He looked down to check it. "It says Princess Kate; got it, let's go get Wasabi."

Before Kate could reach for the door handle, Wes was at her door.

"Gosh, you're fast," said Penny, stepping out of the sport utility vehicle rather ungracefully. She tripped over her boot and landed in Wes's arms. Her face smacked right into his chest.

"Whoa, ballet dancer, thanks for falling into my arms," said Wes.

Penny's phone started to ring. She grabbed it out of her purse. "Sorry, got to take this; it's Rachel, the Yorkies' mom. "Hi, how's everything in the country?" She paused, listening to the voice on the other end of the call. "No, it can't be true," said Penny frantically. Her face turned a lighter shade of white.

"Penny, what's wrong?" questioned Wes, grabbing the phone out of her limp hand.

She steadied herself against the side of the SUV. "The puppies have been stolen. They're gone. The babies are gone."

He's more myself than I am. Whatever our souls
are made out of, his and mine are the same…
—EMILY BRONTE, *WUTHERING HEIGHTS*

Chapter 5

"Hello," said Wes into the phone. "I'm Penny's friend and a fireman in New York City. She's pretty shaken up; could you give me more information?" Wes listened to Rachel and wrapped his arm around Penny to steady her.

"I have a lot of friends in the police department. Please tell me exactly what happened." Wes listened quietly for several minutes. "Penny and I will be at your house in a few hours. Does she have the address?"

Penny shook her head yes.

Wes hung up the phone and took Penny in his arms. "I'm sorry, but don't worry; we'll find them; we'll get them back."

"Is that possible? I mean what are the chances? I can't believe this. Who could do this? Maybe they're lost. They're fragile; they couldn't survive one night on their own in the wild."

"Penny, listen to me," said Wes firmly. "Let's get into the clinic, pick up Wasabi, and get to Connecticut as soon as we can."

"You've had no sleep."

"I'll be fine. Do you have someone who can take care of your afternoon walks for you?"

"Kate will do it." Kate didn't enjoy walking dogs. She had better things to do, but Penny knew she would help out in a pinch.

"OK, step one, let's get Wasabi," said Wes. "Are you with me?" Wes clutched her hand and led her toward the clinic.

"Yes. Thank you." Penny grabbed his arm. "Wes, do you really think we'll find them?"

"Penny, listen to me, we'll find them," said Wes as he pulled her down the sidewalk.

⚜

Wes scouted the radio channels for a good road-trip song but finally settled on a Beethoven CD he kept in the glove compartment.

Penny felt strangely content sitting in the passenger seat, although she despised riding shotgun. "It's a control issue," thought Penny. She always used air brakes for whoever was at the wheel. She leaned the seat back and closed her eyes. The Yorkies danced through her mind, playing ball and wiggling their tails. Her thoughts were disrupted with a startling fear. "How was Wes so sure he could help them? Wasn't it a promise he knew he couldn't keep? Sure, he was used to saving people, but how could he help them find the puppies?" She squeezed her eyes tight, trying to visualize Harold, Darlene, and Toby running toward her jumping into her arms, reunited.

"Penny," said Wes. "I hate to wake you."

Penny, startled, reached for the lever and pulled her seat up.

"You can rest; it's fine. I just wanted you to know we're only a few miles away."

"Oh yeah, thanks for letting me know. Gosh, let me warn you, Rachel will be completely distraught. If you think I'm a mess, she'll top me two times." Rachel was a relatively new client, but Penny knew her well enough to know she'd be frantic. Her intentions were always good; she was a lovely person but typically a bit dramatic under entirely normal circumstances. Her goal would be to keep Rachel focused and calm. Penny knew it would be a challenge.

"Understood. Listen, I reached out to the chief in Greenwich. They're sending over a few of their top detectives. I expect they'll be waiting for us when we arrive."

"I'm not sure how you're doing this, but I can't thank you enough," said Penny. She reached over the console and gave him a kiss on the cheek.

Wes took his eyes off the road for a two-second eye lock. His eyes twinkled with pleasure, and Penny fell back into her seat, feeling light-headed.

"Seat belt back on, please," said Wes with authority.

"Of course." Penny closed her eyes again. "Geez," thought Penny. "Wes was certainly demanding when it came to the rules of the car. She had no idea firemen were such goody-goodies." Penny knew better than to complain about it, since he was driving her to Connecticut and lining up a team to help them.

When they approached the Abernathy estate, Penny noticed two cop cars parked outside. Wes parked his SUV behind them.

"Perfect, they're right on time. The detectives are going to be our ticket for getting your pups back." He unbuckled his seat belt, and one second later he opened Penny's car door for her.

"He's like superman," thought Penny, quickly matching his speed as Wes sprinted from his car to the officers. This was all happening so fast. It was surreal, like a dream, and Wes was leading the band.

"Thanks for coming so quickly," said Wes, reaching out to shake the detective's hand. There were four police officers, two sets of detectives, both a male and a female in each car. Wes made introductions to the officers and relayed the information as concisely as he could. "I can't thank you enough for getting here quickly. We appreciate the help." Wes was in superhero mode, and Penny couldn't help but be impressed.

"Let's all go in and meet with Rachel; she's going to give us the most accurate time the pups went missing," said Detective Simon, a petite blonde with a kind face.

Penny felt a bounce in her step. A team of professionals had been assembled with one aim: bringing the puppies back home.

Rachel met them at the door. Her eyes were swollen, and she embraced Penny with a gasp. "I can't believe it, Penny; who could take our dogs? Who could do something so horrible?"

"I know, Rachel. I can't believe it. I feel like I'm in the middle of a nightmare."

Detective Simon interrupted their exchange. "Ladies, time is a sensitive matter when it comes to a puppy snatch. Let's get busy with details." She pulled out a chair from the kitchen table and motioned for the others to join her.

The information flowed. Rachel explained she had no reason to believe this was personal. Perhaps it was a random act. Rachel took the pups with her to pick up her dry cleaning early morning and then proceeded home. Rachel and her husband, the Abernathys, had fashioned a large enclosed dog run in their backyard so the pups could play outside unattended. When Rachel went outside to play with them, they were gone.

"How long after you arrived from your errand did the pups go out to the run?" questioned Detective Wright.

"Almost immediately," whimpered Rachel. "I thought they'd like to run for a while, since they were in the car with us driving in from the city yesterday and then with me running errands this morning. I took them outside right after I came home from the cleaners."

"What time was that?" questioned Simon.

"Here's my receipt from the cleaners. I picked up my clothing at nine fifteen."

"Can I take a look at the receipt?" questioned Simon. Wright leaned over her shoulder so he could get a look at it. "I know the owners of Courtier Cleaners. I'm pretty sure they've got security cameras at that location. We need to secure video from any nearby businesses as well—the yogurt shop across the street, the restaurant on the corner—see who and if someone seemed interested in your vehicle," said Simon.

The other two detectives remained quiet, watching Simon and Wright as they gathered and questioned.

Penny's fingers were crossed tightly under the table while they talked. They were good, she liked them, and it was clear the detectives were invested in solving the crime. Their mission was to find the criminal and rescue the puppies. Penny felt her heart leap. It was inspiring to watch them work; they were serious about getting the culprit.

"Like I said before, time is an issue, so we need to get over to the cleaners quickly. We'll be in touch with you soon," said Simon, pushing her chair under the table and hustling out the door. The other three officers followed.

"Wow," said Penny. "I'm hopeful. They made me feel optimistic. Thank you, Wes." She gave him a hug. Rachel walked over and put her arms around the two of them.

"One of the detectives told me they've had a lot of pup theft in Greenwich over the past six months. It's so serious they gathered a task force to investigate. What I'm saying is… they have leads which could work in our favor."

"It's hard for me to understand. What kind of person steals puppies? It's incredibly sad and extremely evil," said Penny, sitting down at the dining-room table.

"Can I make you both some coffee?" said Rachel.

"Wes, you could take a nap in the guest room. I'm sure Rachel wouldn't mind."

"Of course," said Rachel.

"Wes had to work all night, and now I've got him invested in our drama," said Penny. "You must be exhausted, Wes."

"Actually, that's a great idea. I could use a little sleep and then we can get back out on the street and start our own search." Wes joined Penny at the table.

"I can't tell you how much I appreciate your help," said Rachel. "Come with me and let me get you comfortable in one of the guest rooms. Penny, I'm not sure where you found this guy, but he's a keeper." Rachel led Wes down the hallway.

Rachel got Wes comfortable in a room upstairs and met Penny back in the kitchen. "Let's get ourselves a bite to eat. I picked up a lot of goodies in town yesterday. I couldn't eat a thing this morning, but suddenly I feel like I must have food."

"Yeah, I'm pretty famished too. Wes and I ate a big breakfast this morning, but it feels like a day ago already. Do you know anyone who would want to take the puppies?"

"No, I've searched my mind for anything or anyone I've encountered lately. Nothing comes to mind. It's really scary. I had little hope until the detectives arrived. Now, I feel absolutely certain my babies are coming home soon."

"Gosh, Rachel, what if they don't?" Penny didn't want to spread negativity, but she needed Rachel to be aware it was entirely possible the pups were gone.

"Let's focus on the positive and send our babies messages of love and comfort. I'm sure they're terrified. I think it's what hurts me the most, the fear of the unknown. Are they safe? Are they hungry? Have they been mistreated? It's hard to think about."

"I know, Rachel. Professional puppy snatchers want them to be safe and healthy, right? After all, they're probably going to try and sell them. The detectives must find the culprit before they have a chance to do a deal."

"Let's say a prayer of thanks for our lunch and safety for Harold, Darlene, and Toby."

Penny and Rachel bowed their heads and silently prayed for thankfulness and protection.

⁓⁓✼⁓⁓

Lunch was the perfect thing to help calm her nerves. Penny decided to check in with Kate and see how everything was going in the city. Kate answered on the first ring.

"How is everything in the city, and how are the dogs?"

"Regina and I have everything under control." Penny could hear Regina laughing and a dog barking in the background.

"What about Lucy?" Penny asked. Lucy, a cute Russell Terrier mix Penny walked every day, was a sweetheart. Penny and Lucy shared a bond: a dog-walking love affair. Penny was very protective of Lucy, and Lucy of Penny. She was full of love, but she didn't always embrace a new walker. Penny figured if anyone could charm her, it would be Kate.

"I said 'treat' when I walked in and held it out for her. She trusted me, but I can tell she misses you. She looked at me with disappointment and disdain." Kate sighed. "Everything is good, Penny. Don't worry."

Penny was relieved and thankful. Kate was able to take the day off, and Regina was free as a bird. They were hanging out together and catching up. Penny was hopeful she'd be back before Regina hit the road again.

⌒⌒⌒

"What's for lunch, ladies?" said Wes brightly. He found Penny and Rachel sitting on lounge chairs beside the covered pool. Rachel was flipping through an *O* magazine, and Penny was painting her nails a fluorescent blue color.

"Do you need your hands to glow in the dark?" chuckled Wes. He wasn't into sparkly, loud, or fluorescent colors. He liked Penny's style, edgy. The nails didn't fit her personality.

"Maybe," said Penny defensively. "You don't like the color?"

"I might if you were twelve years old and going to a Katy Perry concert."

"Wow, why don't you tell me how you really feel?" said Penny with a bite-me smile. He seemed totally refreshed and full of feistiness after only two hours of sleep. It was hard for

Penny to understand. She needed a full eight hours of shut-eye. If she didn't get it, her mind was cloudy.

"Don't be silly, Wes. All the young girls, I mean young ladies, paint their fingernails wacky colors these days. It's what they do. You should know that, living in Manhattan."

"Oh, I know," said Wes, turning to Rachel with an eye roll.

Rachel giggled. He was interesting, and she liked him.

"Any word from the detectives?" He needed to get these two back to the business at hand.

"Nothing," said Rachel and Penny at the same time.

"We've been tirelessly whining to each other for hours, so I decided we needed to sit outside, clear our heads with fresh air, and refocus," said Rachel. "If crying would bring the puppies home, they'd be here already."

"Copy that," said Penny. She glanced up from her fingernail painting. Wes caught her eye. He was wearing a Harvard sweat shirt. Rachel had pulled it out of her husband's closet. It suited him. Was it possible he got better looking the longer she hung out with him? He'd worked all night and had two hours of sleep. His hair was messy, his chin scruffy, and he was gorgeous.

"Did you get enough sleep, Wes?" asked Rachel, her words breaking up the daze Penny was in. "I'm afraid I'm not being a very good hostess."

"Yeah, I only needed a couple of hours. My body is trained to work as long as I get a little downtime in between."

Penny pondered how this man happened into her life. A day ago, she was a red-faced, nervous, accident-prone maniac in a coffee shop, a winter storm, a ride in a fire truck, a breakfast, and here he was. Could he really be a nice guy? He seemed genuine, but it was hard for her to comprehend. She wasn't a pessimist, but she'd lived in New York City for ten years. Was she street-smart? She thought so. She wanted to doubt his assurance, to wonder what his motives were. Yet, here he was, completely committed to the rescue. He'd never even met the puppies. Her heart believed he was real, but her mind bounced between hero and opportunist. Only time would tell. She felt guilty for doubting his motives, and this guilt worried her.

"I wish Bobby were here," said Rachel to herself. Bobby and Rachel Abernathy were college sweethearts who'd been married for twenty-three years. "He offered to fly back from Atlanta this morning, but I felt awful asking him to do so." Bobby and Rachel were best friends. Although he traveled a lot, Rachel never doubted him. There was no reason to; he was a devoted husband and father. They texted each other constantly and spoke on the phone every few hours. Penny was in awe of their relationship.

"It's going to be fine, Rachel. You have Wes and I," said Penny cheerfully. "He'll be back tomorrow, right?"

"Thank you, Penny. You're right," said Rachel, changing the subject. "Wes, let's get you something to eat." She led Wes toward the kitchen, feeling the need to busy herself. "You look so handsome in Bobby's sweat shirt. He'd love you, I'm sure of it. You and Penny will have to join us for dinner sometime, either here in Greenwich or in the city."

Rachel's affection toward Wes made Penny smile. Rachel Abernathy was a philanthropist, and the list of her foundations was long and worthy. She valued hosting parties at her Manhattan penthouse. Penny had attended a few. She was impressed with Rachel's ability to entertain intimately or with a crowd. She chose her real friends carefully, and everyone in her large circle of friends treasured her. It was clear to Penny; Wes had passed the Rachel Abernathy test.

❧

"That was delicious." Wes placed his plate in the sink, turned on the water, and looked around for the dish soap.

"You don't have to wash your plate," shrieked Rachel. "The housekeeper will be here in the morning. At least give her a dirty dish or two to wash. She has so little to do. I don't even know why we keep one."

"Always good to have a housekeeper," said Penny with a shrug. "At least I've heard it is." Penny had no idea. She'd never had a housekeeper. Kate tried to convince Penny to hire a cleaning service, but she scoffed at the idea.

"Let's get going, ladies. I thought we could go for a drive, take a peek around the town, see if we can spot anything."

"An active dog search?" questioned Penny.

"It'll make us all feel better," said Wes confidently. He wasn't the type of guy to sit around waiting for news. "Even if nothing came of their search," he thought, "it was always a good idea to be hands-on."

"That's a great idea," said Rachel, rushing for her purse and coat.

Rachel, Penny, and Wes piled into his SUV and drove the streets of Greenwich, searching for any signs of the pups. On a drive down Main Street, a chill ran down Penny's spine. The same car she'd seen this morning in the city at the café was parked at the corner. When they drove past it, she saw the same man sitting inside reading a newspaper. "How is it possible?" thought Penny. "Why would someone be stalking me?" There was no way she would mention this to Wes. He would flip out.

It was after 5:00 p.m. when they gave up their search and returned to the Abernathy cottage. "Wes, I can't thank you enough," said Rachel, but her voice quivered, and tears gathered in her eyes. "If my pups were here, they'd give you a big lick and nose nibble."

"Don't give up, girls. I have a feeling good news is headed our way," said Wes, opening the door for Rachel and then Penny.

"How can you still be optimistic? We're exhausted, and you are forever the positive soldier," said Penny, defeated. She knew better than to scold him; it certainly wasn't his fault, but she wanted to yell at him. She wanted to yell at someone.

Wes heard his phone ring. He pulled it out of his pocket and held up a finger to Penny, letting her know this was an important call.

"Thank you, Detective. This is the news we've been waiting for. We'll be there in ten minutes."

Rachel and Penny stared at each other in disbelief.

Wes yelled, "They found them! Thanks to you, Rachel. The cameras at the cleaners and the yogurt shop gave them a perfect shot of the dog snatchers. One of them lives on the outskirts of town. He was recognized, and the police were able to track him down and rescue the stolen puppies. They found twenty-two puppies. Can you believe it? Let's get going!"

Rachel and Penny screamed, hugged each other, and jumped up and down. Suddenly, Penny stopped jumping. "Are they sure Darlene, Harold, and Toby are in the bunch?"

Rachel stopped and looked at Wes in a panic. "What if our puppies aren't in the find?"

When I saw you I fell in love, and
you smiled because you knew.
—WILLIAM SHAKESPEARE, *ROMEO AND JULIET*

Chapter 6

"*L*adies, I wouldn't tell you they were found if I wasn't positive they were found. No doubt about it," said Wes. "A vet is at the police station running all the chips in the dogs. Good thing you had them chipped. It made the identification quick and easy."

Penny ran to Wes, and he picked her up. Without hesitation, she pulled his face to hers and kissed him. It was a long, slow, passionate, lingering kiss. Penny looked at Wes in disbelief. "Sorry, what just happened? My apologies; I'm so excited I think I may have kissed you inappropriately."

"There was nothing inappropriate about the kiss. Please keep celebrating if that's how you do it," said Wes with a chuckle.

"You two have plenty of time for kissing and discussing kisses later," said Rachel. "Let's get a move on. I can't wait a minute longer to see my babies."

Rachel and Bobby Abernathy had one daughter, Pamela. Recently, she moved to the campus of Yale to start her freshman year. Rachel was suffering from empty nest, and the puppies were a gift from her daughter, a farewell-mommy gift. Pamela was smart; she knew her mom needed to nurture, and the puppies had secured a special place in Rachel's heart. Penny was hired to help with the pups due to Rachel's hectic social calendar. Bobby and Rachel often traveled out of town, and Penny took care of the fur babies when they were away.

"Wes, are you driving us?" Rachel was beaming with joy; the anxiety on her face had been replaced with sheer delight.

"You bet." Wes opened the door of his SUV for Rachel and Penny. "Let's get this party started." He was glowing. It was rewarding to bring the puppies home. He thought about his family dog—Fred—a beautiful chocolate Lab. In their youth, Wyatt, Nick, and Wes begged their mom and dad every day for a dog. The pestering went on for a year, and finally on Christmas Eve, when he was eleven, his father showed up with a puppy. He never forgot how delighted he was to see Fred sitting by the tree wearing a big red bow. When he moved out of his parents' home to go to college, leaving Fred behind was incredibly hard. He still felt a pang in his heart when he saw a chocolate Lab.

There was a beam of joy resonating in the car, but no one said a word. Penny was deep in thought about the kiss. She'd imagined her first kiss with Wes and had planned it out perfectly in her mind. She didn't plan for it to be in the driveway in front of Rachel. "What's wrong with me?" thought Penny. But each time she scolded herself, she remembered how good it felt to be in his arms. She was certain she'd never been kissed before. "I'm thirty-one, and I just had my first kiss," thought Penny. She laughed out loud.

"Something you'd like to share?" said Wes, glancing in his rearview mirror and catching a glimpse of a giddy, rose-cheeked Penny. He knew the kiss had affected her. He could see it in her eyes. Step one was complete; she knew the chemistry was real. Step two would be harder; he had to get her to embrace the chemistry.

"Oh, I was thinking about how happy Darlene, Harold, and Toby are going to be when they see us."

"So happy," said Rachel. "I want to snuggle with them all night. Extra treats for everyone!" She put her attention back to her phone, rapidly texting Bobby all the details.

Wes smiled to himself. This girl, woman, lady was like none other. He met and dated many women; there wasn't a time he could remember when he wasn't involved with someone. This someone was different. She was the one he'd been waiting for. Although they just met, he was determined to be part of her life. He felt an urgency to find out everything about her. He needed her to trust him first and then, hopefully, love would follow. He knew Penny had placed an emotional wall between them. He assumed it was for protection; he had to find out why.

Wes pulled into the police station, and Detective Simon was outside the building waiting to greet them. Tonight, the detective had a spring in her step and a smile on her face.

"Rachel, Mrs. Abernathy," said the detective, reaching out to shake her hand.

Rachel avoided the handshake, opting for a hug instead. "Please call me Rachel. Thank you so much for your help, for everything." Rachel made a mental note to add the police department to her list of organizations. A large donation would be in order.

"Thank you," said Detective Simon. "Your information was instrumental in getting the ID on these guys."

"Please let me see them. I can't wait any longer." Rachel didn't have to beg her. The detective was happy to oblige.

"Come on, team, let's get you inside and reunited," said the detective, walking quickly to the door. "It's a great day in Greenwich." Detective Simon had been a police officer for ten years. She'd recently been promoted to detective. In fact, the puppy snatch was her first undertaking in her new position. In her line of work, there was seldom such a happy ending, and she intended to revel in this one.

The police station sounded like a kennel. The dogs had been placed in the back of the building. Several interrogation rooms were turned into a doggy day care. The waiting area was crowded, filling up with anxious owners who'd been contacted with the news. A television crew pulled up outside as Rachel, Wes, Penny, and the detective went inside.

"Gosh, they've got a news crew here from New York," said Rachel, following behind Wes. "I can't believe it. Our puppies are famous."

"Oh yes," said Detective Simon. "This is big news, a real positive bust for Greenwich. They've asked me for an interview. Would you be interesting in joining me? I'd love to have some company. I'm a little leery of the camera, not one who likes to be in the spotlight."

"Oh, not me," said Rachel. "I gave up camera interviews when I turned forty." Rachel chuckled. "But I think Penny could help, right, Penny?" Rachel turned to the detective and whispered, "She's such a blessing to us."

"Sure," said Penny nervously. It wasn't something she was comfortable with, but it was hard to say no to Rachel.

Detective Simon guided the group past the crowded room of patient dog parents and down the hall into the makeshift kennel. Rachel and Penny squealed with delight when they spotted them. Rachel snapped up Darlene and Toby, while Penny grabbed Harold.

"My handsome, strong boy," said Penny, kissing Harold on his forehead. Harold returned the love, licking Penny's face and nibbling her nose. "You're such a lover," said Penny, tucking Harold under her arm and scratching his ears.

"My sweet Yorkie babies," said Rachel. "Let's get you out of here and back to your home; you must be starving."

Wes stood back, watching the shower of affection. It was heartwarming, but he didn't think it was a good idea to share spit with a dog. Fred used to lick his face, but sheer kissing was out of the question. Still, it was nice to see Rachel and Penny so happy.

"Rachel, I need you to step inside the detectives' office at the front of the station to sign some papers. It won't take long, but I've got to get out to the news crew," said Detective Simon.

"I'd pretty much sign anything to get them home quickly." Rachel followed closely behind the detective. "Penny, do you mind helping her out with the media. We should be finished and ready to go soon."

"Wes, wouldn't you like to do the interview instead?" asked Penny. He was the hero. The last thing she wanted to do was stand under the bright lights. On the other hand, maybe Kate and Regina would spot her on the news. They'd get a kick out of it.

"I think you'd look better on camera than me," he said, grabbing Harold out of Penny's arms and giving her a little nudge. "I'll take care of Harold while you're occupied."

"Fine, let's do this," said Penny, turning to the detective.

Network Seven had, what felt like, a small movie set in the parking lot of the station. An overly extroverted reporter with heavy makeup rushed to Detective Simon. "Are you ready, Detective? This will only take a few minutes of your time," said the reporter. She turned back to her crew, shouting something Penny couldn't understand.

"Sure, I'm happy to answer your questions, but we're seriously busy. The shorter the interview, the better." Detective Simon pulled Penny forward so they were side by side. "This is Penny; she helped us find the criminals."

"Wow, that's fantastic! I'm sorry, what's your name again? Penelope?"

"Penny. Hi, I'm Penny." Penny reached out her hand for a shake, but the reporter had turned back to the cameraman and ignored the introduction. "We're so happy to have our dogs back." Penny felt awkward but decided to push forward. Maybe the reporter was listening. It was hard to tell.

"Awesome, follow me, it's easy; I'll ask you a few questions and then we'll be done." The reporter seemed to have her cameraman where she wanted him. "OK, Bobby, we're ready to roll."

Wes and Rachel walked out of the station. Harold spotted Penny and began to bark. The news reporter stopped her speech abruptly, distracted by the noise. She looked toward the dog with frustration and then spotted Wes.

"Wes, is that you? Wes Lane," shouted the reporter, crossing over the entire length of the parking lot in hot pursuit.

The cameraman looked at Detective Simon and Penny standing in front of the lights and gave them a shrug of his shoulders. He seemed confused about whether he should follow the reporter or stay put with the officer and the woman. "Pam, where are you going? We've got a story to tell here."

"Wes Lane, is that you?" The reporter rushed over with her microphone, swinging her arms at the cameraman, letting him know not to record.

"Yep, it's me. How are you, Pam?" asked Wes. He knew this wasn't going to play well with Penny.

"I'm doing good, keeping busy, and you?"

"Great, I'm great; we're great." He glanced at Rachel. "I'm helping retrieve some family pets." If he could redirect her attention back to the story, maybe he could squeeze out of the situation without a huge negative on his player scorecard.

"Right, it's a big story," said Pam.

"Better get back to it," said Wes with a wide grin.

"Right, you still have my number; text me," said Pam, realizing the entire crew was watching her.

"Sure I do," said Wes. "Go get 'em superstar; we'll watch from here. The redhead is with us."

⌖

Penny gave the detective a hug and a pat on the back. "We can't thank you enough for your time, dedication, and attention to detail. You're simply amazing." Penny rushed off to join Rachel, Wes, and the pups at the vehicle.

"You were really engaging, Penny," said Rachel. "I won't forget everything the two of you did for us today. You're officially part of our family."

Wes noticed a tear run down Penny's cheek. She wasn't kidding when she told him she was a crier. He witnessed Rachel's pure, heartfelt praise for Penny, and it was touching. This was a beautiful day. It was this feeling of success that he longed for every time the fire truck pulled out of the station, a happy ending which in turn lead to a happy beginning. This would be a new beginning in the life of Rachel and her dogs, and probably a happy beginning of a lifelong friendship between Penny and the Abernathy family. Alone with his thoughts, Wes almost forgot to open the car door for the girls.

"Thank you, Wes. You're such a gentleman." Rachel climbed into the passenger seat.

On the drive back, Penny tickled Harold's stomach, rubbed his ears, and silently thanked God for bringing the puppies back to their family. After seeing the reporter fawn all over Wes tonight, she was convinced her instincts were right: Wes was a player. No doubt about it. The reporter was practically drooling for him. It was absurd. Her negative thoughts regarding *the gorgeous* were confirmed. There was no way she was falling for a man like Beckett again. She would be nice and courteous. After all, he'd worked a miracle. A hero he was; boyfriend material, he was not. Once they got back to the city, she could avoid him. It was for the best. She had to protect her heart.

꒰꒱

"Please stay with me and spend the night," said Rachel when they arrived back at the Abernathy cottage. "It's really too late for you to drive back to the city, and Wes needs a good night's sleep. There's plenty of room for everyone."

"I'd love it," said Wes. "Can you delay getting back until tomorrow, Penny?"

"Absolutely," said Penny. She wanted to make sure the puppies were in good shape and Rachel had settled down before they left her.

"Great," said Rachel as she opened the front door of the cottage. "I'll order some pizza." She sat down on the sofa with a sigh of relief. Toby and Darlene jumped into her lap.

Penny scooped up Harold and checked his body and face for any signs of trauma. "Thank you, Wes," said Penny, holding Harold to her heart.

"For what?" Wes said.

"For everything," said Penny.

"Yes, Wes, thank you for everything. We wouldn't have them back tonight if it weren't for you."

"I'm happy I was able to help," said Wes with a chuckle. "It's always a pleasure to be part of a rescue."

"I can't believe I'm only now inquiring…how did you and Penny meet?" asked Rachel.

"It's a funny story," said Penny, turning her eyes toward Wes.

"Wait, stop there," said Rachel, gathering the pups in her arms and rushing to the kitchen. "Let me order the pizza first."

"Rachel, you can let the pups down. They can walk," Penny yelled toward the kitchen.

Rachel poked her head out. "I know they can walk, Penny, but I don't want to let them go."

"I better go help her."

"She'll probably be overly protective for a while." Wes knew it was typical human nature. After a near tragedy, it was completely normal for people to be more alert and cautious. He felt Rachel needed time to heal. She'd feel safe with the dogs again, but it would be a while before normal behavior returned.

Penny joined Rachel in the kitchen and gently took each puppy out of Rachel's arms and placed them on the floor. "Run, play, frolic," said Penny to the Yorkies and gave Rachel a hug. "Everything is OK now. They need to know life is back to normal."

"Thank you, Penny," said Rachel, returning the hug. A tear ran down her cheek, and she quickly wiped it away. "I'll call the pizza shop. Could you grab some Perrier out of the fridge?"

⸎⸏⸎

"Cheers," said Rachel as she passed the glasses of sparkling water to Wes and Penny. "Now, tell me how you met?"

Wes and Penny took turns telling Rachel the funny story of their introduction. The pizza arrived, and they dived in, occasionally giving the puppies a small bite. When the pizza box was empty, Rachel took them each to their bedrooms.

"Penny, the bathroom is stocked with everything you need, including a toothbrush and floss. If you need anything else, you only need to ask."

"Such a beautiful room," said Penny. "Thank you, Rachel." Penny's phone rang, and it caused them all to jump.

"Wow, your ringtone is loud," said Wes. "I guess you don't want to miss a call."

"It's Kate," said Penny, grabbing her phone out of her bag.

"We'll give you some privacy," said Rachel. "Wes will be one door down if you want to sneak out and visit him during the middle of the night. We're all adults here."

"Hey, that sounds like a great plan," said Wes. "Thank you, Rachel. I had exactly the same idea."

Penny shooed them away with a wave of her hand and closed the door.

"Hey, Kate, what's up? Is everything OK?"

"When are you coming home?"

"Tomorrow. I texted you; we're coming back tomorrow," said Penny, a little confused.

"Thank God," said Kate.

"Are you OK? What's wrong?" asked Penny, sensing the desperation in Kate's voice. "Why are you whispering?"

"Penny, I think I'm pregnant."

To love at all is to be vulnerable. Love anything, and your heart will be wrung and possibly be broken. If you want to make sure of keeping it intact, you must give it to no one, not even an animal. Wrap it carefully round with hobbies and little luxuries; avoid all entanglements. Lock it up safe in the casket or coffin of your selfishness. But in that casket, safe, dark, motionless, airless, it will change. It will not be broken; it will become unbreakable, impenetrable, irredeemable. To love is to be vulnerable.

—C. S. Lewis, *The Four Loves*

Chapter 7

"*W*hat?" yelled Penny. Did she misunderstand her friend? She looked at her phone, checking the volume button.

"I think I'm pregnant," Kate repeated herself.

"How is this possible?" said Penny. "I don't know what to say. When, how, who? Should I be happy for you? I'm sorry this is crazy. What are you telling me?"

"Remember the townhouse I sold two months ago?"

"Yes, the nine-point-five-million-dollar sale. How could I forget? You were so thrilled with your commission."

"Well, I went out with the seller's agent after the closing." Kate felt as if she was confessing a sin to her mother. She toyed with her thoughts all day, trying to decide if she could wait for Penny to get back before telling her. Finally, she decided to call. She needed her best friend's support.

"You mean you had a date with the seller's agent?"

"No, I mean…no. Two colleagues went out to celebrate a successful deal, had a couple of drinks, and wound up back at his place," said Kate. It wasn't something she was proud to admit. Typically, she wasn't the type of girl to lose control. It had been a temporary lack of judgment. However, it happened, and she had to own it.

"I can't believe you didn't tell me about this."

"I know, Penny; it's awful. I wanted to tell you, but I had to keep firm on the hiatus. I know it's crazy; I don't know. It's complicated."

"Kate, who is this guy?" asked Penny. This news was more than a shock. Penny longed to have babies and was often vocal about it. Kate had always been opposed to the idea of babies, saying they were more hype than necessity.

"I mean he's a business associate. I can't believe this is happening. I can't deal with a baby. I can't deal with the conversation. What am I going to do?"

"Kate, I love you. It doesn't matter that you didn't tell me. I'll be home tomorrow, and we'll sit down and think this through," said Penny. She wasn't sure how to proceed. She wasn't qualified to give advice about babies, but she knew one thing: she was opposed to abortion. It would have to be Kate's decision; she wouldn't judge her whatever she decided.

"OK," said Kate. She felt relief; a huge burden had been lifted. At least she told Penny the truth. However, it didn't help the issue; she was still pregnant.

"Where is Regina?"

"She had a stand-up gig tonight."

"Did you tell her?"

"Not yet. I had to tell you first. I feel like I'm going to explode," said Kate. "I don't want to bring Regina into it until I have a plan."

"Go to bed, get some rest. I'll ring you the minute I get back to the city," said Penny.

⌘

Penny closed her eyes and tried to sleep, but her mind was reeling with thoughts of Beckett, Wes, and Kate. She got out of bed and tiptoed down the hall. He was watching television. "Wes," she whispered, unable to bring herself to knock.

The door swung open, and Wes stood in his boxers with his arms open wide.

"How did you hear me?"

"I have good ears. Do you need a hug?"

"I do actually," said Penny, welcoming his embrace and feeling her knees go weak. He looked like an Abercrombie & Fitch billboard guy modeling the latest line of boxers. His arms were strong but not bulky, and she noticed another tattoo on his left shoulder. She could feel her body melting into his. It was a warm, happy place.

"Something wrong on the friend front?" asked Wes. "I couldn't help but hear you scream."

"It's Kate," Penny whispered. She didn't want him to release her from his arms.

"Do you want to talk about it?"

"I'm not sure." She wanted to tell him, but the lure of his body was too much for her. She had to get out of the bedroom.

"Come, sit," said Wes, taking her hand and leading her to the bed.

"I've got a better idea; let's go for a run," said Penny. It was a brilliant idea. She could get some exercise, have a conversation with Wes, and hopefully come up with a plan.

"A run," said Wes. "I'm trying to lure you into my bed and you want to go for a run?"

"When I don't know what to do, a run usually helps me think. Come on, it'll be fun." Penny jumped up with new-found energy.

"You know what else would be fun," said Wes.

"I don't doubt it," said Penny. "Grab your sneakers. I'll meet you out front in five minutes."

"Pizza and a run—OK, water girl, you talked me into it," said Wes, grabbing his sweatshirt and jacket.

Penny bounced out the door, leaving Wes scratching his forehead. He thought she was about to open up to him, and suddenly she was onto something else. "Patience," he reminded himself. "Patience."

Penny was waiting in the driveway doing stretches when Wes joined her.

"I didn't know you were a runner; you keep surprising me," said Wes. He wished she would surprise him and loosen up a little.

"I'm not exactly a runner, much more of a yogi, but I like running when my mind is cluttered; helps me think. What about you, are you a runner?" She did a sun salutation and remained bent over, stretching for her toes. She could feel the tension in her back fading.

"Not really," said Wes with a shrug. "I work out every day at the house."

"The house?" asked Penny. "Inhale into a flat back and exhale down." She continued to do her back stretches.

"The firehouse," said Wes, kneeling down on one knee to retie his sneaker. He always laughed at people on the street making a big ordeal of the stretch before the run. "Just run already," he thought to himself. Penny was one of those people.

"Oh right, I bet you do," said Penny with a wink. "Let's go!"

Wes was still on one knee, but he jumped up quickly to follow her. "Hey, water girl, wait for me," he yelled. "I thought you were still stretching!"

"What's wrong, FD? Am I too fast for you?" Penny was running backward, toying with him to follow her.

Penny and Wes made their way down the long driveway of the Abernathy estate. The naked tree limbs swayed from the weight of the wind, delivering an eerie texture for the night run.

"It's colder than I thought." Penny shivered and rubbed her hands together. "I should've brought my gloves."

"I think snow is on the way," said Wes. "Let's hope it holds off until we get back to the city."

"Yeah, let's hope," said Penny. "Although I love snow."

Penny and Wes jogged in silence. Finally, Wes spoke, prodding Penny for information. "So, what's up with you and Kate? Do you want to talk about it?"

"Kate thinks she's pregnant," said Penny. It wasn't hard to talk to him. He was a good listener.

"Wow, that's huge. I mean, is this happy news?" said Wes. He'd only known Penny and Kate for two days but already felt deeply tangled in their lives.

Penny stopped running. "I don't know, Wes; I'm confused. I want to be happy for her, but this was unplanned, and I know she's confused. What should I do?"

"You should support her decision. Forego advice and let it play out the way she wants it to. That's the best guidance I can give you." Wes reached for Penny's hand. "Take my hand; let me warm you up. You're freezing." Wes covered his hands around hers.

"Thank you. Wes, I'm glad I met you. You're a great guy. I can see us becoming friends," said Penny, leaning into his chest again.

Wes unzipped his down jacket and wrapped Penny inside it, pulling her closer to him. "Let's get one thing straight. I'm happy to be your friend, but I have no intention of staying in the friend department. I want much more, Penny; that I know for sure."

Penny looked up at Wes. "You only met me two days ago; how are you so sure you want much more?"

"I knew it the moment I saw you. I know it sounds corny, but it's true," said Wes. He looked down at Penny with a goofy grin. "How can I get through to her?" thought Wes. He was certain if Penny wanted them to be friends, it could be much harder moving from friendship to romance. He had to think of something and fast. She was complicated, the most beautiful complicated he'd ever met. He wanted to be a part of her life but not just a friend.

Penny stood perfectly still, enjoying the warmth of the jacket and the feel of her body next to his. She was afraid to speak, afraid to hope for love again.

"Penny?" said Wes. "How do you feel about me?"

"We haven't known each other long. I think you're a great guy, but I know you're a player, so I'd rather we be friends."

"Are you kidding me? You think I'm a player. Why would you say something like that?"

Penny pulled back from Wes. He looked sincere. She could tell her words had hurt him. "Look, Wes. I know you get attention from lots of women. I saw the reporter today; she's one of your many girls." Penny realized she was being cold, but she needed Wes to forget about romance. She had too much on her plate right now. She stood chest to chest with Wes, wrapped up in his coat, feeling the electricity from his body warming her toes. "He's amazing," thought Penny, but she couldn't bring her mind to agree with her body. Beckett was there in the romantic parts of her brain like a tumor, not allowing love or passion to flow.

"The news reporter stopped by the fire station one day working on a story. That's how I know her. We went out to dinner twice. I wasn't attracted to her, so I didn't ask her out again. She gives me her number every time I run into her. It was nothing, really. I guess you assume because I work for the fire department, I have women from all parts of the city jumping into bed with me."

"Well, don't you?" said Penny. She knew she was being cold, but she needed Wes to step away.

"No, I mean. I guess I could if I wanted to. Give me a break; that doesn't make me a bad guy. You're tossing me into the friend bag because of my career and because you've made up an idea about my lifestyle."

"But I think you will admit at least part of my idea is true," said Penny, giving Wes an elbow in the side. She needed to lighten the mood. The conversation had become much too serious. Wes was a tough guy, but he had a fragile side, and Penny had stepped on it.

"What are you afraid of? I feel like you're hiding something."

"Ha, you think I'm afraid. Hardly! I'm not a frightened little girl," said Penny.

"Prove it," said Wes, wrapping one arm around her waist and pulling her to him. "Kiss me," said Wes, tilting her head so he could look into her bright-green eyes.

Penny didn't refuse. Their lips met, and she felt the warmth spread down her arms and into her hands. Every part of her body felt warm. She could feel the adrenaline flowing and her heart beating faster. "Wow, that was intense." Penny backed away.

"How can you run from something like this? I feel it too," said Wes.

"I was engaged four months ago. We were in love. He cheated on me. I can't go through it again. It's too soon. I'd only be using you as a rebound boyfriend, and I respect you too much to let it happen," shrieked Penny.

"I'm sorry, but we've all been hurt," said Wes. He reached out to embrace her again. "You're not the first person to be disappointed by another human. It happens; it hurts, but it's life."

"I don't want to make the same mistake." Penny was the happiest she'd ever been with Beckett. She wanted to spend her entire life with him. Looking back, perhaps she saw warning signs and ignored them. Once he betrayed her, she couldn't look at him the same way. Wes was a beautiful man; she could tell he was sincere, but she was scared.

"I promise not to hurt you," said Wes.

"You can't make that promise," said Penny, pulling away from him. "Let's keep running. I don't want to talk anymore."

Wes didn't want to stop talking. He wanted Penny to confide in him, to release her emotions so he could comfort her. "OK," said Wes. "It's getting late, let's head back."

"We're been running against the wind," said Penny. "We need to run with the wind. Let's turn right."

Wes reached for her hand. "Run with me, Penny, run with my love."

"You're too funny; run with your love," said Penny, laughing.

"I'm not kidding at all, Penny." Wes got down on one knee. "Marry me, Penny Robinson, marry me."

For it was not into my ear you whispered, but into my heart. It was not my lips you kissed, but my soul.

—JUDY GARLAND

Chapter 8

"Yes, get up right now," yelled Penny. "I can't marry you!"

"Why?" whispered Wes. "Why can't you marry me?"

"Because I don't want to get married. You can stop with the proposal nonsense. Knock it off, FD."

"As you wish," said Wes, getting on his feet. He clapped his hands together and started running in place. "I see I'm getting nowhere in the romance department."

"I didn't say you were getting nowhere." Penny looked into his eyes and melted. He was hurt. She was harsh. "Why, oh why, is he so stimulating?" thought Penny. "It would be so much easier to resist him if he weren't so intense." One glance at his lips and she could feel the churning in her stomach, an ache to be near him, to touch him. "I'm grateful for your help with the pups, and I like you, Wes Lane. I really like you," said Penny, running back to him and giving him a quick kiss on the lips. "Now let's get going; we've got a city to get back to in the morning."

"You got that right," mumbled Wes. He straightened his shoulders and took a deep breath. She rejected him, but he was smiling on the inside. He was making progress. "Note to self," thought Wes. "She's extremely stubborn."

They jogged silently under the winter moon back to the Abernathy estate. The tap-tap of their sneakers hitting pavement and a slight rustle of the wind were the only sounds they could hear.

❧

Kate and Regina were standing on the corner of Bedford Street, waiting for Wes and Penny's arrival. They waved like cheerleaders when the SUV pulled up to the corner.

"Look at them, like schoolgirls at a parade." Penny pulled on her uggs and reached for her bag in the back seat.

"It looks like they missed you." Wes spotted a parking space close to the corner and put the vehicle in park. Seconds later, he was at Penny's door to open it.

"How do you do that? One minute you're at the wheel and a second later you're at my door. I think you have a superpower."

"I'd love to show you my superpowers." Wes couldn't help but laugh. He joined Penny's friends on the sidewalk.

"I'd like to see your superpowers," echoed Regina. "Every single one of them." Regina was checking Wes out from head to toe. "Hi, I'm Regina, Kate and Penny's friend." She held her hand out for a shake.

Wes hugged her instead. "I've heard a lot about you. I'm looking forward to seeing your show."

"Thank you; I'd love to invite you, but it won't be this week. I'm heading to Atlanta and then to Boston."

"No way," said Penny. "I had no idea you had to leave so soon. Bummer."

"Don't worry, Penny; you know me. I'll be back soon. Give me a hug. Wow, like how lucky are you to get the puppies back?"

"So very lucky. We couldn't have done it without Wes. He was amazing. He had a whole team of detectives waiting for us when we got to Greenwich. He saved the puppies, no doubt about it. Rachel is completely in love with him."

"Thank you again, Wes," chimed Kate. "We owe you one."

"Great, how about you ladies let me take you out to dinner Friday night?"

"I'd love to; I'm free. What about you, Penny? Can you find some time for dinner with us?" questioned Kate. She could hardly wait for Penny to tell her all about the adventure in Connecticut. Kate wanted to hear the good stuff. She tried to read Penny's face. Right now, she was playing it almost too cool. Kate knew it could mean only one thing: he was having an effect on her.

"I guess I can manage to get a Friday night free." Penny searched her mind nervously, trying to find an excuse. She glanced at Kate and then at Wes. "OK, let's do it."

"Great." Wes smiled, and his face lit up. "I'll call Penny with a time and place."

Kate noticed the childish look on his face. He was a kid at heart, and it was clear he was in hot pursuit. If Kate were guessing right, he wouldn't stop until he was successful.

"I'll be in touch," continued Wes. "I hate to rush off, but I've got to get over to the firehouse and see what's going on with my boys." Wes leaned over and gave Penny a kiss on the cheek. "See you soon, water girl."

Penny felt the electricity from the kiss go straight to her toes. "How does he do it?" thought Penny. It was a strange sensation, not a typical turn-on; something so different she secretly longed for it. A walking, talking electric blanket— that's what Wes was.

Kate noticed Penny's pale face turn light pink. It made her laugh, but she turned away, not wanting her friend to catch the awareness.

Penny, Regina, and Kate stood on the sidewalk and watched him drive away. Finally, Regina spoke. "Wow, how did you find him? You must be saying your nightly prayers and living a life of gratitude. Guys like that don't just show up out of the blue."

"Oh, we met at a coffeehouse," Penny answered her nonchalantly. "Didn't Kate tell you?"

"Well, she did tell me. I couldn't believe it, so I thought I'd see if your stories matched up."

"You're hysterical. Do you have time for lunch?" Penny was looking forward to catching up with Regina. It had been two months since her last visit. She always seemed to be on the road, doing her stand-up gigs. "I don't see how you keep up with your busy schedule. Aren't you exhausted? Surely, you need to take some time for lunch!"

"No, sweetie, I'm on my way to the subway. I've got an eleven a.m. flight to Boston. I can grab a snack at the airport. I love you. Keep your chin up." Regina reached over and gave Penny a big hug, grabbed her suitcase, and headed north on Bedford Street. She stopped a block away and threw kisses back toward Kate and Penny, and they returned the gesture.

"I'm always sad when she leaves." Kate stuck her hand in her coat pocket, digging for keys. "Let's go upstairs; I need to talk to you."

"OK." Penny grabbed her overnight bag off the sidewalk and tossed it over her shoulder. A car across the street caught her eye. "It's the same car again," thought Penny. Her mind wasn't playing tricks on her; this was definitely not a coincidence. The man wasn't sitting inside. Penny glanced at Kate. "By the way, I missed you."

"I missed you too." Kate wrapped her arm inside Penny's arm.

"How about Lucy? Did you bond with her?"

"Oh yeah, she's great. She convinced me to give her a belly rub, and apparently I didn't do it exactly to her liking and she snapped at me," said Kate.

"Oh no, really?" Penny laughed and then tried to take it back.

"She won't trick me into it again, that's for sure. She pulled me in with the nose tilt. Then she dropped and rolled over to show me her tummy. I totally fell for it. Oh, sweet

Lucy, I'll rub your stomach. Snap. I will not fall prey to the bling again."

"She'll learn to love you," responded Penny.

"She better." Kate paused on the first flight of stairs. "I missed an open house because of your dog walks."

"Ugh, now you're making me feel guilty. Why are you stopping on the first floor, Kate? I live on the second floor."

"Hello? I know where your apartment is. I'm winded; I don't know why. Sometimes stairs are a breeze, sometimes stairs are a drag. You know. I've seen you huff before. I'm probably exhausted from all the dogs I had to walk."

"OK. You get one more complaint and then I'm cutting you off."

Kate started laughing. "Good thing we're friends or I'd have to come up there and smack you."

"Thank you, Kate, for walking my neighbors' dogs for me while I went to rescue puppies." Penny opened her apartment door. "Oh, home sweet home. I missed you. Hey, Kate, what about the doodles? Didn't you love the doodles?"

"Look, you know I'm not a huge dog fan, but I have to admit those golden doodles are about the hottest thing I've seen lately. Look at us acting like you were away for months; it was only a day and a half." Kate slowly walked into the living room and sat down on the sofa. "I'm so tired."

"Oh, now I know why you're tired. I can't believe I forgot you're so pregnant. My pregnant best friend!"

"Can you believe it?" Kate started laughing and then she began to weep.

"Kate, everything will be all right. Don't cry. We'll figure this out. Think how lucky your baby will be. His or her mom is amazing." Penny sat on the sofa and cradled Kate in her arms. "Of course, I don't have a tissue. You need a tissue; all I have is toilet paper."

"Toilet paper is fine." Sniffled Kate.

Penny retrieved a roll of toilet paper from the bathroom. "Here you go, a big fat roll of toilet paper."

Kate took it from Penny's hands, rolled a huge piece off, and blew her nose into it. "What am I going to do, Penny?" asked Kate through her tears.

"You're going to be a mom. It's so exciting. You're only feeling the shock right now. We haven't gotten used to the idea yet, but I couldn't be happier for you."

"You think I should have the baby?"

"It's your body and your life. I will support whatever decision you make. I think you already know what you want." Penny was counting on their many years of friendship for her bold assumption.

Kate grew up in a happy home. Her parents were still married, and as far as she could tell, they were still in love. Kate always laughed about the perfect family home she'd been raised in. "I do know, but I'm scared. It's huge." Kate smiled. "You know I didn't know I wanted to be a mom, but now here I am. I didn't expect it to happen this way. I only casually know this guy which makes this odd and uncomfortable."

"Are you going to tell him? I think you kind of have to." Penny was proud of how she was drawing Kate out of her grief and into the happy zone. Perhaps it was trickery but in the most pure form.

"Yes, I know. Don't worry. I haven't totally lost my mind."

"I'll be here for you every step of the way." Penny laid her head on Kate's shoulder.

"I know you will be. I couldn't do it without you." Kate sat up straight and blew her nose again. "I feel better now. Thank you."

"Have you told Luke yet?" Kate and Luke were extremely close. She felt lucky to have a brother living in New York City. He was the kind of big brother everyone would love to have. His support and approval meant a lot to Kate.

"No, I haven't. I wanted to think everything out before I broke the news to him." Kate knew Luke would support any decision she made about the baby. He wasn't judgmental or a doomsayer. If she kept the baby, he'd be blissful. If she decided she couldn't handle the responsibility, he'd applaud her for having the courage to say so. She knew he'd be a great uncle, and because of him and Penny, Kate knew she could handle any uncomfortable times headed her way. Besides Luke, Kate had one other sibling—a sister, Marci, who still lived in Santa Monica only a few miles from their parents. She married right out of high school and later secured a degree in nursing and married an architect. They were proud parents of two children, both girls. Kate spoke with her family every week and took at least one trip to California a year. She had mixed emotions about how her parents would react to the news. If she were married, they'd be ecstatic. But under the circumstances, she was bracing for a negative reaction.

"No need to thank. We are friends. Your joy is my joy; your sadness is my sadness. Now let's get excited about our baby." Penny grabbed Kate's hand and pulled her to the floor. "How about a little happy dance?"

In reality, Kate was closer to Penny than her real sister. She knew she could trust Penny with anything. Their friendship was forever, a steady, calm force. It wasn't seasonal or disapproving. They always said they didn't need blood to be sisters, and it was true.

"Really, the happy dance? Right now?"

"Yep, it's a must-do. Hold on, let me put on a happy song." Penny ran to her purse for her iPhone and clicked on the Bluetooth speaker.

The happy dance originated seven years prior. Kate sold her first listings, a coop. When the check arrived in the mail, Penny snatched it out of her hands, and it fell to the ground. Kate rushed to pick it up, Penny reached for it as well, and their heads bumped, causing them to fall backward on the floor. They both grabbed their heads and roared with laughter. When they saw the amount of the check, they broke into a dance.

"I'll do a happy dance if you'll admit Wes is awesome, sexy, and the one."

"Don't get crazy pregnant, hormone-induced lady. I don't need a man. I have too much to do." Penny clicked on

"Heartbeat Song" by Kelly Clarkson and turned the volume up.

"This is a great song for a happy dance. I'll give it a go, but you'll have to bring the energy." Kate pushed herself up from the sofa and joined Penny in the middle of the living room.

A few minutes later, a thunderous knock on Penny's door startled them and put an end to the dancing. "Do you mind with the music?" yelled her downstairs neighbor.

"Ugh." Penny rolled her eyes at Kate and turned down the volume. She walked to the front door but didn't open it. "Sorry, Mrs. Greenberg, we're celebrating some good news with music. I'll keep it down."

A huff was heard through the door and then the footsteps in the hallway.

"We were loud for five minutes and she puffed up here to chastise me. Really, such a grumpy grouch."

"Every building has one," said Kate. "Luke and Billy are going to be so excited." Kate changed the subject. She didn't want Mrs. Greenberg to steal their joy. "You know they'll spoil the baby." Luke had been toying with the idea of adopting a child. He had so much love to offer, and he certainly could afford the process. Kate encouraged him to look into it. The only thing he was concerned about was his work life. If he adopted an infant, he'd have to cut back on some of his work obligations, and he wasn't prepared to do that. Kate suggested a full-time nanny to help with the child. Other successful single parents worked it out, and she felt he could do the same. He agreed with her. It wasn't a question of getting a nanny to help him; he felt he'd be envious of the time the nanny spent with the baby. It was an internal dilemma, and Kate felt sure he'd figure it out in time. She encouraged him to start the investigative process. Now, he'd be an uncle, which was the second-best thing. She'd have family and friends' support, and the thought excited her. The well-known phrase "It takes a village" came to mind, and although she was only two months pregnant, she understood the meaning so much better now.

"And Regina is going to be so happy. She'll be Aunt Regina, the aunt who occasionally pops into town for fun."

"Promise me you won't tell her yet, Penny. I want to see the doctor, get the sonogram, and be further along before I bring her into it." Kate worried about Regina, the youngest of the three women. She thought it was a lonely existence, traveling all the time. Kate and Penny met Regina years ago when she was bartending. They loved her immediately and brought her into their pack. She was going to do open-mic nights in the city. Kate and Penny went to every club night, laughing hysterically to all the punch lines. They knew she had talent and wanted to encourage their friend in her dream career. She kept punching away, and soon she was getting paid to do out-of-town gigs. Penny and Kate were excited for her, but when she sublet her studio in the Lower East Side because she was on the road most of the year, they were worried.

"I wish she had more time off; it seems like a lonely life out on the circuit, alone. Do you think it ever scares her?"

Kate had voiced her concern to Penny on several occasions. She didn't like Regina living out her twenties with only a small suitcase to call home.

"She has the crowd, you know…it keeps her going." Penny understood Regina's choices better than Kate. She thought it was a romantic idea, following your dream. Personally, she wouldn't want to travel that much, because she loved being home. The thought of living out of a suitcase was dreadful, and yet she understood the choice Regina made.

"I hate to bring this up, but it's got me a little stressed out," said Penny, giving Kate a hard look.

"What? Beckett hasn't been calling you, has he?"

"No, but I think I'm being followed. I know it sounds crazy. Like who would want to follow me?" asked Penny.

"That's bizarre," said Kate.

"C'mon, let me show you something." Penny led Kate to her bedroom and pulled back the curtains. "See the guy sitting in the blue car. He was in Greenwich too, and he was in his car watching while Wes and I had breakfast. I don't have any proof that he's tailing me, but I have an odd feeling."

"This is crazy. Who would do something so bizarre?"

"I mean what if he's a driver for someone who lives around here and they had to go to Greenwich at the very same time I went?"

"Possibly. I mean it would be an odd coincidence but definitely possible. Do you have any binoculars?" Kate wanted to see what the guy looked like. It was hard to tell from so far away.

"Oh, I do. My mom gave me a pair for Broadway shows. I like seeing the actors' faces."

Kate gave her a blank look.

"Right, I'll get them." She went to her linen closet and found them in a basket marked "miscellaneous." "Here you go."

Kate sat for a few seconds, staring at the man. "You are not going to believe this, but remember when we were at Blind Tiger and met Luke and Billy?"

"Uh, yeah."

"It's the guy from the corner. The one who was staring."

"No way, let me see." Penny looked through the binoculars. "I can't believe it. You're right. Who is this guy?"

"I don't know. It's creepy; what should we do?"

"I guess we can take a wait and see, or should I go down there and ask him?"

"Ugh, no, I don't think that's a good idea. Who would want to follow you?"

"It could be the firm. I've been day-trading."

"What? Good for you, Penny! Are you kicking it?"

"I'm doing pretty good."

"I'm impressed! Wait, you think they might think you have valuable information or that you're betraying them in some sort of way?"

"That, or they want to mess with me mentally for leaving."

"Yeah, maybe. Or it could be…" Kate hated to say it.

"Beckett," said Penny. "He doesn't like to give things up. I might have been the emotional one in the beginning, but he would have the greater difficulty letting go for real."

"Have you asked an employment attorney if you're doing anything wrong?"

"Yeah, when I left, we ran over my contract, and he said I was in the clear to work for anyone. There was a noncompete clause, but it was only valid for six months after termination or resignation."

"Then you haven't done anything wrong. Ugh, this really bothers me, Penny. Maybe you should talk to Wes about it or go over to the precinct and talk to a detective."

"I'm not telling Wes about it. I just met Wes, and he's already gone out of his way for Rachel and the puppies, and he wouldn't take a wait-and-see option. I don't want to do anything yet. It could be nothing."

"OK, I'll second that, but pay attention and watch your back. I'd suggest you stay with me for a few days, but I'm guessing you'll say no."

"I don't think it's necessary, but I'll keep you posted. Hey, I've got an idea. How about you bring baby daddy to our dinner with Wes Friday night?"

Penny wanted to stop talking about the man in the blue car.

"Are you joking? I never speak to him. I see him occasionally at an open house."

"Lend me your ear, dear friend," said Penny theatrically. "If you bring Phillip into a casual situation with friends, it would make it easier for you to regain communication with him again. It's the perfect plan."

"I'm listening," said Kate.

"We're a group of friends getting together for dinner. It's easy, and it's fun. You restore some form of contact and then it won't be so painful when you have to give him the news."

"It's tricky. I don't like it."

"Kate, it's not a trick. You have to trust me; invite him to dinner. I said yes to Wes, and now you can pick up your phone and invite him to join us."

Kate knew Penny was right, but she was nervous. What if he said no? What if he said yes? What if he was in a relationship? There were so many obstacles in the way. The biggest one was her fear. "I don't know, P. I'm a little scared he'll say no."

"That's OK. If it's a no, we'll ask him next week. You have nothing to lose. Please do me a favor; pick up your phone and text him."

"I'm trusting your instinct on this one. I have absolutely no idea where this is going." Kate picked up her phone and scrolled through the names. "OK, here goes." *Phillip, how are you? I'm going out with a couple of my friends Friday night. Would you like to join us? Could be fun to catch up.*

Kate and Penny huddled around her phone, waiting on a reply. The minutes seemed like hours.

Finally, Penny got up and went to the kitchen. "Kate, would you like a cup of tea?"

"Yes, please," said Kate, wringing her hands and staring at her phone.

Ding.
"OMG, Penny! It's a message from Phillip."

⁂

Regina walked out of the subway station on Roosevelt Avenue and found the line for the express bus to LaGuardia Airport. She didn't love traveling, but it was a part of her life, so she tried to embrace the long lines, the shuffling of bags, and loud children running around the airport. She brought her Kindle with her everywhere and was an avid reader. It was a habit she picked up as a child, getting lost in a book. Regina grew up in Smyrna, a small town on the outskirts of Nashville, Tennessee. She was born Regina Thigpen but used Regina Rae as her stage name because she loved the Sally Field character, Norma Rae, in the movie *Norma Rae*. In fact, she was completely in love with Sally Field and her work. Regina Rae was twenty-nine years old and fell in love with Sally when she was fourteen. While her friends were at the skating rink, she was sitting at home watching Sally Field's movies. When she needed a break from movie watching, she checked out books from the local library and immersed herself in the words on the page, acting out scenes in the privacy of her tiny bedroom, which was actually a closet. Her parents weren't poor; they were considered middle class, but with so many children to feed and house, she felt lucky for whatever she had. Her father worked at a local car factory, and her mom was a cashier at a grocery store. They worked hard to provide a good life for their children. It wasn't always easy. Regina considered herself odd and didn't mind it when her friends at school reminded her. Looking back at her childhood and high-school days, it didn't surprise her that she found comedy. It was her way of coping with being different. She saved a little money working at Burger King her junior and senior years, and after she graduated, she bought a bus ticket to New York City. Her parents didn't try to stop her. "We'll be here waiting for you, sugar, if you want to come home," her mama said. "With open arms, baby," her daddy chimed. They gave her a hug and a kiss and waved good-bye.

Regina got a job at a restaurant, waiting tables, the first day she arrived in the city. It took her three months before she was able to find a place to live. The restaurant manager never suspected she was living on the street for the first three months of her employment. The money she arrived with was enough to buy her a gym membership, which is where she showered. Fortunately, she moved to the city in July and didn't have to worry about freezing when she napped on a park bench. An ad on Craigslist caught her eye…*NYU student, Lower East Side—seeking female roommate.* She answered it and moved into a studio with Valerie, a junior studying premed at NYU, the next day. It was perfect. She loved everything about the tiny apartment and the trendy, yet grungy, neighborhood. It was a third-floor walk-up, and the room measured about eighteen feet by sixteen feet, which left plenty of room for two twin beds, a small sofa, dresser, and television. There were two large closets, plenty of room for the few items Regina owned. The bathroom, which was separate from the main room, had black-and-white 1960s' ceramic tile throughout. Regina found it charming. Valerie stayed at her boyfriend's apartment all the time, so Regina had the place to herself. When Regina arrived home from a long shift at the restaurant, her tiny home gave her joy. Occasionally, Valerie would stop by to pick up some clothing or toiletries, and they became close friends over time. Regina went out with Valerie and her friends for drinks and clubbing. They loved hearing her stories and her self-deprecating jokes.

"You should totally do an open-mic night," said Valerie one night, roaring with laughter over Regina's tale. Her friends agreed. "You have to, Regina; it's your calling."

A week later, Regina took the stage at a club near campus in the East Village. She rocked the crowd, which consisted mainly of NYU students, including Valerie and her friends. Regina was hooked; she couldn't stop writing comedy and performing. She went to every open-mic night in the city as often as she could and slowly began to receive real bookings at clubs in New York City, which were coveted spots for all co-medians. Her career began to take off, and whenever she had a few extra dollars, she would fix something in the apartment, giving it a fresh coat of paint, replacing the old coffee maker, or getting a new stove installed.

After Valerie graduated from NYU, she applied to medi-cal school and was accepted. Regina was sad to see her leave the city but knew their friendship would last a lifetime. Regina continued to hang out with Valerie's friends, the ones who stayed in New York. She traded waiting tables for bartending, which gave her a better income. After Valerie moved out, Regina was able to put the rent-stabilized apartment in her name. Her landlord had noted her appreciation of the building and the improvements she made to her living space. When her agent insisted she had to spend a solid year on the club circuit, Regina found a trusted friend to babysit her apartment. Kate and Penny worried about her, being on the road doing comedy all the time. They were only a few years older than Regina but treated her like a little sister. The comedy tour was fun, but she could hardly wait to move back to the city in May, back to her tiny apartment. She missed the comforts of home, waking up in her own bed. It was the only adult home she'd ever had and couldn't imagine ever giving it up.

She placed her MetroCard in the slot, dragging her small suitcase up the steps and making her way to the back of the bus. In a few hours, she'd be in Atlanta. She was booked to perform seven nights in Atlanta and then she'd go to Boston for a week. Valerie was living in Boston, doing her residency at a hospital downtown. Regina could hardly wait to see her again. It would be a delightful reunion.

And above all, watch with glittering eyes the whole world around you because the greatest secrets are always hidden in the most unlikely places. Those who don't believe in magic will never find it.

—ROALD DAHL, *THE MINPINS*

Chapter 9

"What did he say?" Penny put her cup of tea on the counter and joined Kate on the sofa.

"He said he'd love to meet us for dinner," said Kate, staring at her phone.

"What else? What else does he say?"

"OK, I'll read you the whole text." *Kate, it's so great to hear from you. I've been thinking about you. Time gets away. Well, you know, you're an agent. But, yes, I would love to meet for dinner. What time, where?*

"Great, sounds like he's excited. I like him already."

"Penny, I have to text him back. Where are we going, and what time?" Kate paced around in circles, wringing her hands. Kate felt she was in a dream. She didn't expect to get pregnant, not now, not this way. How could she have been so irresponsible? She was meticulous about everything. Every decision she made in her life was carefully thought through. The universe was laughing in her face. She kept replaying the night in her mind. What could she have done differently? For starters, she could have toasted with Phillip over one drink and then gone home alone. She didn't want to regret the experience, which would be the same as regretting the baby. She wanted to be happy, to forgive herself for being irresponsible in one of the biggest ways possible. This wasn't like buying the wrong pair of tennis shoes or even purchasing the wrong home. All of those things could be remedied. This could not. If she had an abortion, she'd never be able to fully forgive herself. Why hurt an innocent child for the mistake she made? Wouldn't that be two mistakes? If only she could turn the guilt around and see it as a blessing! Penny often said everything happens for a reason; don't fight the universe if you don't have to. It was easy to say but hard to do. She had to put one foot in front of the other and deal with the issue. There was no running away.

"Tell him you'll get back to him with details and then text Wes and ask him. Kate, don't be nervous. I'll text Wes if you want me to."

"Yes, please," said Kate with a sigh. "I'm so nervous. Hi, Phillip, thanks for meeting us for dinner, and by the way, I'm having your baby."

"That's not exactly what I said. Let's get to dinner first, please, and then we can plan the next step." Penny picked up her phone and texted Wes. She couldn't decide whether to let him in on the details. Not now, but later she'd have to tell him. He already knew Kate was pregnant. She'd have to tell him not to say anything. Although, he wasn't an idiot, so she wouldn't have to worry about him blurting something out. While Kate was busy with her phone, Penny ducked into her bedroom and called Wes, letting him know the plan and getting the information for the Friday-night dinner.

"Penny, where are you?" Kate yelled from the living room. She was jumpy and nervous. "This is happening to me" kept running through her mind. "Penny, could you come in here and pinch me, please?"

`"I'm talking to Wes," yelled Penny. She stepped out of her bedroom and grabbed a pen and paper off her desk, scribbling down the name of the restaurant and time. "OK, speak to you soon, Wes. Kate and I will meet you there." Penny hung up the phone and handed the paper to Kate. Then she gave her a big pinch on the arm.

"Ouch," yelped Kate. "It's me; I'm not dreaming. Thanks, Penny." Kate eyed the piece of paper. "Oh, that's cool. He wants to go to Raven? I haven't been there in a long time."

"I suggested it. He wanted someplace quiet. Maybe we can sit in the outdoor garden."

"It's December, remember? I don't think we'll be able to sit outside."

Penny laughed. "You're right. I don't know what I'm thinking. Well, it doesn't matter; in or out, typically it's not a loud restaurant." She'd never seen Kate so worked up. It was totally understandable. It would be a huge event for anyone, but the fact it was happening to Kate made it extra huge. Her life plan was mapped out meticulously. This had not been part of it. She watched Kate trying to digest the enormity of it all.

"Yeah, I like it. The dinner burger is good. Don't we usually order the hamburger when we go there?" Kate paused to think. "Last time we went there, I think we ordered burgers."

"The salads are good, so is the chicken. Look at us; we're such New Yorkers, we're planning what to order a day before we go to the restaurant."

Kate laughed. "You know it's true." She picked up her phone. "OK, I'll text Phillip and let him know." She glanced again at the paper on the counter. "He wants to meet at six? Are we senior citizens going for the early-bird special? What's up with dinner at six o'clock?"

"I don't know. I guess he has a reason. I didn't get into the how or why? Maybe he has to work a late shift?" Penny was relieved Wes would be with her at this occasion. She watched him work like a pro under pressure in Connecticut. He truly had a gift for making people feel relaxed. She smiled to herself, feeling confident Wes could make Phillip feel at ease.

"You're right. I bet he has to swing an all-nighter. OK, no worries." Kate started to text Phillip. "I wonder if he'll think I'm nuts asking him to a six o'clock dinner!"

"Text him please and stop complaining," said Penny, handing Kate a glass of water. Penny went back to her bedroom and pulled the curtain so she could get a look at the street. The blue sedan was still parked across the street. The man was sitting in the driver's seat, again, with a newspaper. How could it be a coincidence? She pondered, "Who would want to know what I'm doing every minute of the day, and why?"

‹·›

"Look, Kate, I saw a snowflake." Penny looked up at the winter sky. "It's so pretty, the first flake of the season."

"It's snowing. I wanted snow and it's here! It's really coming down now." For a moment, Kate thought it was romantic, standing on the corner waiting on the baby daddy. Then reality tapped her on the shoulder. "This isn't a movie; this is real life, and there isn't always a happy ending."

"I hope we get six feet." Penny held out her hand, trying to catch a flake. She glanced at Kate and noticed a scowl on her forehead. "Don't think about it too much, Kit-Kat. It'll be fine." She used Luke's term of endearment for Kate. It made her smile, and she gave Penny a side-by-side hug.

Wes spotted Penny as he fast-stepped it down Grove Street. He snuck up behind her, reaching his arms out, pretending to catch a flake too.

Penny jumped. "Wes, you scared me. Don't you know it's not polite to sneak up on girls?"

"Oh, tonight you're a girl. That's great news, a young innocent girl. I think I might have a chance getting you to say yes to marriage instead of no."

"What?" screeched Kate. "Am I missing something?" Kate couldn't believe her ears. "Are you telling me you asked Penny to marry you?"

"I did, and she turned me down." Wes was letting Kate in on his secret. He knew she was a fan; he could tell. In his mind, he figured, it could only help, not hurt. What woman didn't love a guy who asked her best friend to marry him?

"Penny, you didn't tell me any of this."

"He's kidding with you, Kate. Wes likes to play games. He doesn't want to marry me."

"Bite your lip, Penny. There's nothing else in the world I want more." Wes started to get down on his knee, but Penny grabbed his coat collar.

"Wes, stop it right now. I swear I will turn around and walk home." Penny gave him a hard look. He was being ridiculous.

"Penny, stop being mean!" Kate reached out and pulled Penny's arm toward her. "What are you doing?"

"Kate, he's being silly. He's figured out how to push my buttons. Don't encourage him, please." Penny spotted a handsome guy walking toward them. "Is that Phillip?" asked Penny, distracting Kate from the marriage talk.

Kate whipped her head around to check out the man approaching. "No, that's not Phillip. But I see him crossing Bleecker Street. He's the tall guy in the black coat."

"Dark brown hair?" questioned Penny.

"Yep, that's him. Ugh, what am I going to say? Maybe this was a bad idea." Kate wanted to run away. She thought of jumping in a cab and going to her brother's house. He'd hold her in his arms and tell her everything was good. She was too hard on herself. She was human; humans make mistakes no matter how hard they tried to be perfect. Her big brother always had the right words at the right time.

"This is not a bad idea. You didn't tell me he was so handsome and tall. Play it cool, Kate. He doesn't know what we know. We're four friends meeting for dinner."

Before Kate had a chance to run, Phillip appeared in front of them. He reached out his arms and gave Kate a warm hug and a gentle kiss on the cheek. "I was so glad to hear from you, Kate. Thanks for reaching out. It's so good to see you."

The hug was nice. She felt her body relax and went into full professional mode. "It's great to see you, Phillip. Let me introduce you. This is my best friend Penny and her friend Wes. We're so happy you could join us."

"Great to meet you, Phillip," said Wes as he reached out his hand for a shake.

"Kate mentioned the two of you work together, or at least you're in the same business, right?" asked Penny. She knew exactly what Phillip did and whom he worked for, but she thought she'd pretend he was only casually mentioned.

Kate gave Penny a thumbs-up smile. She could feel her hands growing sweaty in her gloves. It was cold out; how could she possibly be sweating?

"Kate and I don't exactly work together, but our paths do cross on occasion. I'm with Simon and Blackwell Realty. We have multiple listings in the West Village and Chelsea right now. Didn't Kate tell you about the townhouse we sold a couple of months ago?"

"I think you mentioned something about a brownstone," said Penny, turning to Kate for validation.

"I told you, Penny. I was so happy with the commission, remember?"

"Oh yeah, you treated me to a mani-pedi the following Saturday."

"Exactly." Kate directed her attention back to Phillip. "That was a nice one, wasn't it? Hopefully something even better is right around the corner."

"You've got a four-story brownstone in the meat-packing district. I've got a prospective buyer, so it might happen faster than you think," said Phillip. He reached for Kate's hand.

"I love that brownstone. I think it's going to sell fast." Kate was comfortable discussing business. She could talk about brownstones and penthouses in her sleep. Perhaps, she should have labeled this meeting as "business." It would have been safer. Now, she was on a date, or at least the resemblance of a date. She was completely at a loss. There was no other occasion in her life she could draw from. This was absolutely a stand-alone moment.

"I hate to interrupt the real-estate conversation, but could we continue it inside? I'm starving," said Wes, opening the door for Penny.

"Of course," chimed Kate. "We're being rude with the shoptalk."

"Not at all rude. I'd love to hear more about it after we sit down," said Wes. "A table for four, please." Wes smiled at the hostess and had her in his corner immediately.

"Of course, follow me." The tall, slender brunette blushed.

Penny leaned over to whisper to Kate. "Unbelievable, is everyone in this city a model? Look at her; she's completely beautiful."

"I know and totally smitten with Wes. You and I are going to have a long talk later. I can't believe you didn't tell me about the proposal."

"Kate, he's not serious. He's kidding. You know we just met, and big exclamation point: I don't want a boyfriend."

"Ladies," said Wes. He pulled out a chair from the table, offering it to Penny. "Or should I say, 'Here's a chair, young fragile girl'?" Wes chuckled.

"Ha-ha, thank you, FD." Penny had to admit his silliness was a welcomed distraction. Phillip didn't seem uncomfortable, but Kate was a ball of nerves. She was covering it pretty well, but Penny could tell she was anxious.

"FD?" questioned Phillip.

"Wes works for the fire department," said Kate. She couldn't believe this was actually happening. Phillip was here. She had to take a deep breath. A stay-calm mantra was running through her mind.

"You're kidding." Phillip's eyes lit up. "I have so much respect for you guys. I wanted to be a fireman. I went through all the initial tests and paperwork, but I didn't make the cut."

"That's hard to believe," said Wes. "I think you'd make a great addition to the fire department. If you're still interested, I could try and help you out."

"It's a dream. Thanks, man; I really appreciate it. We'll exchange numbers. I've got a great gig now with real estate, but my first choice was your career."

The conversation between Wes and Phillip made Penny smile. It was always fun to eavesdrop on a guy-on-guy conversation. She could sense the positive energy between them and thought it was sweet. Phillip was extremely handsome. She could understand how Kate was taken with him. She knew they'd been toasting their good fortune with martinis, thus letting down the walls of reason and good judgment, which was foreign to Kate. If first impressions meant anything, he was a catch. Penny was excited Kate's baby daddy was a ten.

"We've got a huge fire-department bonfire cookout planned next Friday night. You could all come as my guests. How about it, everyone? Want to experience a party like you've never experienced before?"

"A party? In the country?" Kate was mouthing words to appear interested in the conversation.

"Yep. My brother Nick has a place in the country, eighty acres of sweet solitude. This is our sixth year in a row, a tradition. It's mad, crazy fun, and it's for the kids. We turned the party into a toy-and-food drive. It's awesome." Wes was proud of the event he created, and organized and appreciated his brother's involvement. When he first mentioned it to Nick years ago, Wes thought it would be a great party space. He wasn't thinking of charity; he was thinking beer, band, and brothers. It didn't occur to him until later in the planning that it would be a great tool to bring in a huge amount of goods for those in need. Years later, Nick and Wes were amazed and proud of what it had turned into.

Kate glanced at Penny with a let's-go look. "It sounds amazing. Where do the toys and food go?"

Penny couldn't believe Kate was interested. Surely, she was only making small talk.

"It's grown into a huge event. A few years back, we took in so many donations we had to ask for help. We reached out to the church of New York, and they partnered with us. We truck all of the contributions to their warehouse in the Bronx, and they distribute it to the kids of Greater New York. You wouldn't believe how many people we've reached." He knew from their trip to Connecticut that Penny didn't like to leave the city. It was like an allergy to her. She got wired, itchy, and stressed out just thinking about getting in a car and leaving Manhattan. He found it adorable, but she took it serious. Her comfort level was the city, and he could tell it was going to take all of them to convince her that it would be fun.

"Is it the whole fire department?" questioned Phillip. He was intrigued.

"Yep, everyone is invited, friends and family as well. Of course, a lot of people have to work; we can't shut the city's needs down. A full staff will be at each firehouse, but anyone who's lucky enough to have Friday and Saturday off will be there. We have a band, parking, and full security. It's like a fire-department Woodstock for charity."

"Live musicians or a wedding band?" asked Kate. She narrowed her eyes back at Penny and nodded her head toward Phillip.

"Live musicians," said Wes.

"Sounds like a blast. I'd love to go," said Phillip. "I can take the weekend off, especially since Kate and I are going to nail a brownstone deal in the meat-packing district."

"How far out of the city are you talking? I'm not fond of leaving the island."

"It's about an hour-and-half drive. It's totally worth it, water girl. We can all sleep at my brother's house. He's got plenty of room. The hotels and inns in the neighborhood have been booked up for months. We have buses and vans taking guests to their sleeping quarters. There's no drinking and driving. In fact, we're so strict about it; the guests have to show their hotel receipt to the bus driver before they're allowed to go to the party."

"It sounds like a huge wedding reception." Kate laughed out loud. "I love big weddings."

"Typically about three to four hundred people show up," said Wes proudly.

"Shut up. You're kidding us," said Penny. "Don't you have to have the town's approval or something?"

"They love it. It's completely legit. It gets bigger every year. We plan a year in advance. They look forward to it. We bring a lot of business to the little town, and my brother's house is so remote, no one ever complains."

"What does your brother do? Is he in the fire department too?" Phillip thought it was a genius plan. He'd been working nonstop for months. A weekend out of town was exactly what he was looking for. Plus, it would give him some alone time with Kate.

"Nope, he's a dentist on the Upper East Side. Six years ago, I spent a weekend at his place. 'This would be a great place for a party,' I told him. He said, 'Let's do it.' That's how it all began." Nick was the oldest of the three brothers. He was their mother's favorite son. Wes and Wyatt grew up closer because Nick was always clinging to their mom. Now, as adults, the three brothers laughed about it. The event brought Nick and Wes closer as brothers and friends. It forced them to work as a team, and they enjoyed it. The event was so successful for its charitable contributions that even the fire-department brass endorsed it.

The waitress approached the table with her hands full.

"I ordered some appetizers for the table," said Wes with an uncomfortable snicker. "Sorry, I was starving. Let's all share; dig in, everyone."

"Here's your fried calamari, tuna tartare, and vegetable dumpling," said the waitress, sliding some water glasses to the side to make room for the food.

Kate took one whiff of the fried calamari and felt her stomach turn. She tried to fend it off but with little success. "Penny," mumbled Kate. "I've got to go to the ladies' room." She dropped her napkin and ran to the back of the restaurant.

"Gosh, I better check on her!" said Penny, jumping up from the table to follow Kate. She didn't even think about food making Kate sick to her stomach. "Darn, why did Wes have to order something like fried calamari? It was yummy, but clearly there was a pregnant woman at the table," thought Penny. "Whatever, how could I expect him to think of which food were appropriate for pregnancy?" She found Kate hovering over the toilet in the ladies' room and tried to console her.

"Thanks for ordering the food. I love this stuff." Phillip plowed into the calamari. "I guess the smell of it didn't suit Kate. Did you see her? She was really pale. I wonder if I should go check on her."

"No, let Penny do it. You know how chicks are. They like to team up in the bathroom." Wes knew exactly what was going on. He tried to play it off as if it was nothing, but he could tell Phillip was fascinated. He silently wished he'd ordered something bland.

"Yeah, I guess you're right. I'd love to swing the weekend party, though; sounds like a lot of fun." Phillip was calculating how many business cards he could pass out. He was succeeding as an agent, but it was always good to meet a new group of people, and he was sure there would be plenty of potential homebuyers in the crowd.

"You and the girls can ride with me. I plan on heading up around four in the afternoon next Friday. The bonfire and party start at eight. It's so much fun, you'll meet a lot of cool people." Wes knew he was playing a little dirty. He figured

Kate would want to go if Phillip was interested, and in return Penny wouldn't let Kate go alone. Mission accomplished.

"Sounds awesome. You don't think Kate is coming down with something, do you?"

Wes glanced behind him and spotted Penny heading back to the table. "Here comes Penny." Wes looked like an eight-year-old schoolboy with a big crush and a secret.

"She's fine. A little nauseous, that's all." Penny wondered if she should come up with some story about Regina having the flu and giving it to Kate. She decided to play it off and hope no questions were asked.

"Are you sure? Should I go check on her? I feel bad; I haven't spoken with Kate in two months, and I just, well… I'm happy to see her again."

"Aww, incredibly sweet. Maybe you'll rub some sweetness off on FD here."

"Whoa, I'm as sweet as Southern iced tea," said Wes, "as long as you don't pour it on me."

Wes and Penny both laughed out loud.

"Am I missing something?" questioned Phillip. The two of them were like a comedy team without even knowing it. There was a lot of sexual tension between them. Phillip could see Wes was totally into Penny, and she was soaking it in like a sponge.

"First time I met Penny, she poured an entire cup of ice water on my shirt," said Wes.

"I was so embarrassed." Penny giggled, thinking about the weird experience in the coffee shop. It seemed as if it were months ago. "You'll find out, if you hang out with us long enough, I'm a little clumsy. My friends don't call me clumsy, though; they refer to me as 'body control challenged.'"

"That's a great first impression," said Phillip, chuckling. "I see it didn't keep you from asking her out."

"She had me at hello," said Wes, laughing.

Phillip gave him a high five. He liked Wes—a tough guy, for sure, but also easy to talk with. Kate told Phillip about Penny on their drunken night together. She was exactly how he pictured her: spunky, edgy, and extremely attractive in a weird sort of way.

"I'm sorry to break up the bro party. Here comes Kate now. She's looking fresh and calm. I wonder if Regina gave her the flu. Let's hope not." The moment she said it, she regretted it. She was coming up with lies to cover for Kate's nausea.

"I'm so sorry, everyone. The smell of the calamari hit me the wrong way. I've always had a thing about calamari. It's a long story; trust me, you don't want to hear it."

"Kate," said Phillip, getting up to pull out her chair, "are you sure you're feeling better? I can take you home if you don't feel well." Phillip had thought about Kate for two months. She had a reputation in the real-estate world for her ability to close deals like nobody else in the business. He was intimidated by her success and standing in the real-estate community. He knew the martinis were the reason they wound up in bed together, and it embarrassed him. It wasn't planned; he hoped she knew that. He'd picked up the phone to call her several times and lost his nerve.

"No, it's OK. I wouldn't mind having something to eat, but an early night would be awesome. I'm exhausted; thank you for being so understanding." Kate's eyes locked with Phillip's.

"Oh my God," said Phillip. He froze in his chair.

"What?" said Kate. "What's wrong?"

"You're pregnant!"

I would rather spend one lifetime with you,
than face all the ages of this world alone.
—J. R. R. TOLKIEN, *THE LORD OF THE RINGS*

Chapter 10

Penny and Wes sat in silence, neither taking a bite of food or a sip of water. All eyes were on Phillip.

"Kate, I have three older sisters; I've seen this. I know this. You're pregnant."

"Phillip, I don't know what to say," Kate mumbled.

The look on her face told Phillip he was right. "Kate, I'm so sorry I haven't been around. I've thought of you every day since we spent the night together." He got up from his chair and walked around the table to Kate. "This is huge. Can we get out of here and talk?" His words were steady and calm.

"That would be great. Yes, thank you." Kate turned to her best friend. "Penny, I'll speak with you later tonight. Everything will be fine; don't worry." She took Phillip's hand, and they walked out of the restaurant.

Penny wanted to run after her. She wanted to stop them from leaving without her. There was a pang in her heart, and she buried her face in her hands.

"Penny." Wes nudged her. "It's going to fine; don't worry. She knows what she's doing. I know it's a hard moment for you." He reached under the table and grabbed her hand.

"What if he hurts her? What if he's angry? What if he blames her for being irresponsible?" Penny's mind was reeling with negative thoughts.

"He seems like a solid guy to me. Also, he was surprised but definitely not angry. Remember, he took the risk along with her. I'm sure he knew there was a chance this could happen. Trust me, guys always think about the possibility."

Penny's eyes filled with tears. "This is so huge for Kate. She didn't even want to ask him to dinner. I forced her to; it's my fault this is happening." Penny was searching her mind for a solution. "If only I could go back to yesterday, I'd never put her in this situation."

"Penny, tomorrow you might say, 'This is the best thing I ever did for my friend.' She had to tell him eventually. I know you weren't planning on telling him tonight, but things happen sometimes to push the plan forward. I think it's a good thing; it's out in the open. Now Kate won't have to worry about how she's going to tell Phillip. Let's focus on the positive; the romantic wheels are in motion. Penny, get out of your head and into your heart. You did the right thing for your friend and for Phillip. Now, how about some dumplings? The food is getting cold, and you need to eat."

"I'm not sure I can eat now," said Penny with a pout. She contemplated Wes's words. "I guess you're right, but I'll be a nervous wreck all evening until I hear from her."

"You know there is a tried-and-true activity between two people which has been proven to take your mind to other places and relieve stress."

"Really?" Penny looked at Wes with exasperation. She was in pain, and he was hitting on her. "You're so predictable."

"I'm just saying. I'd be willing to participate in order to help you relax." Wes knew he had no chance of getting Penny into bed tonight, but he was aspiring for the wear-her-down option.

Penny picked up a dumpling and popped it in her mouth. She couldn't really taste anything. Since the collapse of Penny and Beckett, she hadn't been able to taste food. She continued to eat but got little pleasure from it. It occurred to her, she hadn't thought of Beckett for days. Kate was pregnant, and Wes was a distraction, both interrupting her constant thoughts of the breakup.

"Well, if I can't get you to spend the night with me, how about I order you a glass of wine?" The stressed look on Penny's face led Wes to believe he'd have to be extremely charming this evening. She was worried about Kate, and he'd have to come up with something entertaining to keep her distracted.

"I didn't say I wouldn't spend the night with you. I'm not ready for intimacy. Wes, I think I've made it clear; I'm not ready for a relationship. I'm not ready to lose my best friend." Penny looked at Wes with a shocked look on her face. "I can't believe I said that."

"Penny, you're not losing your best friend." Wes put his arm around her. "I can see how attached you and Kate are; the baby won't take that away, nor will the man."

"Wow, I'm really a case for a therapist, huh?" Penny wasn't aware she was scared of losing Kate until she spoke it. She felt a mix of emotions about the pregnancy. She wondered if the baby would alter the easy ebb and flow of her relationship with Kate. Change was always a hard pill for Penny to swallow.

"Nah, it's modification. You know, it can be stressful and alarming." Wes had witnessed the bond of friendship between the two women. He wasn't really great with girl talk, although in his line of work he had to ease emotions in stressful situations. Penny needed his strength tonight, and he was going to be there for her.

"How are you so good at this? I know I give you a hard time FD, but I'm glad you're here with me. Thank you for stepping into my screwed-up life."

"I don't think it's so screwed up. Let me see now. You take care of pets, which you love. They give you great love in return. You have a best friend with whom you share a special bond, and you met a great guy recently who's crazy about you."

Penny loved hearing the words. She pondered what Wes was saying. He had no idea how deeply Beckett had hurt her. She wanted to let him in, but she couldn't. It was too soon, and she was tired of hearing herself talk about it. "It sounds pretty good when you describe it for me."

"Look, I know you had an intense relationship end, Penny. We're in our thirties. Most everyone our age has loved someone and lost. What's the saying? It's better to have loved and lost…"

"Nope, you are not quoting the nineties standard love-and-lost blurb, are you?"

"Are you impressed I know it?"

"Not in the least. Yes, let's order a glass of wine and make a toast to Kate, Phillip, and the baby. Maybe it will bring them good luck." She was trying to stay positive about the baby, but Penny knew a lot of things could go wrong in childbirth. A chill ran through her.

"You got it, water girl. Did you know the love-and-lost quote is from Hemingway?"

"Get out, I didn't know that. How do you know that?"

"I'm smarter than I look?" Wes laughed. "I'm not sure, but it was Ernest Hemingway. You're making fun of Ernest Hemingway."

"No way." Penny laughed but felt a little embarrassed. "I'm not sure I believe you. I'll google it."

"Google away and you'll see." Wes caught the eye of the waitress. She bounced over to the table with a wide grin.

"The other two people in our group had to leave, but we'd love two glasses of wine." Wes stopped and looked at Penny. "I don't even know whether you like white or red." He had never wanted to know every single thing about a woman until he met Penny Robinson. He wanted to know her favorite color, food, vacation spot, movie, and music. The list went on and on.

"I like both, but let's go with white this evening. A glass of Chardonnay would be lovely." Penny had her face in her phone, but she looked up quickly and managed a "Thank you" to Wes.

"I will have the same," said Wes. "Note to self," thought Wes. "She likes wine, both red and white."

Penny couldn't help but smile as she watched the waitress mesmerized by his words. She knew it was his eyes. Wes could put anyone under his spell with his magnetic eyes. He was so perfect; it was hard to keep batting him off. She'd love to get tipsy and take him home with her.

"Penny," said Wes. "Wes to Penny, can you read me?"

"Sorry, Wes; I was drifting, lost in my thoughts. You are correct; it is a quote from Hemingway. I'm impressed with your knowledge. By the way, are you sure you should be drinking wine? I thought you had to work tonight. You can't have alcohol before you clock in, can you?"

"First of all, we don't say 'clock in.' Second, I did have to work when I made this early dinner date for the four of us. But I traded a shift with a buddy of mine. You've got me all night. I'll keep you company until you hear from Kate, so you don't have to worry alone."

"Well, that's incredibly kind of you," said Penny. "I appreciate your concern and your company." Penny thought, "Perhaps, he wasn't a player after all, or was there a time in every player's life when he decided the game was over and wanted to settle down with one woman?"

"I'd also like to bring up one important fact. Clearly, you can date me now because I'm pretty sure getting pregnant on a three-month hiatus from men means Kate lost the bet." Wes chuckled.

"Oh my gosh, you're right, Wes. The hiatus is a bust." In the hustle and bustle of the news of the baby, the dinner date, and Phillip, Penny had given no thought to the wager. She'd won the bet.

Wes grinned from ear to ear. "You're just realizing it? It's true! You're a free woman, Penny Robinson."

The waitress arrived with two glasses of wine. She carefully placed them on the table in front of Wes, making sure he got a glance of her boobs.

"Seriously, could she have been more obvious?" Penny wasn't the jealous type, but it was clear the waitress was hitting on Wes. It was annoying.

"I didn't even notice." He noticed, but he wasn't going to admit it to Penny. She wanted every reason to put him on the friend list. He had to get off that list and onto the romance list. It was going to be difficult enough without him acknowledging a nice rack.

"You didn't notice her putting her boobs in your face?"

"Look, I mean, I think maybe she's proud of her appearance, but hitting on me would be taking it a bit far. I think she shows a little to all the men customers. Probably helps her tips at the end of the night."

"Hmm, that's a thought, but I don't think so. I think she's got her eye on you. I guarantee if I left now, she'd be over here in a second, writing her number on a napkin."

"Ha-ha, Penny, I'm flattered. You're jealous." Wes believed Penny's distasteful reaction to the waitress was a positive sign.

But he didn't plan on going along with it. He'd ignore the waitress's advances no matter what.

"No, I'm not jealous. I think it's rude. I'm sitting here, and we're clearly on a date. Doesn't she understand that? Can't she see it?" This was exactly the kind of problem that came along with dating or hanging out with a man who looked like Wes. Everyone noticed him. He wasn't a guy you'd pass on the street without glancing back to take another look. The waitress's overt display of cleavage confirmed her fear of getting involved with Wes. He couldn't be trusted. Penny was starting to let her guard down, but a reality check was in order.

"I only have eyes for you, Penny. Let's make a toast to the new couple and their healthy bouncing baby girl or boy."

"Gosh, it's hard to believe Kate is pregnant. It seems like a dream. It's going to take some getting used to for sure. To Kate, Phillip, and the baby." Penny held her glass up, and Wes clinked his to hers. "Oh no," said Penny.

"Oh no, what's oh no?" Wes was confused. He couldn't imagine what it was this time.

"She broke the hiatus, and it's bad luck. Let's double toast. She's going to need all the luck we can send her."

"Are you serious? You really believe it's bad luck?" Wes found it ridiculous but charming. She was convinced losing a bet would give Kate bad luck. It was beyond his comprehension.

"I do, but let's pretend it isn't."

"Penny, the news is all good," said Wes, clinking his glass to Penny's again. "All the luck in the world for the couple and the baby. They're both young and healthy, and I'm sure a bouncing baby is only seven months away."

Penny looked at Wes, and his eyes pierced hers. It took her breath away. She opened her mouth to speak, but no words came out.

"Are you all right?"

Penny cleared her throat. "Oh, I'm fine. I think I took a huge gulp of the wine. Totally rude, guzzling wine, not very ladylike."

"Spend the night with me, Penny." Wes nudged closer to Penny and looked straight into her eyes.

"OK, you can sleep over, but here's the deal—we're not having intimate relations."

"Intimate relations?" He laughed out loud. "You're kidding me? You think I can sleep in the same bed with you and not put my hands on your body?"

"I don't know, can you? Those are the rules of the game." Penny had to admit to herself that she needed and wanted his company tonight.

"I don't know. I'm willing to give it a try. I can't promise my toes won't make out with your toes."

"Toes can touch. Want to take a walk? I love the city when it's snowing."

"I would love to take a walk with you. You didn't have much to eat. Are you sure you don't need a proper dinner?" Penny assured him she had a hearty appetite, but he wasn't convinced.

"Maybe we could pop into Joe's for a slice."

"Or two," said Wes. Pizza wasn't a proper dinner, but it would give her some carbohydrates. "By the way, I can't wait to touch your toes."

Penny laughed out loud. "You're a tragedy, Wes Lane. I mean that in the most loving way possible."

"I'll take it." Wes hailed the waitress for the check. He barely glanced up when she brought it over. When they walked out the front door of Raven, the sidewalk was completely covered in snow.

"Isn't it beautiful, Wes? The first snow of the season, it's good luck you know."

"You've got to stop with the good- and bad-luck stuff. It's bad luck." Wes laughed. "It's beautiful. Let the shoveling begin!"

"You can't mess around with the universe. We have to respect it for the laws it sends our way."

"Oh, I respect the universe, but I don't stifle it into good and bad luck; unless, of course, you pick up a penny on the wrong side."

She looked at him sideways. "You know about the penny?"

"Of course, everyone knows you can't find a penny and pick it up on the backside; it's bad luck for sure. If you pick it up when it's on the front side, you'll be blessed with the luck of the Irish."

"Did you know if you find a penny and it's on its backside, you can turn it to the front side as long as it doesn't leave the ground and then it's good luck to pick it up?"

"You then force the good luck to happen." Wes decided to play along with her silliness.

"Exactly," said Penny with a serious tone in her voice.

"You look beautiful with snowflakes in your hair." Wes took Penny's hand and pulled her down the street.

"What's your hurry? Where are we going?" Penny ran to keep up with Wes's stride.

"Let's swing by the firehouse. It's almost eight, and my buddy Frank is getting off. I want you to meet him. Do you mind?"

"Of course not. I'd love to meet another masculine fireman," said Penny, picking up her pace.

"Hey now, don't get any ideas. I'm not trying to hook you up with someone."

Penny grabbed Wes's arm. "I know you aren't. I'm only messing with you." Wes made her laugh. He had a great sense of humor. Maybe if she thought of him as her brother, he'd become less inviting physically.

"I want to ask Frank to look into Phillip's fire-department application. What do you think about that?"

"Geez. How do you do this? How do you know what I need before I actually know what I need?"

"I thought a little background information couldn't be a bad thing."

"It's perfect."

You should be kissed and often, and
by someone who knows how.
—Margaret Mitchell, *Gone with the Wind*

Chapter 11

*W*es and Penny rounded the corner of Bedford Street onto Sixth Avenue as Frank was getting off work and walking to his truck.

"Frank," Wes yelled. "Hurry, Penny," said Wes, grabbing her hand. "He can't hear me."

"Hold on." Penny stopped in her tracks, put her fingers to her mouth, and sent out a magnetic whistle.

Frank spun his head around in their direction, spotting Wes. "Wes," yelled Frank, picking up his step in their direction. "I thought you took the night off, buddy. What are you doing hanging around the house? Miss me?"

"That's it. I couldn't stand a Friday night alone without you." Wes grabbed his friend and gave him a bear hug. They exchanged a few manly pats on the back before Wes realized he was there with a purpose. "This is Penny."

"Aww, Penny. It's nice to meet you." Frank took Penny's hand and kissed it. He then bowed slightly. "Now I understand what's got Wes in a lather."

"A lather," said Penny with a thick, fake Southern accent. "What do you mean, Captain?"

Frank and Wes chuckled. "Well, let me say Scarlet. A lather is a tizzy, and if I may, I can see what the tizzy is about."

"Nice to meet you," said Penny with her normal voice.

"Nice to meet you." Frank took a deep breath of air. "Where you headed? Can I give you both a lift? I'm heading to the East Village to meet Brian and Sam for a beer or two."

Penny was intrigued by the apparent close relationship between Frank and Wes. It seemed they shared a history. She'd have to remember to ask Wes about it.

"No, Penny wants to walk around in the snow. Apparently, the first snow of the season is good luck." Wes smiled and squeezed Penny's hand. "I have a favor to ask you. I don't know if it's asking too much, but I'm going to ask."

"Whatever you need. Don't I always say whatever you need?"

Frank's smile was kind and contagious. Penny found herself smiling from ear to ear.

"Well, I want to know if you can look into an application. Penny's best friend is involved with a guy. I met him tonight, and he seems like a solid man, but we'd like to be sure. He applied to the fire department. I think it was last year, maybe the year before. We don't know a lot about him, and it's complicated, but we need to get a feel of his background. Wondering if you could see if there's anything that stands out. You know, any red flags."

"Sure, I'll check it out tomorrow, fast enough?"

"Yep, tomorrow is great; I really appreciate it."

"No problem," said Frank, reaching into his backpack to pull out a small piece of paper and a pen. "What's his name?"

"His name is Phillip," said Wes and hesitated.

"Patterson," said Penny. "His name is Phillip Patterson."

"Shouldn't be a problem. Do you know the middle initial? It's a pretty common name, right?"

"Edward is the middle name," said Penny. "It's either the first or the middle, not sure which order. I think it's Phillip Edward Patterson." She was proud of herself. Kate had shown Penny Phillip's business card from the real-estate company. She'd imprinted it into her mind.

"Thanks so much, Frank. I owe you one."

"You owe me nothing."

"Hey, are you coming to the party Friday?"

"I wouldn't miss it. You kids keep it safe, and I'll call you tomorrow," said Frank. He opened the door to his truck and climbed in.

"Thanks, buddy; say hello to Brian and Sam for me."

Penny and Wes turned on their heels and headed north on Sixth Avenue.

Frank sat in his truck for a minute, watching them walk away. He'd never seen this kind of look on Wesley's face. It was about time. He thought his friend would never find the right girl to settle down with. Frank had a feeling the road to happily ever after was going to take some work. Call it intuition, but Wes had finally met his match.

Penny had a spring in her step. She needed to know more about Phillip Edward Patterson before she could stand by and watch her best friend fall in love. "Thank you, Wes. Can I buy you a slice at Joe's?" Penny elbowed him in the side. She knew Wes wasn't the kind of guy to let her open her wallet even if it was only a few bucks.

"No, you cannot, but I'll buy us both one," said Wes, reaching out his hand and messing up Penny's hair.

"Watch it, pal. You're on thin ice messing with a girl's hair." The words had just left her mouth when she felt herself in a snow-ice slide across the sidewalk.

"Penny, watch out!" Wes grabbed her from behind and caught her, but his right foot slipped, and he landed on his knees with Penny balanced on his upward-facing hands.

"Whew, that was close. Are you OK?" Penny regained her balance. The full brunt of her clumsiness was about to be out in the open.

"Yeah, I'm all right; maybe a bruised kneecap but no big deal. I'm guessing you didn't study ballet growing up in San Francisco?"

"No, I'm not ballet-dancer material. I'm skinny enough but not at all graceful." Penny didn't mind admitting it. He was going to figure it out anyway. "You did it again, you know. You continue saving me in the most unusual ways."

"Nothing unusual about a slip and slide on the sidewalk, but I'll take it."

Penny and Wes turned onto Bleecker Street, passing a small park on the corner. The skateboarders were out, annoying folks who wanted to sit on the park bench and enjoy the snowfall.

"Eddie would yell at you," Penny mumbled.

"What?" Wes was already used to her habit of mumbling or talking to herself out loud, but he wondered what she was saying.

"Oh, I was thinking about Eddie, a mini dachshund I walk. He doesn't like skateboards. He would totally put those guys on the defensive. I often think he's yelling something like 'Hey, that noise hurts my ears. Why don't you get a job or take your stupid skateboard to an empty parking lot?'"

"I think a lot of dogs have issues with skateboards, am I right?"

"Yeah, it's the noise. Also, frantic activity bothers them. With the skateboard, you have the two annoyances rolled into one. Why would they be skateboarding in the snow anyway? Aren't they asking for a visit to the emergency room?"

"I see it all the time. It doesn't make sense. Maybe it's the danger of the skate that turns them on."

Joe's Pizza was squeezed in between several other busy takeout joints. A few people milled about outside. The interior of Joe's was small. A wooden countertop lined two and a half walls, allowing about twelve people to hang out on stools while they dined on a combination of tomato sauce and cheese on soft thin crunchy crusts. Since it was a bustling Friday night, the stools were taken.

"Want to sit in the park outside?" said Wes.

"Sounds like a good plan. Maybe the skateboarders have left."

"We'll take two cheese slices to go," said Wes, pulling out his wallet and handing the guy at the counter a ten. "Hey, how is Wasabi doing?"

"He's as feisty and obstinate as usual. He's spending time with his family uptown this weekend."

"That's cool. He's pretty old, right?"

"Yeah, he'll be eighteen next month, an old man. I know he won't live forever. I guess it's an occupational hazard, loving dogs and then losing them."

"Hemingway again? See it's not such a corny quote after all."

"Hmm, I guess you win that one."

Wes chuckled. Penny continued to intrigue him. She was beautiful, but he knew it was more than her appearance that made his heart beat faster. She was a strange combination of princess and tomboy. Could the wall around her emotions be from the previous breakup? He felt it was more than a man. He couldn't figure out how to get her to share with him. Patience, he reminded himself again; she was worth the effort.

"What about the puppies we rescued? How are they doing?"

"The puppies you rescued. Thank you again. Rachel is completely in love with you. She asked about you yesterday. The puppies are great, but Rachel has become obsessive. She's with them all the time, never lets them out of her sight. I used to see the pups when Rachel and Bobby were staying in the city. Now she's decided to keep them with her in Connecticut all the time. I don't see how she can commit to her charity events if she doesn't come into the city."

"She's still reeling from the experience. Give her some time; it's only been a few days."

"Exactly. Hey, this pizza is so good." Penny pulled a layer of cheese and sauce off the crust and put it in her mouth.

"What are you doing? Why aren't you eating the crust?" Wes was appalled. For a New Yorker, Penny had no idea how to eat a pizza.

"I eat some of the crust, not all of it; too many carbs, white flour, that sort of thing."

"That's the craziest thing I've ever heard. You can't be a New Yorker and eat pizza like that."

"Oh, hush. I'm as New York as it gets," said Penny flatly. "Did you grow up in the city?"

"I did. It was great, but we had a place in the county, upstate, my grandfather's farm. We spent a lot of weekends there. How was it growing up in San Francisco?"

"I loved it. Hey, let's do something different tonight. Let's mix it up; head uptown, downtown, maybe Lincoln Center or Central Park."

"In the snow?"

"Why not?" Penny knew Wes was a warrior. He wasn't scared of a little snow.

"OK, let's go to Times Square, walk around, and pretend we're tourists."

"Gosh, Times Square drives me crazy; can't stand it. OK, let's do it." She wanted to get out of the neighborhood. Times Square would be a great distraction.

"I'll be Ted from Omaha, Nebraska."

"I'll be Tammy from Memphis, Tennessee."

They both laughed at the idea.

"How are you killing the Southern accent? I definitely believe you, Tammy. Are you married?"

"No, but I'm thinking about getting hitched to my high-school sweetheart. I'm here in New York City to have a wild one before I put the ring on."

Wes laughed out loud. "I hope the wild one includes a spin with Ted."

"Why, Ted, I meant a wild one, shopping and sightseeing."

"Oh right." Wes chuckled. "You can see what my mind is focused on."

❧

Penny and Wes exited the subway station on Forty-Second Street and Broadway, entering the chaos of Times Square.

Penny always avoided Times Square. The frantic energy stressed her out. Normally, she'd walk five to ten blocks out of her way to avoid it. Perhaps tonight the hustle-bustle would take her mind off Kate. It was hardly the place for deep brooding or enlightenment.

"OK, we're here," said Wes. "Now, what?"

"Let's check out the naked cowboy."

"Seriously, that's the first thing you thought of doing in Times Square? Is that Tammy or Penny talking?"

"Tammy; c'mon, it'll be fun."

"Maybe we could get our photo taken with one of those silly people in character outfits. Hello Kitty perhaps?" Wes had zero interest in getting a photo with a character. He wasn't a big photo taker. As a fireman, he watched people on the street every day obsessed with their phone and selfies. It was completely foreign to him. He wondered what they did with all the photos and why they felt the need to document every moment of their lives with photographs. He secretly hoped Penny wasn't obsessed with her phone. So far, he'd seen her take not one photograph, and that was a good sign.

"I love Hello Kitty."

"I am so surprised."

"What? Hello Kitty is brilliant! Do you know why Hello Kitty doesn't have a mouth?"

"No, but I think you might tell me."

"Hello Kitty doesn't have a mouth because she speaks the language of love."

"Did you make that up?"

"No, it's part of her thing. You can read it online if you research Hello Kitty. Hey, look, there he is."

Penny and Wes stood at a distance to watch the naked cowboy engage his audience. He strutted around in his underwear in the middle of Times Square during a snowstorm, strumming his guitar and singing "God Bless America."

"He's got to be cold. OK, we've seen him; what next?"

Penny surprised herself. The noise, people, and lights weren't giving her stress. In fact, she felt completely at ease. Was it Wes? Did he make the noise go away, or was her mind so overwhelmed that the noise was a welcomed distraction?

"Hey, I think there's a Heartland Brewery around the corner. How about a pint?"

"How do you know that?"

"Honestly, I'm not sure why. I've lived here a long time. Care to join me?" Wes didn't mind the chaos of Times Square, but he'd rather share a few intimate moments with her.

"I'd love to, FD."

Wes cleared his throat. "I don't know what you're saying, Tammy; my name is Ted."

"Gosh, I'm sorry I broke character." Penny giggled. Her mood was upbeat, and it felt refreshingly good. Maybe everything was going great with Kate and Phillip, and the energy was floating her way. "I really should get out of the village and enjoy the sights in the city more. This is fun."

Wes opened the door for Penny into the brewery, and they found a pair of stools at the end of the bar. Penny kept forgetting it was Friday night. The place was packed, and a loud constant murmur of voices serenaded the guests. The bar murmur was always a comfort to Penny. She loved sitting in a bar or restaurant and listening to the sound of the clinking silverware and the incessant hum of voices.

"I love New York City, don't you?"

"I do. Maybe you should move here, Tammy, and enjoy the city full time, every day of the year."

"Well, maybe I will, Ted." Penny spoke in a thick Southern drawl. "You know what, Ted? Let's go back to being Penny and Wes. I like us better."

"Oh, good. Ted was running out of things to say. But I, Wes, have lots of interesting tidbits to amuse you with. Want to try a favorite beer of mine?"

"Sure; I'll give it a try."

The bartender leaned over the bar and put his ear close to Wes's face so he could hear his order. "Sure thing, two coming right up." He tossed a couple of coasters on the bar, and seconds later two large mugs arrived.

"Cheers to you, Penny. Health and happiness to you and yours." He would have chosen a more romantic setting for their conversation, but he'd take what he could get. They were alone together even if it was a loud, crowded bar. He could tune the others out and focus on the woman he was with.

"Cheers to you, Wes. Everything good, everything bright, may it be yours every morning and night."

Wes leaned over and kissed Penny on the cheek. "You're the best."

Penny felt the warmth of his kiss on her cheek. It felt so good, like a glowing white light entering her being and running from her cheek to her toes.

"How is it possible?" Penny blurted and then pretended she was confused.

"How is what possible?"

"Oh, nothing; I was drifting in my head. You'll have to overlook my weirdness."

"Your weirdness is very attractive; I like that you're unpredictable."

Penny smiled at him and took a gulp of her beer.

"You've never told me anything about your family in San Francisco, and yet I've bored you with so much talk of my brothers."

"It's pretty simple—Mom, Dad, and brother." Penny didn't like talking about family. It felt too personal.

"Are they still living there? Do you visit them?"

"I mean, yeah, we're close. I talk with them often. I don't fly back a lot, but I'm busy, so I never really seem to find the time, you know."

"I love San Francisco. It's one of my favorite cities."

"Really? It's a pretty city. Of course, after living here, it seems small, comfy almost."

"I'm glad you're here." Wes smiled sweetly. He didn't want to make her uncomfortable, but maybe talking about family would help her open up. The idea of getting into Penny's head thrilled him. He wasn't used to these feelings. His last girlfriend was fun and interesting, but their relationship was based on physical attraction. During the six months he spent with her, he never found himself the least bit curious about her interests or her past. At the time, he called it love, but after their breakup, he realized it was only her presence he missed, not actually her. Penny was different. He knew it from the moment he met her. "Is your brother still in San Francisco too?"

"My brother lives in Portland; he's three years older than me. He's working for a tech start-up. He's pretty wrapped up in his career. What else? My dad is an attorney, and my mom is an artist. I mean not a famous artist, but she paints. She has a small following, but really she just likes to create stuff for fun and relaxation."

"Cool; what's their names? The mother, dad, and brother." Wes was prodding. Something told him the answer to Penny's reserve was through her past. He wasn't sure if the past was ex-lovers or family.

"Mom is Carol and Dad is William. Brother is Eddie." Penny took another long hard drink of her beer. "This is so good. I may be drinking it too quickly."

"No such thing. I can order two more; drink up. Are Carol and William happy with your career choice, your city choice, and all that stuff?"

"Oh sure. They've always been supportive of everything I put my energy into. They didn't understand why I left Wall Street, but they don't judge. They're complete hippies hiding under the image of ordinary."

"So they're cool?"

"Completely."

"Nice. Cool parents must be fun. Our dad was always on us to overachieve, and of course, Wyatt and Nick made him happy. Wyatt and Nick were always at the top of their class. Me, I was something of a disappointment compared to them."

"I don't think anyone with a brain would call you a disappointment. Why would you say that?"

"I'm not sure, really. I felt compelled to serve as a fireman, but Dad would have liked me to be a doctor. He never said it, but it was unspoken. After college, I thought about going to grad school or medical school, but my best buddy, Frank, he joined the FDNY. I was in awe of him. That's how it happened."

"So you and Frank go back to college or high school? The Frank I met tonight?"

"Yeah, Frank and I went to high school together; he was two years ahead of me. We went to different colleges, but we never lost touch. I was trying to decide what to study next, and he said, 'Wesley, join the fire department; you'll love it.'"

"And you did!"

"I did, and I never looked back. Frank was the key. Dad wasn't thrilled, but Mom said, 'Let the boy do what he feels he needs to do,' and the conversation was over."

"That's awesome. Frank sounded like a great friend, like Kate is to me."

"Yeah, we're brothers." Wes stopped talking, and his mind drifted back to the summer after his graduation. He and Frank were playing basketball. Wes was going on about where he was going to apply. He was in pain about the choice because it didn't feel organic. Frank was on a high about his new job as a firefighter. His excitement was contagious. Wes had never even considered the possibility until Frank suggested it. The memory brought a smile to Wes's lips.

"What are you smiling about? Where are you?"

"Thinking about Frank and I on the basketball court, that's all."

"My mother died in childbirth." Penny blurted it out. She'd never said the words out loud.

We delight in the beauty of the butterfly, but rarely admit the changes it has gone through to achieve that beauty.

—MAYA ANGELOU

Wes was stunned. "Penny, I'm sorry; did you say your mom died in childbirth? What about Carol? I thought Carol is your mom."

Tears welled up in Penny's eyes. She couldn't believe her words. It was a huge secret she'd been carrying around with her for a while. "Wes, I don't know why I'm telling you this. I've never shared it with anyone. Kate doesn't even know. I guess I convinced myself it didn't happen, or at least I've been trying to pretend it's not true. Carol is my mom, the only mom I've ever known, but my real mom, my birth mom, is dead. She died bringing me into the world."

"Gosh, Penny, I'm sorry. When did you find out?" Wes took Penny's hand in his. This could explain her extreme anxiety over Kate's pregnancy. He wasn't a psychotherapist, but even a simple man could put those two thoughts together.

"Carol and William told me about a year ago. I guess they figured, since I was living on the other side of the country, they should let me know. In many ways, I wish they'd never told me the truth. My dad said they felt I should know for many reasons but mainly health. They thought with the advances in technology, somewhere down the road I'd find out I wasn't their biological child. They wanted me to know in case something happened to them. Surely, I'd be angry with them someday if they weren't around. Who would be there to tell me the truth? My brother doesn't even know. When Carol and William told me, we decided it was a secret we'd share between us. William, my dad, is my real mom's brother. When my birth mom passed away, my real dad freaked; he couldn't handle it. Carol said he tried real hard, but every time he looked at me, all he saw was my mom, Nora. Nora was her name." Penny paused, not really knowing if she should continue. Why was she telling Wes this? It was a secret she planned on telling no one. Now it was out there. She couldn't take it back.

"Penny, this must be difficult for you to discuss. I'm sorry. Have you tried to find your real dad? Do Carol and William know where he is?"

"They haven't heard from him in years. William and Carol legally adopted me right after I was born. You can understand why I never questioned anything; they were the only parents I'd ever known. Anyway, Carol said my dad used to send me gifts when I was a toddler. He dropped in occasionally to see how I was doing, but he never told anyone what he was doing or where he was living. Of course, I'd probably be able to track him down, but I'm not sure I want to. Who does that? Who gives their baby away? On the other hand, I feel sorry for him. He lost his wife, and there I was, tiny and needy. Do I blame him for loving my mom so much he couldn't bear me?"

"That's a tough question. It must have been a complete heartbreak. Can you imagine sharing the happiest time of your life with your wife and then losing her? It's heavy, but I agree, on the other hand, who could turn their back on a child? Do you know if he asked Carol and William? Was there anyone else in your circle of family? What an amazing couple they must be."

"William was the only sibling my mom had. Carol and my mom were very close, so the loss was hard for them as well. They were two young couples living in the same neighborhood, several blocks away from each other. Carol had Billy three years before, and she told me my mom loved playing with him, she wanted a baby so bad. She was young, twenty-six years old, when she delivered me. It was a freak event. Nobody saw it coming; she was healthy and had a normal pregnancy, but something went wrong during birth. It makes me feel weird talking about it. It feels like it's someone else I'm speaking of. I don't know if that makes sense."

"It makes a lot of sense." Wes shifted uncomfortably on his barstool. This was a total shock. He felt sorry for Penny and wasn't sure if he was qualified to give advice, but his heart told him to keep talking. She clearly needed to tell someone. "It's like it happened to someone else. I get it. You grew up in a loving home with parents and a brother. Why would you think anything was wrong or missing?"

"Exactly. I mean I gotta tell you, sometimes I would look at my mom and wonder how I got red hair and green eyes. She's a blue-eyed blonde. Of course, my dad and I do share some features, but it was only my appearance, which I questioned, from time to time. Other than that, everything was happy and normal. I consider myself lucky to have them. They're wonderful. But, now that I know, I do think about my real mom. I wonder who she was, what she loved, what made her happy—you know, those kind of things."

"Did Carol and William show you any photographs?"

"Yes, they had a few of my mom and dad when they got married. She was pretty, and he was handsome, but it was like looking at a portrait of people you find in a frame when you buy one at a store. My father was an only child, so there was no other family around. My grandparents on both sides knew at the time. Both his parents passed away, and I never knew them. I still have my me-maw; she's seventy-eight and like a second mom to me as well; so, you see, I was never alone. There was a lot of love."

Wes was impressed with her courage. It was a tough story to hear. He tried to imagine how he would feel in her shoes. His mom and dad were a rock in the family. Sometimes, he resented the pressure they put on their boys to achieve, but he was proud of the closeness he shared with his brothers. His mom always said, "Family is first." It was pounded into his head from as long as he could remember. His grandparents reinforced the same tune as his parents. If the boys got in a fight, they were grabbed by the shirttail and re-minded that "brother" was another name for "best friend."

"It sounds like Carol and William are awesome people. I think you should find your dad!" The minute he said it, he regretted it. It wasn't his place to tell her to do something so personal.

"I knew you would say that." Penny smiled and drained the last swallow from her beer mug. "I've toyed with the idea a lot."

"I mean he must think of you all the time."

"No, I don't think so. He knows where Mom and Dad live. If he wanted to see me, he would have contacted them. Like I said, they haven't heard from him in years."

"Do you know if he changed his name or is it the same? I wonder what he's doing for a living."

"Gosh, you sound as bad as me. I think it must be the warrior in you, probably the part that makes you a great firefighter."

"Whoa, did I get a compliment? How do you know I am a good firefighter?"

"I didn't say good; I said great, and I can tell, that's all."

"Well, thank you, water girl. I appreciate the acknowl-edgment. Now, back to you please." This beautiful woman sitting next to him was getting more beautiful every minute. When she blinked her emerald eyes and a tear ran down her cheek, he felt his heart ache. He felt the actual physical pain, and it scared him. It wasn't a feeling he was used to. His whole being longed to take her in his arms and protect her. She was a strong independent woman, living in a big city. She was smart; she didn't need of a knight to rescue her.

"I think I've laid enough 'me' stuff on the table tonight for the both of us." She was surprised; she'd shared something very personal with Wes. She felt a sense of relief. "Maybe that's why people have therapists," she thought. It was cathartic, getting something out in the open.

"I never stop wanting to hear about you. But, if you insist on stopping the talk, we could go to my place and touch toes all night long."

"I thought we were going to my place," said Penny with a wink.

Wes wanted to grab her hand, drag her to the street, and get a cab to the West Village as fast as he could. Instead, he remained calm. He couldn't let her see how eager he was to be alone with her. "I'm all right with your place. Should we continue our adventure through Times Square?"

"Let's walk over to Rockefeller Plaza and look at the tree." Penny loved Christmas; it was her favorite time of the year. Everything was sparkly and festive; how could anyone not love it? New York City embraced Christmas like no other city. All you had to do was glance to your left or to your right. The lights, the decoration, the music on the street—she loved it all.

"Great idea! I haven't seen the tree in person this year. It's the biggest tree we've ever had."

"I heard that too. Don't you love Christmas? And now it's snowing, which makes it even more perfect. I wonder how many inches of snow we're up to now!"

"Let's go see. Does the luck get better the bigger the snow fall?" Wes settled their check with the bartender, and the two of them headed out into the cold bitter air.

"Look, it's beautiful! I think we'll get a couple of feet." The snow was pilling up. The wind blew Penny's hood off her head. "Whoa, good thing it's attached to my coat."

Wes pulled his skullcap out of his pocket, put it on, and zipped up his jacket. Penny reached for his hand, which caused his heart to leap. Wes chuckled to himself. "I feel like I'm in high school or maybe even junior high."

"Really, why?" asked Penny. His brilliant eyes looked deep into hers. She felt her body tingle. He was undoubtedly the hottest man she'd ever dated. The energy from his hand could warm her entire body. She wanted to be with him; she admitted it to herself.

"You make me feel things. I don't know how to say it. You make me feel like I've never dated anyone before. It all feels wrong, and you feel right. C'mon, let's go see the big tree."

"Thank you." Penny stopped and pulled him close to her. "Will you kiss me?"

"I thought you'd never ask." Wes put his hands around her waist, pressing her body to his. Gently, his lips met hers, and they melted into each other. In the middle of Times Square, with the billboards flashing and the lights blazing, they were lost in each other.

Penny released her clutch on Wes and immediately had to grab his arm. "My head is spinning, FD. That was an amazing kiss."

"Let's do it again, you know, for good luck." Wes laughed and pulled her in again. Tonight he intended for more than their toes to touch. He knew he had to be cautious. Penny was akin to a deer. "Move slowly," he thought. He could tell she wanted more, but if he pushed her, she'd dart the other way.

Penny stood on the tiptoes of her platform boots and wrapped her arms around his neck. She could feel his body lock into hers. Wes kissed her again, and the passion sent a wave of desire through her body. The air was icy, but the heat from Wes's body rippled through hers. For a moment, her mind was completely free; there were no worries, no concerns, only Wes and Penny spinning around in a golden white light of desire.

"It's magical," said Penny, gazing up at the Rockefeller Center Christmas tree. The crowds and the noise seemed to blur when Penny was with Wes. She didn't feel the need to rush around or avoid the crowd; she focused on the beauty of the tree and the magnificence of Christmas. She hadn't expected to have such a good time with Wes. He continually surprised her.

"I could stand here with you forever," said Wes, giving her hand a squeeze.

"Let's get home now," said Penny. "Thanks for sharing this with me. Let's walk across the city to the one train," said Penny.

"Excellent," said Wes.

They held hands and navigated through the thick crowd of people. Before they reached Sixth Avenue, a man bumped into Penny, startling her.

"Sorry, miss, I apologize," he said, tucking his newspaper under his arm and darting quickly across the street.

"That's him," said Penny. It happened so fast. "The man from the blue car."

"What? Do you know that guy?" asked Wes.

"Oh no, I'm sorry; I don't know what I'm saying," said Penny, looking confused and frightened.

"You said, 'It's the man from the blue car.'" Wes grabbed her arm. "Are you OK?"

"Oh yeah, I'm fine. Let's go," said Penny, laughing it off.

∞

The one train was packed with people. "I haven't been out on a Friday night in a while. Have I gotten too content in the comfort of my everyday routine? Perhaps."

"Did you ask yourself a question and then answer it yourself?" It was something he'd observed on numerous occasions. He didn't want to embarrass her, but he wondered if she realized the habit.

Penny laughed out loud. "I did. I think since I'm around dogs all day, I sometimes talk out loud to them, and they don't talk back, so I answer myself. I guess it's an odd habit."

"It's quirky and very Penny," said Wes. "Don't apologize; your oddness is charming."

"I'm going to thank you for calling me odd. Thank you." She rumbled through her purse, looking for something, but she wasn't sure what—a peppermint, a bottle of water, a stick of gum perhaps. The subway car rumbled, and the smooth rocking was enough to make her sleepy. Her fingers found the peppermint in her handbag, and she unwrapped it quickly and put it in her mouth. "Oh, I'm sorry; how rude of me. Would you like one too?"

"Maybe, but it took you a long time to dig the first one out of your bag. Sure you have the energy to search again?"

"Ha-ha. I'm perfectly capable of finding a peppermint for you if there's another one in my bag." She continued to search.

"Don't worry about it. I'm OK. Hey, I'm curious, did you quit your finance job after finding out about your mom?"

"Yeah, shortly after finding out. I know what you're going to say. I made a life change because my past was a lie, and I needed to regroup and make sense out of everything."

"Yeah, something along those lines. Do you miss working in the corporate world?" Wes had never worked in a large office. He interned in college, but it was in a hospital; corporate world was not for him. He needed a flexible environment. He couldn't imagine Penny in a suit working on Wall Street. She seemed much too rebellious for that.

"No, not really. I miss my coworkers, but other than that, I'm glad I made the change. It doesn't have to be forever. I'm still young. I can reinvent myself time and time again if need be. Right now, I'm happy where I am." Penny pulled her hand out of her bag, revealing a red-and-white peppermint. "Ha, I told you I'd find it."

"Thank you." Wes pulled the clear wrapper off the candy. "Refreshing."

"Next stop, Houston Street," said the conductor of the train in a muffled tone. The wheels of the train squealed to a stop. Penny put her fingers in her ears. She had a pair of earplugs in her handbag, but she always forgot to pull them out in time.

"After you," said Wes, getting up from his seat and offering his hand to Penny. The noise didn't bother him. He figured his hearing was already damaged from the sound of the fire sirens.

When they exited the subway, the sidewalk snow was up to six inches. The snowplows were out on the streets, and several people were scraping the sidewalk with shovels.

"It always makes me laugh. When it snows, it's a mad rush to fight it. The supers, the shop managers, and brownstone owners are in a rush to scrape it off the sidewalk. The city sends out the plows and the salters. I sometimes wonder why we don't let it win and frolic in the beauty."

"Well, let's see; slip and fall is one. Two, would be crash and carry. Three, would be emergency care."

"No, I know all that. I guess it seems funny to me. I'd like all of us to get out and throw snowballs and build snowmen, take Monday off and enjoy the snow. That's why I always hope for six feet. I love it when the snow wins. Remember the blizzard last year. It was wonderful. New Yorkers were forced to take a day off and rejoice in the beauty of Mother Nature. I loved it."

"It was a pretty awesome blizzard; I have to agree with you." Wes and Penny slowly made their way to Bedford Street. The light from the streetlamps cast a sparkly glow across the snow. He put his arm around Penny and gave her a squeeze. "Are you cold?"

"No, I'm OK," said Penny. She pushed her hands into her coat pockets. There was an object in her pocket. She pulled it out and looked at it under the streetlamp. "It's a bug," thought Penny. "Blue-car guy left a listening device in my pocket."

"What are you doing?" said Wes, pausing on the sidewalk to wait for her.

"Oh, checking out the lucky penny I just found in my pocket. Lucky me!"

Wes chuckled. "You and your luck stuff."

"Hey, hold my hand; yours are so warm. Do you have hand warmers in your pocket?"

"No, I don't. You know what they say? Warm heart, warm hands."

"That's not it at all."

They both laughed.

Penny felt her phone vibrate. "It's my phone, Wes. Hold on, wait up; maybe it's Kate." She stopped and read the text out loud.

Penny, everything is good. I can hardly believe it. Everything is everything. Have fun; I'll call you tomorrow. K.

"Wow, that's good news," said Wes, giving Penny a radiant smile. "I told you there was nothing to worry about."

"She said everything is everything."

"Is that some sort of Penny-Kate code?" asked Wes.

"It's something I say to her all the time. Kate hates it; she always says, 'That makes no sense, Penny.' I tell her it makes perfect sense. If you think about it, everything is everything. Nothing is nothing, but, well, you see where I'm going?"

"I don't follow, but if she's saying it, is that good?"

"It's great. She's happy, everything is everything!" Penny and Wes turned onto Bedford Street.

"Penny," said Wes, "I don't really understand; care to elaborate?"

"I'd love to explain it, if I can. We get tied up in our everyday routine and forget to express gratitude for the small things. When everything is going well, we carry on our journey with no expression of thankfulness. The minute something bad happens—the flu, a broken bone, a lost loved one—we long for our ordinary life. Nothing is everything. Everything is nothing. Everything is everything means every day is special. Does that make sense?"

"You know what? It kind of does."

"I'm so glad you get it."

Wes shook his head. It made his head hurt to contemplate this hard. "I think what you're saying is every day, whether it's ordinary or not, is a great day to be alive. No real drama is nothing, and nothing is everything. When you experience a special moment or event, you stop and think that everything is everything."

"Gosh, FD, you explained it better than me. She opened the front door of her building. "I should check my mail," said Penny. She stopped at her mailbox, opened it, and dropped the listening device inside. "No mail tonight. Now, let's go upstairs, and I'll make you a cup of tea." Penny giggled. "You like tea, don't you?"

"Sure, who doesn't like a good cup of tea?" He hesitated. Was she really speaking of tea? Penny Robinson had her own language. He wanted to find out how to speak it.

Believe in a love that is being stored up for
you like an inheritance, and have faith that
in this love there is a strength and a blessing
so large that you can travel as far as you
wish without having to step outside it.
—RAINER MARIA RILKE, *LETTERS TO A YOUNG POET*

Chapter 13

*P*enny and Wes had a cup of decaffeinated green tea and fell into bed. Every bit of strength she had to withdraw from him was lost. When he kissed her passionately, she felt her bed levitate. Every excuse she used since the day they met didn't seem to hold any value.

Penny woke up regretting nothing. Wes was out of bed early; she heard the water from the shower. She considered getting up and joining him, but she needed a few more hours of sleep. Penny wasn't a short sleeper. Wes could generate energy on only two hours of shut-eye. "I could accomplish so much more every day if I didn't need nine hours of sleep," Penny thought to herself. The squeak from the water values whistled throughout the apartment. Penny heard the radiator click on and the pipes whistling, sounds she found romantic, the roar of heat generating through an old walk-up apartment. When she first moved to New York City, a boiler in a basement of a building generating heat to its inhabitants was foreign to her. Her San Francisco home had none of this eccentric charm. She fell in love with New York City winters and the cozy sound of the clunk tick from the pipes. It was comforting like a bowl of chicken soup or the roar of a football game on television. Wes turned the shower off, and Penny longed to call him back to her, but he'd be late for work. "That would be so wrong," thought Penny. She rolled over, closed her eyes, and drifted back to sleep.

The warm shower felt good; it was slowly bringing him back to reality. A long shift at the firehouse was ahead of him. It horrified him to leave; he wanted nothing more than to get back under the covers and embrace her. Normally, he was excited to go to work, but today was different. Penny exhilarated every part of him, and he didn't want the feeling that he woke up with to end. He dried off quickly, got dressed, and quietly closed the front door behind him. Wes paused in the hallway, came back to the door, and checked to see if it was locked. When he started down the stairs, he felt his heart ache. He quietly cursed himself for not taking the day off. "I'll be back soon, Penny," he said under his breath, almost in a whisper, and then stepped quickly to the stairwell.

When Penny finally woke up, she sat straight up in her bed, suddenly remembering the man and the listening device. "This is crazy," Penny thought. "Why would anyone be following me or wanting to hear my conversations?" She made herself a big bowl of oatmeal and sat on the sofa to ponder the situation. Now she knew the man in the blue car was watching her. He'd followed her and Wes to Rockefeller Center last night. That question had been solved. It was not her imagination or a paranoid delusion. Penny threw on a pair of yoga pants and a sweat shirt, slipped on her flip-flops, and went downstairs to her mailbox. She pulled out the small device. This was not her area of expertise. Maybe it was a decoy. Was this all a ploy to mess with her mind? She put it back in the mailbox and went back upstairs. "Ivan would know," thought Penny and pulled out her phone to scroll names. Ivan was an old friend who worked in a pawnshop in the East Village. After confirming he was at work, she assured him she'd stop by with an interesting object for his inspection. He couldn't wait to see it, which made Penny laugh. Only Ivan would find a listening device fascinating.

Penny wanted to pick out her Christmas tree without worrying about being followed. "Go ahead, follow me to the market," thought Penny as she walked quickly to the corner of Six Avenue and Bleecker Street. Tree hunting was a treasured, yearly tradition. Her eyes scanned the people passing on both sides of the street, searching faces for the man with his newspaper.

Rick Early, the tree guy and loyal Vermont citizen, greeted her when she arrived at the market. His lodging, a sleeping camper, wasn't five-star, but it didn't seem to bother him and his two sons. He showed up every year with a Kris Kringle attitude, and devoted customers embraced him with a purchase.

After browsing the selection, Penny picked a tree she thought would look perfect in her living room. It only took her ten minutes to make the decision. Kate would look at each and every tree before picking the same one. Penny's parents always bought a large, fresh tree and spoiled her and her brother with gifts from Santa. It wasn't just the gifts she loved at Christmas time but the entire holiday season. Several boxes of ornaments sat on the top shelf of her hall closet. Each year, she retrieved them from their hiding spot, turned on holiday music, and decorated the tree. Some of the ornaments were from her childhood, and each one had a story or special memory. Kate liked to help Penny with her tree. She never got one for her apartment because she didn't like the needles falling off and making a mess all over her house.

It was a beautiful Saturday morning in New York City, only a few weeks from Christmas, and the tree market was bustling with activity.

"I'll bring the tree to your place in about four hours if that's OK, Penny," said Rick Early, glancing at his watch. "You're still at the same address, right?"

"Yep, I'm still there. That's fine; no rush, Rick. Looks like you're going to have a busy day. Everyone is in the mood for a tree today."

Rick chuckled and tagged Penny's tree with her address. "We like it busy. I don't want to leave too many trees on the sidewalk when I head back to Vermont."

Kate called, sounding happy and content, and Penny was relieved. She looked forward to hearing details when Kate could pull herself away from Phillip. Wes texted her, and she sent him a heart emoji; she didn't feel like sharing a lot of sappy texts back and forth, and she needed to get to the East Village and meet with Ivan. She didn't have time for texting.

Ivan's pawnshop was tucked away on Fourth Street near Third Avenue. He was reading a comic book when Penny walked in. The bell on the door startled him.

"Penny, shiny, happy, lucky Penny! How are you?" Ivan greeted her with a hug.

Penny held up her finger to her lips and waved a Ziploc bag with the device inside.

"I don't care if anyone hears me. Give it to me. Let's see who's messing with my girl. I've missed you and Kate. Where've you been hiding?"

"Oh, here and there. I'm sorry I haven't stopped by in a while. How's the band? Are you gigging anywhere? I promise we'll come see you. Oh, wait! Don't tell me yet. Maybe you can disable this thing."

"We can smash it into bits, you know. But first, let me take a look at it." Ivan pulled the device out of the bag and put it under a magnifier. "This isn't big brother if that's what you were worried about. It's something you can get online; just an ordinary, everyday listener."

"OK, let's smash it," said Penny cheerfully.

Ivan pulled a hammer out from under his desk. "Sure you don't want to take it to the cops for fingerprinting or evidence?"

"Nope, smash it."

"With pleasure," said Ivan and pounded the small device into bits. "Now, you can talk freely. Do you have any idea who would want to hear your conversations?"

"No, it's creepy. A guy has been tailing me. I have no idea what's going on. I'm guessing it's either the firm messing with my head for leaving or Beckett."

"Either way, maybe you should go to the cops, no?" Ivan put the hammer back in its spot and straightened up the watches on the counter.

"I'm hoping if I ignore him, he'll go away. Is that a Rolex?" Penny picked up the ladies' watch and put it on her wrist.

"Yeah, it's a real one but eight years old. A Rolex isn't really your style."

"I know." Penny laughed and put it back on the counter.

"I have friends who can put a tail on the guy who's following you. No charge for the service; I'm worried about you."

"Ivan, that's sweet of you. I'll think about it. Now, how are you, and where is the band playing?"

"I'm great. The band is kicking it at Lucille's every Thursday this month, and we've got Friday nights at the Bitter End."

"In the West Village?"

"Yep," said Ivan. "How convenient is that?"

"Very; I'll see you there, but I warn you in advance a middle-aged man with a newspaper sitting in a blue car might show up." Penny frowned. "I feel like I'm dirtying my friends if I bring him along."

"This friend isn't worried. Maybe we'll invite him in for a cocktail." Ivan laughed and gave Penny a hug. "Seriously, let me know if I can help."

"Thanks, Ivan; I appreciate it."

❦

Penny decided to stroll through Washington Square Park on her way back home. It was fun to be out walking around the city in the sunshine. Most of the building supers, landlords, and homeowners had scraped and shoveled their snow off the sidewalk; mounds of it lay on the street in piles. She kept walking and wound up in Abingdon Square, where local farmers showed up every Saturday with fresh vegetables, breads, honey, pastries, and cheese. The farmers were at their outdoor tents in the square. The snow from Friday night hadn't stopped them from showing up. She browsed the aisles of offerings, choosing some apples, gala and fuji, some fresh whole-grain bread, and salad greens. Penny put the items in her backpack and headed home feeling invigorated.

She was unpacking her items when her Christmas tree arrived. Rick helped her put it into the tree stand. "Thank you so much," said Penny, handing him a generous tip and closing the door behind him. She found the perfect angle for the tree in its location next to her chocolate leather sofa and was digging her Christmas-tree lights from the closet when Kate buzzed her. Penny met her at the door. "Your timing is perfect; I just got the tree set up."

"Penny, it's gorgeous. I thought you'd wait for me, but you picked a winner." Kate admired it from each direction and gave her friend a high five. "OK, we have to talk."

"Should I make some tea?" asked Penny.

"Yes, that would be great," said Kate. She could hardly believe her eyes. Penny seemed normal. There wasn't a cloud of grief over her. Maybe it was temporary, but she'd take it. "I think you must have had a good time with Wes; you look refreshed."

"Let's not dwell on me. You have to tell me all about it; sounds like you had a happy reunion."

"Phillip is amazing. I mean I was scared; I didn't know what his reaction would be." Kate paused, thinking about what to tell Penny next. "We decided to start dating and see what happens. I don't want to pressure him into being something he's not. We don't really know each other yet. It's odd to start a relationship under these circumstances, but no matter what happens between us, he wants to help with the baby. He offered emotional and financial support. I told him I don't need financial support but being involved would be great. It's a little overwhelming. I still feel I'm watching it, like a movie. Does that make sense?"

"I definitely understand those feelings. I kind of feel the same way." Penny was pleased with the news. "He seems very kind and responsible. I was frightened when you left the restaurant. Wes kept telling me to relax, but it was stressful. I'm relieved. It sounds like a good plan. When are you going to see him again?"

"Tonight, can you believe it? We want to spend as much time with each other as our schedules allow." Under normal circumstances, Kate would've been excited about dating Phillip, but it felt odd courting the guy who got her pregnant on a drunken afternoon. "I've been thinking a lot about Matthew," Kate said.

Penny almost dropped the cord of lights she was unraveling. "I haven't heard you mention his name in years."

"I know. It's weird, right?" Matthew was the first man Kate fell in love with. She was in graduate school and overwhelmed with her move from Santa Monica to New York City. She accepted an invitation to a jazz club with some friends, and he was there. Matthew was charming and wooed her with exciting dates. He was a native New Yorker and gave her a behind-the-scenes look at Manhattan. Matthew was sixteen years older, a surgeon, and everything about him was exciting. Kate was young and impressionable, and he was confident and successful. He loved entertaining and took her with him everywhere. Once he felt confidant Kate was in love with him, he began to pull away. She was devastated. "You know it was an eye-opener for me to see how a person could change so quickly. I felt certain he was the man I was going to spend the rest of my life with. I desperately wanted a wedding and a baby in that order. It was a huge blow to my ego and my heart."

"You're scared the same might happen with Phillip? Is that why you're thinking of him now?" She met Kate in the early stages of her relationship with Matthew. Penny was there to pick her up and dust her off.

"No, I don't think so. Honestly, I've been thinking about the irony. I was so in love with Matthew and wanted to have a baby with him. Years later, I don't want a relationship or a child, and now I have both. I guess I have to trust fate." Kate didn't want Phillip to feel trapped. She made it clear to him; he didn't have to stick around. There was a wonderful energy between them, and she was willing to give it a try. It felt like they'd known each other for years.

"Like you said, don't say you'll only live in a loft in Soho or you'll be buying a condo on Central Park West." Penny grinned at her. Kate was completely calm and serene. "At least you can say you were young when you fell for Matthew. I wish I could use that excuse. Ugh, talk about not seeing the whole picture." Penny laughed. "Hey, can you believe it? I'm just laughed about Beckett."

"Yay, stage five. Maybe it's finally stage five, Penny. I'm so happy for you!"

"Could it be? I hope so." Penny knew Kate was referring to the five stages of grief, denial, anger, bargaining, depression, and finally acceptance.

Kate helped Penny pull ornaments out of the storage boxes. "Look, Penny, I gave you this one years ago. It's Santa Claus doing a yoga tree pose!"

"I love that one. It's so cute," said Penny, hanging it on the tree. "Can you believe this is our tenth year sharing Christmas together? Next year, we'll have a baby cooing in a crib or bouncy thing while we decorate for the holidays. It's so exciting!" They were growing up; it caused a tear to form in her eye. "Again, with the tears," thought Penny.

Kate noticed the touching moment and gave Penny a hug. "Promise me, no matter what happens down the road, we'll always spend Christmas together. I know we may have boyfriends or husbands and kids and who knows what, but let's blend it all together."

"I know we will," said Penny. "Let's have a cup of tea and finish the tree later."

Kate and Penny spent the afternoon decorating the tree. Later in the evening, Penny went out with Wes. Frank had gotten back to him. The background check on Phillip turned up nothing odd or suspicious; he was squeaky clean.

Kate cooked dinner for Phillip at her place. She, the takeout queen, gave it a try. When she pulled the charred roast out of the oven, she threw her hands up in disgust and called her favorite restaurant. A few minutes later, two beautiful meals arrived. Phillip was captivated with her efforts. He knew Kate Wesson didn't spend time mashing potatoes in her kitchen. Her penthouse apartment on Sixteenth Street was impressive. It was fashionable but comfortable. Ironically, the kitchen was a chef's kitchen with a huge white marble island and a Viking professional oven, which made him chuckle. The living room, with a fireplace, was exposed to the kitchen for an open-concept feel. There was a separate formal dining room, three bedrooms, and two bathrooms. One of the bedrooms Kate used as an office. The penthouse had a beautiful outdoor terrace, which was about the size of Phillip's entire apartment.

"I had no idea you had such a huge condo." Phillip was shocked at how massive it was and slightly embarrassed that he was still living in a studio apartment. He was making progress in his field. The first big deal was with Kate two months earlier, and he felt confident he was on the right track. Phillip was thirty-two years old, the same age as Kate, and bewildered at the wealth she'd acquired at their age. He grew up in Columbus, Ohio, and did his undergrad at Ohio State, where he was active in his fraternity. He had such a good time in college; he stayed there six years, switching majors three times. Graduate school wasn't an option due to his delay in graduating. He was hired out of college as a media planner for Procter & Gamble and relocated to New York City. Phillip enjoyed his colleagues, and three years flew by before he pondered if media and advertising were a long-term fit for him. He put in his application for the fire department but wasn't selected. It bummed him out; he'd been a baseball player in college and missed the physical activity as well as the camaraderie. At a dinner party, he met Tom Blackwell, the owner of Simon and Blackwell Realty, and they talked about sales. A year later, Phillip passed the realtor exam for the state of New York and joined Tom at his small, boutique company.

"I didn't intend on buying something this big. Four years ago, a potential client called and asked me to stop by her condo. I'd been recommended by a friend, a mutual friend. She trusted me to take a look at her place and tell her what

I thought she could get for it. Of course, she had some idea; she wasn't clueless about the market. I was familiar with the building; I sold a one bedroom on a lower floor the year before. I knew it was a full-service luxury doorman building, and I was curious what the penthouse looked like. I took the meeting, and when I walked in, I felt a tickle in my stomach. I love everything about it, and I've seen a lot of condos and co-ops in this city. Not to mention the brownstones; I always pictured myself buying a brownstone. The look of an old brownstone suits me, regal and comfortable at the same time. Anyway, I didn't see myself being in a penthouse. But, when I walked in, I knew it was home. I spend a lot of time running around the city, and when I come home, I feel pampered and secure. It's silly really, but I love it."

"Who wouldn't love it? It's amazing. I think I'll stay here forever." Phillip stretched out on the cream-colored velvet chaise lounge and grabbed Kate's hand, pulling her to him. "Didn't you tell me on our first date you often spend the night on Penny's sofa in the village?"

"Yeah, I do, on occasion. Isn't it hysterical? We always go out in her neighborhood, and I don't know; it feels fun to hang out there. By the way, her sofa is incredibly comfortable." Kate laughed at herself. She knew it was odd that she enjoyed staying at Penny's when she had such a spacious, beautiful home.

"What are you thinking about?" Phillip noticed her thoughtful look. Since the news of the baby broke, he felt different. He was going to be a dad, and it excited him. Kate was beautiful, successful, and generous. Although they hadn't spent a lot of time together, he was extremely fond of her. He could see them spending the rest of their lives together, but he didn't want to startle Kate by professing his love and adding to her anxiety. He had two older sisters, each with a child. He was already an uncle and loved it. Phillip thought he'd be more apprehensive about taking on such an enormous responsibility, but he was euphoric. His parents would insist he propose to Kate immediately; they were extremely conservative. Of course, he wasn't a child anymore, which he would remind them. They couldn't refuse him his trust fund because he didn't have one. He'd never heard more people talk about their trust fund than his colleagues in New York City. In Ohio, it wasn't common for children to live off their parents, at least not in the circles he ran in. He didn't care if Kate was rich or poor; he wanted nothing more than to love her.

"You'll laugh; I was contemplating what color to paint the nursery." Kate smiled at him.

"Are you going to ask about the sex of the baby at the sonogram?" Phillip already imagined playing baseball with his son. It was too soon to be having daydreams about the great time he'd be having with a boy. He scolded himself for doing it. On the other hand, he imagined holding the hand of a cute toddler girl with brunette curls meandering down the sidewalk. People would stop and comment, "Oh, isn't she adorable?" and he'd smile. He realized he didn't care if the baby was a girl or boy; he would be proud. How could a simple guy from Ohio be so lucky?

"They won't know the sex yet but later, maybe. What do you think?" Kate didn't like surprises; everything in her life was neat and organized. She knew she'd have to know whether it was a girl or boy, but it was too soon to think about it.

"I think it would be good to know, but I will leave that up to you." Phillip stood up and reached for her again. "All that matters is that you and the baby are healthy and happy." He pulled her close to him and gently kissed her.

Kate looked into his eyes and kissed him again. "Thank you, Phillip, for being here."

"There is nowhere else I'd rather be," Phillip whispered in her ear. He was falling in love with Kate Wesson.

❧

Regina had two more shows in Atlanta and then was booked on a plane to Boston. She planned on spending Christmas with Valerie. Henry, Valerie's boyfriend, would be there too. It would be an enormous love-fest reunion, and she was looking forward to it. The crowds in Atlanta were awesome. The roar of the audience laughing was a high, which gave her strength and fortified her sacrifices. She'd been opening for one of her favorite comics, Doug Cullman. He was a seasoned comedian, with numerous appearances on Conan and Fallen, and she almost fainted when she saw the lineup. He drew the biggest crowds, and they came ready to laugh. She'd seen him around, but they'd never officially met. He was far too famous for her group of comedians, the ones she spoke with on a regular basis.

Regina was staying with her cousin, Angela, who lived in Virginia Highlands, a quaint-downtown section of Atlanta. Regina loved the neighborhood, full of cute restaurants, bars, coffee shops, and bookstores. Regina took Marta, the subway system, to the club in Buckhead every night, but Angela insisted on picking her up and driving her back home.

Tonight, Regina arrived at the club wearing a pair of shredded jeans, black hoodie, and platform black leather boots. She was five foot three and petite. The boots added two inches to her height and made her feel tough. When she arrived the club was closed, but the bar manager was inside. She tapped on the window and caught a glimpse of her reflection. Her wavy blond hair was tousled, and she subconsciously tucked a few stray strands behind her ear. She was surprised to see Doug Cullman sitting in the bar area alone with his notebook. He glanced up when she walked in. Regina didn't want to bother him; he was clearly working on his set. "Maybe he's going to try some new material on the audience tonight," thought Regina. The crowds had been awesome; it was a good time to throw in some new jokes and see if they worked. She planned on doing the same.

"Regina Rae," shouted Doug from his table in the corner.

"Yes," she said timidly. Had she done something wrong? Was he going to fire her? She wasn't even sure he could fire her, but maybe he could have the club owner fire her. She froze in her steps.

"I'm Doug; nice to meet you." He stepped forward, offering his hands for a shake. "You've been killing it out there every night. I'm absolutely impressed."

"Thanks. The crowds have been really accommodating, but I appreciate the vote of confidence."

"You don't need any votes of confidence. You rock. Who writes your material?" Doug noticed Regina the first night. He couldn't understand how he'd missed her in the comedy circles. He called a few of his friends, and they'd seen her perform and thought she was an up-and-coming star. Not only was she hysterical, but also she was beautiful.

"Oh, thanks, Doug. That means a lot coming from you. I write everything myself. Don't you?" Regina longed for a staff of writers who'd come up with continual fresh material for her to try.

"Oh yeah, I create it all. Sometimes a writer tries to sell me a joke, but it's never worked out for me. I don't think they know me as well as I know myself. Can you sit for a few minutes, or are you in a rush to get backstage?" He arrived early tonight, hoping to run into her. His strategy worked.

"Sure, I'm in no rush. I was thinking of putting some new material into my set tonight, but I've got everything worked out, I think." She laughed and joined him at the table.

"Would you like anything to eat or drink? I could get something for you from the kitchen." He chuckled at himself for sounding so cavalier.

"No, I'm good, thanks! You've got a solid collection of groupies; you must be proud of your following." Regina couldn't think of anything better to say. He was a huge star as far as she was concerned, but stardom had never impressed her. She wasn't a stargazer. She thought it was odd people worshiping other people. Some guy or girl got a break and wound up making a lot of money. What was there to idolize? This guy had skill and talent, and she found him intriguing, but her interest had nothing to do with his television appearances. A famous actor lived across the street from her building in the Lower East Side. A steady line of tourists would stop every day in front of his building to take photos of themselves standing near his residence. They'd even photograph his newspaper lying on the steps of his home. She thought it was ridiculous behavior. She could understand respecting someone's talent, but in her eyes worshiping other human beings didn't make a lot of sense.

"I've got a great group of loyal followers, but I'm not an overnight success. What about you? Where did you start your career? Where do you call home?"

"I'm from Tennessee originally, but I moved to New York City after I graduated from high school. I did my first stand-up gig at an open-mic night in the city."

"So did I." Doug smiled. "We have something in common already."

"New York City, I can hardly wait to move back. I've been on the road for almost a year now." Her agent assured her that once she moved back to the city, she'd still be doing a little traveling to Jersey, Connecticut, upstate New York, and Los Angeles. Regina didn't mind as long as she could get back to her apartment and feel grounded again. Hotels, guest rooms, and sofas were getting old.

"I believe they call that 'paying your dues.' I was wondering if you'd be able to have dinner with me after the show?"

"I'd love to, but my cousin will be here after my set to pick me up. I've been staying with her this week in Virginia Highlands. I'd hate to change plans on short notice. I could tomorrow night if you're free."

"I am now," said Doug with a bright smile. "If you don't mind waiting until the end of the show tomorrow night, we can leave from here. I know a fun place in Virginia Highlands and then I can drop you off at your cousins afterward."

Regina and Doug talked in the bar area for an hour, before Regina realized an audience was beginning to gather outside. Doors would open in five minutes and the performance would start in thirty. She needed a little time to clear her mind and focus on the show. They hurried backstage, and Regina went to her small, unglamorous backstage room to prepare. She was really looking forward to hanging out with Doug Cullman. Rarely did she socialize with other comics. It seemed pointless, since they were always trying to get someone, including her, to criticize or praise them. It was an observation she made early in her career, and she promised herself no matter how lousy or fantastic she did onstage, she'd never seek colleagues out to weep to or rejoice with. It was a sign of weakness, and she never wanted to feel weak. Later, when she walked onstage, she noticed Doug standing in the wings. Her stomach took a leap, and her knees began to tremble until she felt the cold aluminum microphone in her hand, and then it was business. This was her job. For a few minutes, the audience forgot any trivial problems they might be enduring and simply laughed.

Just in case you ever foolishly forget;
I'm never not thinking of you.
—VIRGINIA WOOLF, *SELECTED DIARIES*

Chapter 14

*W*es got off work at seven in the evening and stopped at the corner of Sixth Avenue and Bedford Street to see Rick, the tree guy. He was fascinated with Penny's love of Christmas. Her tree was awesome and made her apartment feel cozy and cheerful. He wanted to surprise her with something festive. A fresh wreath was on his mind when he showed up at the market.

Rick Early was wearing a plaid shirt and jeans. His moustache and beard, along with his wardrobe, made him look like a lumberjack. Wes had to grin when he saw him. The guy looked as if he was born to sell Christmas trees. Wes pictured Rick out in the woods, chopping down the trees and loading them into a wagon.

"I'm buying this for a woman, someone special; she's very fond of Christmas," said Wes as he browsed the various wreath arrangements with Rick at his side.

Rick looked at him hard for a moment. "You're not talking about Penny, are you?"

"How could you possibly know that?" Wes glared at him in disbelief. "You do know this is a city with ten million people, right?"

"Sure, but how often do you meet a woman like Penny?" Rick flashed a big smile.

"When you put it that way, I have to agree. I'd say she's special, but that would be an understatement."

"I think this one would be good for her," said Rick, picking up a large, fresh wreath with a fat red bow. "I'll throw in some mistletoe."

"Mistletoe, great; I'll put it on every door entrance." Wes handed Rick some cash and shook his hand. "Nice to meet you, Rick, and Merry Christmas!" Wes walked away wondering how Rick was so familiar with Penny. It felt strange. Maybe he was being overly protective, but it bothered him out, and he'd discuss it with Penny.

Wes was at Penny's door fifteen minutes later. "I've got a little gift for you." He stepped out into the hallway and came back with the wreath.

Penny squealed with delight. "It's wonderful! Let's hang it up now."

Wes found a hammer and a nail in Penny's toolbox, and minutes later the wreath was on the door.

"Thank you; it's so pretty."

Wes was pleased with himself. Her troubles seemed to be dimed by the joy of the season. "My mother is the same way; she loves the holidays. Wyatt, Nick, and I wore matching Christmas pajamas every year until we were old enough to refuse them. We always went to my grandfather's farm upstate to pick out a tree the weekend after Thanksgiving. My dad would bring it home a few weeks before Christmas, and the whole family would gather to decorate it. My mom insisted we spend quality time together as a family at Christmas time."

"Were the pajamas red-and-green plaid?" Penny giggled.

"Close, they were red-and-white plaid." The both laughed.

He wanted Penny to meet his parents on Christmas, but he was waiting for the right time to ask her. She was still opposed to a relationship, so he wasn't sure she'd agree to family dinner.

"Isn't it beautiful?" asked Penny, standing back to look at the tree again. "Oh wait, let me turn the lights on. It's even more magical with the white lights."

"Penny, how well do you know Rick, the Christmas-tree guy?" He couldn't shake the weirdness. New York City was a big city, and it seemed a little small townish for Rick to know Penny.

"He's been showing up on the corner for the past eight or nine years. He's from Vermont, and his two sons come with him. Did you see their camper? They actually sleep in that thing for the entire three weeks. Did he sell you the wreath?"

"Yeah, he did. I found it strange that he knew who you were. I mean I barely mentioned a woman I was seeking a gift for, and he guessed it was you. You're beautiful and unique, but for some reason, I found it peculiar."

"Oh, don't be weird. I've been buying my tree from him for years. Sometimes, I take him a Christmas gift or hot-spiced cider when it's really cold outside. He knows a lot of people in the neighborhood. Remember, Greenwich Village is a community, even though it's in the middle of New York City. That's part of the charm of living here; it's a small town feel in the middle of an enormous city."

"All right, maybe it's the firefighter in me, looking for a situation when there isn't one." Wes smiled, but he made a note to himself; he'd look into Rick or have one of his buddies at the NYPD do it. "I'm glad you're coming with me to the fire-department event. Phillip and Kate are hyped about it, and Nick is looking forward to meeting you."

"Ugh," said Penny. "I really despise leaving the city; two hours in a car, blah." She hadn't willingly joined in on the event. Kate and Phillip were superexcited about it. "How could I say no with all the peer pressure?"

"I promise you, you'll have a great time. Also, I have a surprise for you; we added something to the lineup, especially for you."

"Wes, you know you can't promise me I'll have a great time. It's impossible for you to predict how I'll feel about your toy-drive festival." Penny hesitated and looked at his boyish grin. "What kind of surprise? You're not going to get onstage and ask me to marry you again, are you?"

"I would if it would work! You'll see when we get there. Now, where's that hot-spiced cider you were promising me?"

❧

On Friday late afternoon, Penny, Wes, Kate, and Phillip climbed into Wes's sport utility vehicle and made their way to Kent, Connecticut.

"It's the cutest town I've ever seen," squealed Penny. "Look, Kate, Main Street is covered in lights, and there's a tree in the town square. I can't believe I'm going to say it, but it's magical." She felt as though she was leaping into a storybook and each page provided another beautiful backdrop.

Wes spotted the signs directing the fire personnel and their friends and family to Nick's home. It appeared everyone in the municipality was happy to see the participants arrive. "See, all we have to do is follow the signs," said Wes proudly. "The van drivers shouldn't get lost."

When Wes made the turn into his brother's driveway, Penny gasped at the sight. The winding driveway, surrounded by tall white trees, beckoned the fairies out from their hiding places. She squinted to see if she could catch one with her eye. Nick's home was immense, and thousands of lights had been draped around each window and gable. On the roof, Santa Claus, his sleigh, and reindeers were ready for flight. The home was hidden on eighty acres of forest. The land immediately surrounding the home was groomed, and Penny spotted a stage and a large pile of sticks, twigs, leaves, and wood waiting to be turned into a bonfire. On the far right of the stage, an enormous Christmas tree was glowing with bright white lights. Penny was breathless; she never imagined it would be so beautiful.

Nick greeted them when they arrived and led them into his house. Kate and Penny weren't surprised at how handsome he was. They gave each other a glance that needed no words. He looked nothing like Wes and Wyatt. Penny remembered Nick was the Greek one, like his mom; while he and Wyatt were Irish, like his dad. It made her laugh out loud.

"Penny, so nice to meet you," said Nick when they entered the front door. "Wes hasn't stopped talking about you since you poured water on him."

"Nice to meet you, Nick. Thank you for hosting us." Penny liked Nick immediately. He was warm and friendly. The three brothers, besides being incredibly good-looking, had one thing in common: coziness.

Wes and Penny took the large bedroom on the second floor with a view of the grounds. She could see the Christmas tree from their window. The house was designed to feel like a tree house. The windows were large and open, creating a feeling of the outdoors blending inward. The bathroom attached had a huge soaking tub sitting beside floor-to-ceiling windows. The large tree directly outside the windows created a curtain of privacy. Phillip and Kate had a room on the opposite side of the house, with amazing views of the forest. Kate was captivated by Nick's home. Her real-estate expertise was specialized in New York City, and she contemplated if she should expand into Connecticut.

The guests began to arrive around seven in the evening. Vans and buses carted people from the town square to the secluded oasis. The vans were red, white, and green, and each van driver wore a Santa hat and was instructed to play the Christmas music they were given. Fifteen NYPD officers roamed the property, while dozens more plainclothes cops mingled in the crowd. Keeping the event orderly and crisis-free was top priority for Nick and Wes. By ten o'clock there were at least four hundred people on the lawn. The band played an assortment of Christmas music, and the partygoers sang along. A team of volunteers, dressed like elves, gathered the toys and canned food as the guests arrived. Twenty golf carts with dump beds were decorated to look like sleighs, and the elves were in charge of loading the food and toys onto their carts and driving them away. An eighteen-wheeler parked nearby, when full, would leave for a warehouse in the Bronx. Later, the church would distribute the goods to children and families in need.

There were five bars with beer kegs and four tents where red and white wine was served. Santa's helpers, dressed in red and white, passed out hot chocolate, eggnog, and apple cider. Two local restaurants were grilling hamburgers, roasting chestnuts, and serving hot pretzels.

Phillip worked the crowd; he was the perfect combination of partygoer and businessman. Kate, who was mesmerized by the entire workings of the event, had little desire to speak with anyone professionally. She and Penny floated around, laughing and chatting with guests and sipping hot cider.

Penny snuck up behind Wes and hugged him. "This is wonderful! You must be so proud." She regretted her blasé attitude the previous day and understood why he wanted them to experience it.

"Thank you, Penny. It means a lot to me." He grabbed her hand and led her to a group of his friends. "Frank, you remember Penny?"

Frank bowed as he had the first night they met. "Penny, it's nice to meet you again." He picked her hand up and gently kissed it. "Wes puts on quite an event! What do you think?"

"I think it's magical. I can't believe the massive amount of toys and food being donated." She knew it was fun for them to socialize in the woods, away from the stress of their jobs. They lead demanding lives, and for one night, they were free to celebrate with their friends and family in a safe, festive environment.

"A good cause, for sure; thanks for coming. I hear the tree was added this year in your honor. Wes says you're fond of Christmas and trees." The other people standing around chuckled.

Later, Penny pulled Wes aside and asked him why they were laughing.

"Everyone knows I'm trying to impress you, and they think I went overboard on the size of the tree."

"They're laughing at you for doing something thoughtful for me?" asked Penny. She thought his friends were being rude.

"They're laughing with me, not at me," said Wes. "There's a big difference. Relax, Penny; we're a family."

Wyatt interrupted their conversation. "Great turnout this year, bro," said Wyatt as he passed by with two drinks in his hand.

"Yeah, awesome," said Wes, but Wyatt was already on his way to his date, Carmella.

"I see Wyatt brought a date," said Penny. "She's stunning."

"Stunningly smart," said Wes. "She's a doctor, a surgical oncologist, with on office on the Upper West Side. They'll be staying at the house tonight, too."

"Wow." Penny was having a hard time keeping her eyes off Carmella. "Maybe I'll get to speak with her tomorrow at lunch. Looks like your brother isn't going to let her wander too far."

"No, he's smitten." Wes laughed. "Look at him; he's like a puppy."

The bonfire was lit at ten o'clock, and the crowd cheered with delight. Penny found it ironic that a bunch of firefighters would choose to have a bonfire at an event. They were praising the fire like heathens. Didn't they fight fire, not applaud it? Perhaps, there was an inside story; she'd have to remember to ask Wes about it.

At midnight as the fire burned down, Santa's helpers passed out marshmallows, chocolate, and graham crackers so they could make s'mores by the fire. The crowd dwindled to a hundred people and felt more intimate. At two in the morning, an elf walked onstage and read a Christmas poem.

Twas the night before Christmas and all through the town,
the fire siren echoed blaring its sound.
The firefighters came running from far and from near,
and raced to the trucks quickly donning their gear.

And I in my bunkers my boots and my hat,
jumped to the engine to see where the fire's at.
Down at the corner of Fifth and of Oak,
the dispatcher informed us of a house filled with smoke.

Smoke poured from the sides, from up and from down,
yet up on the roof there was none to be found.
So up to the rooftop we raised up a ladder,
and climbed to the top to see what was the matter.

I came to the chimney and what did I see,
but a fellow in red stuck past his knees.
Well we tugged and we pulled until he came out,
then he winked with his eye and said with a shout.

"These darn newfangled chimneys they make them too small,
for a fellow as I, not skinny at all."
With a twitch of his nose he dashed to his sleigh,
and called to his reindeer, "AWAY now, AWAY."

As we rolled up our hoses he flew out of sight, saying
"God bless our firefighters" and to all a good night.

The elf took a bow and whished everyone a safe trip back to their hotel.

When the last of the vans and golf carts had diminished from the property, the brothers and their guests headed back to Nick's house for a nightcap. A few officers stayed behind to ensure the bonfire was completely hosed down. They also searched the property for anyone who might have been left behind.

Penny couldn't believe how perfectly orchestrated the event was. It was a massive undertaking, and Wes and Nick made it look easy.

The overnight guests slept late the following morning. Brunch was scheduled for noon, and Penny was surprised to see it was catered. There was an omelet station with a chef who'd prepare your eggs exactly as desired. The table was beautifully decorated, and each setting had a nameplate. Kate and Phillip were the last couple to arrive, and everyone stopped talking to welcome them to the group. Penny saw Kate's cheeks turn rosy.

Nick was the only married Lane brother. Annie, his wife, was caring for their two young sons, who'd come down with bronchitis. They skipped the event, choosing to remain in Manhattan. Annie sent her best wishes to everyone that Nick announced when he gave the toast before brunch. Penny watched the three brothers chatting over the meal, and the bond between them captivated her.

Carmella, Wyatt's date, was seated in between Wes and Wyatt. She was tall and beautiful with creamy brown hair. She wore dark black-rimmed eyeglasses, cream-colored slacks, and a black turtleneck. Wyatt lingered on her every word.

After brunch, the couples and Nick gathered in the large living room. Nick, Wyatt, Wes, and Phillip were pumped to watch the giant's game. Kate suggested the girls go for a walk.

"I want to watch the football game," huffed Penny, joining Kate in the kitchen.

"Don't you want to talk to Carmella? It's the only way we'll get a minute with her. Wyatt doesn't share her."

"Yeah, good idea," said Penny. "Let's grab our sneakers."

It was a five-mile hike into town. Carmella captivated Kate and Penny with talk of her medical practice. It was clear to them; her work was rewarding but demanding. They stopped on Main Street to shop at the charming stores. Penny bought a large hooded sweat shirt with the name of the town on it.

Carmella picked up a pair of black leather gloves. "I always leave a pair of gloves in a cab at least once a year. It's good to have an extra pair."

"I remember my gloves; I leave a lot of hats. I wonder what the cabbies do with all those hats and gloves!" Penny and Carmella giggled about it.

Kate bought an ornament at a Christmas store to remember the weekend. "Look, Penny, we can add this one to your tree next year!"

"Kate, you're supposed to buy a gift for yourself, not for my tree."

"All right, I'll find something for myself. Or maybe I'll buy something for Phillip."

"For yourself," insisted Penny.

Kate selected a red cashmere scarf. "Now, I look ready for Christmas," Kate said as she tried it on in the store. Carmella and Penny gave her a thumbs-up, and the three of them started out on their five-mile walk back to the mansion.

"I didn't expect Nick's home to be so elaborate," said Penny, picking up her pace in order to keep up with Kate and Carmella. "He must be an amazing dentist."

"You do know the Lane brothers are part of the Nabisco fortune?" asked Carmella, stopping for a moment to let Penny catch up.

"Excuse me? Did you say the Nabisco fortune? I don't think so. Wes is a fireman in New York City."

"Oh, I know. They've all chosen outstanding careers. I guess Wesley's is the most sacrificing. Their great-grandfather was the founder of Nabisco." Carmella laughed. "I can't believe Wesley didn't tell you. I'm sorry for letting the cat out of the bag. I assumed you knew."

Penny and Kate stared at each other with blank looks on their faces.

"I'm totally shocked. I can't believe he didn't tell me." Penny was trying to process the information.

"Maybe he didn't think it was important." Kate was stunned, but she felt the need to take up for him.

"Of course, the company was sold years ago, so they have no involvement with it. But, as you can imagine, it was a remarkable buyout. Wyatt told me Wes wants you to come to Christmas lunch with the family. He'll have to tell you; wait until you see their parents' home in the city." Carmella felt bad for spilling the beans. "Maybe you shouldn't tell him I told you. I don't mean to sound like a teenager asking you to keep a lid on it. What do you think? Could you keep the secret until Christmas?"

"Don't feel bad; I'm glad you told me. I would've been in complete astonishment at Christmas dinner. I'll keep the secret. It'll be interesting to see him squirm. I wonder if he'll try to explain it away or come clean."

Kate laughed out loud. "I love it. Let him suffer in silence. How much fun! I'm sorry I won't be able to see the expression on his face." The three stunning brothers were multimillionaires. It surprised her. They were the sweetest, down-to-earth people Kate had ever met. She never would have guessed.

"Thank you, Penny; that's very kind of you. By the way, you'll love his parents. I'm so happy you'll be there."

"Well, he hasn't asked me yet. But when he does, I'll say yes. This is going to be so much fun." Penny was lighthearted; she couldn't believe he didn't share something this important with her. On the other hand, she completely understood why he didn't.

The girls were so engrossed in their conversation, they didn't notice the blue car pull up beside them.

"Excuse me, it's awfully chilly to be walking. Can I offer you ladies a ride somewhere?"

You pierce my soul. I am half agony, half hope. Tell me not that I am too late, that such precious feelings are gone forever.

—JANE AUSTEN, *PERSUASION*

Chapter 15

*T*he Saturday-night crowd at the Atlanta Comedy Club proved to be as outstanding as the previous nights. Regina felt a surge of energy when she left the stage. Every new item she put in her lineup worked. The audience was pumped up to see the headliner; she was in the right place at the right time. However, she promised herself she'd try the same material in Boston and see if it worked as well there. Her Southern self-deprecating jokes worked much better in the east than in the Midwest. She tried to learn something each time she stepped onstage. Being on the road was a learning experience, and she understood why her agent wanted her to travel around the country. It made her stronger. Regina took a seat at the back of the club and settled in to watch Doug perform. He worked the crowd with precision, and they loved it. She wondered how he handled hecklers. It was something she feared, although she was learning how to take power away from them. Typically, the person creating the disturbance was drunk. Club owners always had bouncers prepared to escort an unruly person out of the club. Her fear wasn't dealing with the heckler as much as being able to get the crowd back to her monologue. Once someone interrupted her set, the audience became distracted and unable to focus on her words until he or she was either taken out or embarrassed enough to force them into silence. Ad-libbing was a gift and a skill, and she'd love to see how Doug handled it, but she didn't wish a heckler on him.

Doug and Regina planned to meet each other at the backstage door after he exited the stage. If he waited for the crowd to disperse, he'd wind up getting dangled up with fans. He told her what his last bit was in his act. When she heard it, she got up quietly and left the club. Regina walked around the corner and stood outside the door. Minutes later, Doug walked out, and they both laughed at how clever they were. His rental car was parked across the street, so their getaway was quick and easy.

Doug chatted easily with Regina on their drive from Buckhead to Virginia Highlands. She was relieved he didn't talk about himself the entire time, which was common for a performer. Regina was guilty of it as well. It was an occupational hazard. Performers ran their own business, and their business was themselves. She hated that actors, musicians, and comics were often touted as egotistical. It was true, perhaps; however, it was the nature of their business.

"Have you tried Taco Mac?" Doug asked. He had favorite places in all of the twenty cities he frequented. Comedy kept him on the road, and it helped him feel like a resident of each city when he found a few spots where the locals hung out.

Taco Mac was a beer-and-wing joint that he loved. Doug's manager booked him hotels in every city he did stand-up in. He didn't mind the hotel experience. Sometimes it was nice to order room service and enjoy the solitude. However, in Atlanta, he had a college buddy who lived in Midtown. They enjoyed hanging out together and catching up when he was in town.

"I've been to Taco Mac, love the wings," said Regina enthusiastically. "And the beer," she added with a snicker.

"Great! We get to share an Atlanta-food experience together." Doug looked for a parking space along the crowed street. "Looks like it's going to be tough finding parking on a Saturday night."

"I don't mind walking if you want to park in the residential section." Regina was surprised at how many people were out. "If you can't find anything, you can park at my cousin's. She lives a few blocks from here."

"That would be awesome. Do you need to ask her?"

"I'll text her so she won't wonder who's parked in the driveway."

Regina and Doug found a corner booth at Taco Mac and settled in for beer and wings. The manager recognized Doug from his appearances on the Conan Show and told them whatever they ordered was on the house. Doug was gracious but explained he was more than happy to cover the bill. The manager insisted, and Doug conceded.

"The perks of being a celebrity," said Regina, giving him a boost of confidence. He seemed embarrassed by the attention.

"I'm flattered. It rarely happens, but I guess I should be grateful when it does. I don't think I handle it well. I should ask my manager for advice." Even though Doug was a seasoned comedian, he was shy. It was only onstage or on camera where he felt comfortable. In everyday life, with other people, he was timid and unsure of himself.

Regina found it endearing. "I think you handled it like a pro."

⁕⁓⁕

Penny and Kate froze in their steps. It was the same man in the blue car.

"No, we're fine," said Carmella. "Thanks for your offer, but we enjoy walking."

Kate quickly decided to push back. "Don't you live in the West Village in New York City?"

"You do," said Penny. "I've seen you on multiple occasions." She gave him a hard look.

"What brings you to Connecticut?" asked Kate.

"It's good to get out of the city from time to time," he said with a devilish grin on his face.

"I'm sorry, I didn't get your name," said Penny. How dare this man interrupt a beautiful weekend in the country? It was really starting to make her angry.

"I'm Samuel," said the man. "Nice to finally meet you. Have a great day."

"The nerve," said Kate.

"Do you know that man?" asked Carmella, noticing a touch of anger in Kate's voice.

"Sort of," said Penny. "I've seen him around my neighborhood. It's probably just a coincidence. He seems like a nice guy." Penny turned to Kate and rolled her eyes.

Once back at the mansion, Kate pulled Penny into the kitchen. "Penny, this has gotten out of control. You've got to go to the cops or let Wes know; he can help you."

"I've got Ivan handling it."

"Ivan, when did you see Ivan?"

"The other day. Don't worry; he'll have his people get to the heart of it. I'm not scared, Kate. You shouldn't be either."

∞

Luke decided to throw an intimate Christmas Eve dinner. His decorator finished ahead of schedule. He understood she was leaving for London the week of Christmas and wanted to get all her clients settled before she left. Whatever the reason, he was delighted. Luke knew Kate would tweak each room and was prepared for her eagerness to help. They didn't always agree on style, but, without a doubt, she had impeccable taste. He invited Kate and her new boyfriend Phillip, whom he was yearning to meet. It had been so long since Kate brought a man to a family dinner. He couldn't imagine who caught her eye. She was too busy and focused on her work to worry about men. Luke and Penny were the only two people she consistently made time for. Penny was bringing Wes. He heard from Kate that Wes was a handsome fireman. Was it a perquisite for the job? Luke chuckled as he assembled the table with his treasured Spode Christmas china. Billy would be joining them. He was an excellent cook and had a simple, elegant dinner menu planned. They'd start with fresh shrimp and crab for the appetizers. Prime rib with roasted potatoes, carrots, and brussels sprouts for the main meal. The only item not being baked in Luke's innovative, fully renovated kitchen was the cake. They opted for a German chocolate cake from Amy's on Bleecker Street. It was so delicious; they knew everyone would be pleased.

At seven in the evening, the first guests arrived. It was Kate with Phillip. Luke greeted her at the door of his new home with a hug and a kiss. "I can't wait for you to see what the decorator did with the space," Luke said enthusiastically.

Kate was thrilled to see Luke excited. He looked like a kid in a candy store. "I'm sure I'll want to change a few things," said Kate. "After all, it wouldn't be right if I didn't complain about something."

"Exactly," said Luke. "It's a family tradition. Come in. Come in. Don't just stand on the doorstep." Luke offered his hand to Phillip. "I'm Kate's brother, Luke; nice to meet you."

"Thank you for inviting me. I'm honored." Phillip helped Kate with her coat.

"Billy's in the kitchen cooking. Let's take your coats into the guest room on this floor, and I'll start with the tour. We can circle back downstairs to talk to Billy when we're through. He gets testy in the kitchen when he's under pressure."

Kate and Luke laughed together. After they put their coats and Kate's purse in the guest room, Luke took them upstairs to show Kate the master bedroom.

Kate was enthralled with the master and every other room. She couldn't find one thing to change. "You have to give me the name of this woman; she's done an amazing job. I'll have to recommend her to some of my clients. Honestly, I'm trying to find something to complain about or to challenge her on, and I'm completely speechless."

"I'm so happy you like it, Kit-Kat," said Luke lovingly. He didn't want to say he was stunned. This was a kinder, gentler Kate. He wondered if Phillip had something to do with her serenity.

Phillip tagged along without saying much. He'd add a "terrific" and a "wow" occasionally to make it seem like he knew what he was talking about. After seeing Luke's home and Kate's penthouse, he was thinking he should tidy up his bachelor pad.

"I think that's enough talk about my new home," said Luke. He was interested in getting to know Phillip. It was exciting; Kate had a man in her life. He seemed like a gentleman, and the way he looked at Kate, it made Luke think he was already in love with his sister. What a wonderful Christmas this was going to be. "I think that's enough talk about my new home. Let's go downstairs and annoy Billy. His hair is probably standing straight up. I'm predicting he's worked himself into a seven on the one-to-ten stress monitor."

Penny and Wes arrived a few minutes later, and everyone gathered in the living room, chatting about last-minute shopping and holiday traffic in the city.

"I've got a wonderful bottle of Italian red. Let's all have a glass, shall we?" Luke dashed to the bar in the adjoining room.

Ten minutes later, Billy appeared in the living room looking somewhat tattered. He calmly announced dinner would be served if they'd join him in the dining area.

The food was amazing. Chef Billy stood up and took a bow. The chocolate-cake dessert received a five-star review from the guests. They all settled back into the living room for after-dinner coffee. Billy was sharing a story about Sherri Court, a famous supermodel. He acted out her refusal to wear a black bikini at a photo shoot. "Black bikinis are so eighties," said Billy in a high voice. "I refuse to wear it or be photographed in it." They were roaring with laughter when Kate suddenly stood up.

"I have an announcement to make." Kate cleared her throat. "Thank you, Luke and Billy, for such a beautiful dinner. This has been an amazing year, and I'm so happy we're together on this special day." Kate glanced at Penny and gave her an encouraging smile. "I didn't plan on making this speech tonight, but after being here with you all, I decided it's time to let everyone in on a secret. Penny, Wes, and Phillip already know, and it would be wrong of me to leave you two in the dark." Kate paused and looked directly at Luke and Billy. "Phillip and I are having a baby."

Luke almost fell off the sofa, and Billy reached to catch him.

"Woo-hoo!" Penny yelled to erase the awkward silence.

Luke regained his balance. "I couldn't be happier. It's simply the best Christmas ever." He got up and hugged his sister.

"I'm only a little more than two months. It's still early, but it felt wrong to keep it from you."

"I'm going to be an uncle. Could it be any better?" Luke turned to Billy with nervous excitement. "I'm going to be an uncle, Billy. Can you believe it?" Then he went to Phillip and gave him a pat on the back. "I look forward to getting to know you. Congratulations to you and my beautiful sister."

"We're so excited for you both," said Billy. "I'd like to think I'm going to be an uncle too." He hugged Kate and shook Phillip's hand.

"Of course, Billy, you're part of our family." Kate was glowing with joy. She was relieved. She didn't like keeping secrets from her brother. It was early in the pregnancy, but she knew she'd need everyone's support. It was important to her to have Luke and Billy's blessing.

"I propose a toast," said Penny. "Luke, help me with the glasses." She wanted to distract Luke and give him a job. It would give him a few extra minutes to process the information.

"I wondered why she wasn't drinking wine," Luke said to Penny. "I can't remember the last time my sister refused an exquisite red. This is the most wonderful news. I never would have guessed it. I mean where did Phillip come from? How long have they been seeing each other? Why hasn't she told me about him until now?"

Penny put both her hands on Luke's shoulders and looked him in the eyes. "Don't worry about all the details right now. Kate will fill you in later. Let's celebrate!"

❧

The text read as follows: *Wes, buddy, need to speak with you soon. I heard back from the lieutenant, and I've got some very interesting information.* Wes glanced at his phone as he put the last piece of tape on his mom's Christmas present. The message was from Frank. Wes cringed when he read it. His instincts were decent after years at the FDNY. He quickly replied, *I've got Christmas dinner with Penny and my folks. I'll call you later today—thanks, buddy.* Wes wanted to pick up the phone and call Frank immediately, but he knew Penny was dressed and waiting for him. He didn't want to be late for lunch. His mother liked everyone to be prompt, and prompt he was going to be.

Kate helped Penny pick out the dress. It was green with an Empire waist and long sleeves. She insisted Penny wear a string of her pearls as well as her diamond and pearl earrings. Penny stood back to look at herself in the mirror. It wasn't something she would typically wear. The lunch would be proper. She couldn't show up in black, which was almost only color of clothing in her closet. The color green looked great with her auburn hair and brought out the color of her eyes. It felt perfect for Christmas.

"You look beautiful," said Wes when he opened the car door for her.

"Thanks, Wes. You look handsome as well." Penny smiled at him.

"They'll probably have the lunch catered," Wes said as he pulled away from the curb. "Typically it's a really good meal. Don't be shy, water girl; eat as much as you like."

"Oh, I intend to." Penny was waiting for him to explain why his parents had an impressive home on Central Park West. It seemed as if he was toying with the idea of letting her in on the secret of his family's wealth.

"You know Wyatt and Carmella will be there." Wes glanced at Penny again. It was hard for him to keep his eyes on the road. He'd never seen Penny look so stunning.

"I know. I'm looking forward to speaking with Carmella again. She's incredibly smart and interesting. I like her."

"You'll finally get to meet Nick's wife. Apparently, the boys are feeling better, and they'll all be coming to lunch."

"Great. I'm sure your mom will be happy to have all of you under the same roof at the same time. Hope they have a large table," said Penny with a chuckle.

Wes stopped at a red light and glanced at her again. "There's something I should tell you."

"You forgot my Christmas present?" Penny laughed. "You don't have to get me anything."

"No, I didn't forget your present. It happens to be in the back seat with the others." Wes hesitated. The light turned green, and he focused on his driving. A few minutes later, he pulled over into an empty parking space along Sixth Avenue. "My parents have been pretty lucky in the business world. They've accumulated a comfortable nest egg."

"That's wonderful. I'm guessing your father's work as an attorney provided your family with a decent upbringing."

"Well, yes," said Wes. "But my father's father left him a substantial fund. I'm only telling you this because I don't want you to be alarmed at their lavish home or lifestyle. They really are simple folks, but it may appear a bit excessive on the outside."

"Are you embarrassed by them?"

"Not at all," said Wes. "Remember, they're simple people really." He put the car in drive and cautiously pulled back into traffic.

Penny chuckled on the inside. It was cute how he handled it. She was certain he didn't want her to feel intimidated. "We're all simple people, right, Wes?"

"Everyone but you, Penny. You're the most complicated individual I've ever met." Wes looked at the scowl on her face. "I meant that as a compliment."

Wes, Penny, Wyatt, and Carmella arrived at the same time. Penny was glad she'd been warned about the location and size of his parents' home. It was elaborate from the outside; she could hardly wait to see the inside.

The housekeeper greeted them at the door and took their coats. Moments later, Mrs. Lane appeared with hugs and kisses for her boys. "It's so wonderful to have you all here today." She turned to Penny and Carmella. "Please call me Emma."

After Nick and his family arrived, everyone was seated for lunch. Mr. Lane, Thomas, led the family in prayer and then gave an amusing toast.

Penny could see where Wyatt and Wes got their looks. Thomas was extremely handsome. Like Wes told Penny, Nick took after his mom. After an enormous lunch, they gathered around the Christmas tree to exchange gifts. She was surprised when Thomas and Emma presented a gift to her and Carmella.

"Just a little something," Emma said as she handed the package to Penny.

Inside the beautifully wrapped gift was a blue box from Tiffany's. Penny opened the small box and discovered a set of solitaire diamond platinum earrings. She gasped. Carmella glanced at Penny with a broad smile. They both got a pair.

"Thank you so much," said Penny. "They're lovely." She could only imagine how much they cost. Penny tossed those thoughts aside and decided to be appreciative and gracious.

Wes helped her remove them from the box. "Would you like to wear them? I'll help you. Thanks, Mom; your taste is flawless. These will go perfectly with the gift I got Penny."

Penny took Kate's pearl and diamond earrings off and put them in the small box while Wes helped her put the new diamonds on. He gave her a box, which was under the tree. She guessed the housekeeper had taken everything out of the back seat of his car and put it under the tree. When she opened the box, she discovered a waterproof raincoat from Lululemon, her favorite. There was also a pair of cool yoga pants and comfy sweater from the same and a gift card to the store. It was a great present, and she was thrilled. "You're right, Wes; the earrings will go perfectly with my yoga and dog-walking gear. Thank you for being so thoughtful." Penny pulled him aside. "You didn't tell me we'd be exchanging gifts. I should have brought your mom and dad something, and I left your small gift at home for later."

"Don't worry; I've got you covered," said Wes, nodding his head toward the gifts under the tree.

"Thank you," Penny whispered.

Emma insisted on giving Carmella and Penny a tour of the garden and then afterward, the rest of the home.

While his mom kept Penny busy, Wes snuck upstairs to his old room and opened the double glass doors leading to his terrace. He had a few minutes to call Frank. They'd never miss him if he worked quickly.

Frank answered on the second ring. "You aren't going to believe this," said Frank.

"Try me," said Wes.

One of Frank's best friends was a lieutenant at the NYPD. He had their detective look into Rick Early, the Christmas-tree guy.

"He's Penny's birth dad," said Frank. "No doubt about it."

When Wes hung up the phone, he felt nauseous. Had he stepped over the line? He found Penny's father by sheer accident. When he met the guy, he had an overwhelming suspicion Rick was hiding something, but he didn't expect this. He followed a hunch and stepped into something huge. Penny would assume he was out hunting for her father. He needed time to think of how he was going to handle this information. He couldn't keep it from her that would be wrong. But telling her might wreak havoc in her life. Even though Penny would never admit it, she was vulnerable and confused about the loss of her real mom. He knew Penny left an amazing job and changed careers suddenly. She plunged into a relationship with a guy who was wrong for her and who broke her heart. Finding her birth dad was big news. Wes had to take some time to contemplate the pros and cons of letting her in on the discovery. He was in a pickle.

"Wesley, what are you doing up there?" his mom called him from the garden. His terrace overlooked it.

"I'll be right down, Mom," yelled Wes. He had to decide what to do with the information. How a guy wound up in Vermont from San Francisco was his first question. Why did he sell Christmas trees? Was he really the bearded lumberjack, or was that an act? The other part he understood. Appearing in Penny's neighborhood once a year gave him a chance to see his daughter without being intrusive. Was the guy stable? Did he have alcohol or drug issues? There was so much information he had to sift through. He couldn't tell Penny anything until he had the missing pieces. Frank said the detective would meet with Wes to give him all the details. They couldn't get together for several days. It was, after all, Christmas.

Before everyone left the Lane house, Emma pulled Wes aside and whispered, "Your girlfriend is delightful. Please bring her around more often."

"Thanks, Mom. I'll try," Wes said and kissed her on the cheek. He treasured his mom; her advice and opinions meant a lot to him. Growing up, he and his brothers always jockeyed for attention from her. She was always present. They had nannies and housekeepers, but she was their main caregiver. Emma made breakfast, lunch, and dinner for them, read them books at night, and tucked them into bed. The Lanes were wealthy and always had a full staff at their disposal, but their mother never let them take her place. Wes admired her for it. He knew she could have relinquished more of her duties to others, but the fact she didn't meant the world to him. Their nanny had been with them for eighteen years, and the housekeeper for twenty-five. They were important people in his life. He loved both of them, but they could never replace his mother. Thomas and Emma appeared in love after all the years. If they had any issues, their sons never saw it. Wes longed for the kind of love the two of them shared. Nick believed he found it when he married Annie. Wyatt was in love with Carmella, but it was too soon to know if she felt the same way. Wes knew Penny was the one. He was making progress. She trusted him now, but there was still a part of her that was unavailable. "Patience," Wes reminded himself each day. It was his morning, afternoon, and evening mantra. The fact he added mantra to his vocabulary was odd. He had Penny to thank for that.

∽◌∾

Regina was stunned when Doug Cullman reached out to kiss her when he dropped her off at her cousin's house in Virginia Highlands. They had a great time at Taco Mac, but she was under the impression they were two comics getting together to talk business and have a few laughs. Without thinking and responding automatically to another person's advances, she kissed him back. He said, "Call you tomorrow." She was confused. Were they dating? She wasn't opposed to it. He was interesting, and she found his offstage personality charming and unexpected. Onstage, he was the life of the party. Privately, he was soft-spoken and somewhat shy. Regina was elated when she found out he was flying to Boston the next day. It appeared they were going to be performing at the same venue again. Her agent never gave her the lineup when she was performing at a club. Usually, she found out the first night of the booking. Another great crowd was her first thought, since his fans always came ready to laugh. It would be a great week. They'd have two days off for Christmas, which she planned on spending with Valerie and Henry. She was homesick for her apartment in New York and counting the days until she could move back in. It was lonely being on the road all the time, living out of a suitcase. She didn't complain about it to her friends. It would worry Kate and Penny if they knew she was tired.

Kate woke up on Christmas day to the smell of fresh coffee and pancakes. Phillip was in the kitchen preparing a full meal for both of them. He'd gone shopping before Luke's Christmas Eve party and stocked the refrigerator with fruits, vegetables, sushi, and fresh fish.

"Good morning," said Phillip when Kate emerged from the shower.

"Merry Christmas," said Kate. "Wow, look at you. You made breakfast!"

"I know how much you love takeout, but none of your favorite places are open on Christmas morning."

"I know. There are only a few occasions in this big wonderful city when I can't get food brought to my door, and this is one of them." Kate poured herself a cup of coffee and sat down at the table with Phillip.

"I made oatmeal, pancakes, bacon, and eggs with whole-wheat toast. What would you like?"

"I'll start with oatmeal and then pancakes." Kate laughed. "I'm starving."

Phillip and Kate enjoyed a big breakfast and decided to go back to bed. They planned on binge watching movies on Netflix. Kate knew Penny would be busy with Wes, and besides she wanted to hang out at home with Phillip.

Late afternoon, after watching two comedy romance flicks and one adventure film, Phillip went into the kitchen, put on his Santa Claus hat, and came back to the bedroom with a gift for Kate to open.

"Oh," said Kate, "you got me a present. I love presents. Thank you." She took it in her arms and shook it like a child would. "Hmm, let me guess."

"You'll never guess it," said Phillip. "Penny helped me pick it out."

"Did she? I wonder when the two of you had time to go shopping. Now I'm really curious."

"Open it," said Phillip. "I hope you like it."

Kate opened the medium-sized square box and discovered another box inside it. "I see. You've made this a puzzle. Cute," said Kate. She opened the other box, which was wrapped, and found a smaller box inside it. "This better be good," said Kate, giggling. Finally, she opened the small box and found a sterling silver baby rattle. Tied around the rattle was a pretty yellow ribbon and attached to the ribbon was a ring. Kate looked up at Phillip, afraid of what was going to happen next.

Phillip got down on one knee beside the bed. "Kate Renee Wesson, I knew the moment I met you, I'd never be the same. Regardless of how we came together, the most important thing is we are. I want to spend the rest of my life with you. Will you marry me?"

I want to love you wildly. I don't want words, but inarticulate cries, meaningless, from the bottom of my most primitive being, that flow from my belly like honey. A piercing joy, that leaves me empty, conquered, silenced.

—Anaïs Nin

Chapter 16

Rick Early pulled his secondhand Roadtrek camper van into his driveway. He was grateful Vermont was spared a blizzard while he was in New York City. The dirt road leading to his house could get dicey after a big snowstorm. Often, he was forced to leave the camper at the edge of the highway and walk the mile in the snow back to his house. It was remote, no neighbors in sight, and he liked it that way.

Mary, his wife, was waiting on the porch for her husband and two boys to arrive back home. It was lovely to have them home for Christmas even if it was in the middle of the night. Rick and the boys packed up their Christmas-tree business around ten on Christmas Eve night and drove the six hours straight back to Vermont. It was four in the morning. The plan was to get into bed quickly, sleep late, and have a Christmas lunch together. A big snowfall was predicted for the next day, and Rick was thankful they'd beat it. The firewood had been stacked behind the house before he left on his trip. They had all they needed to keep them warm. Mary always made sure the cupboards were full in the wintertime. They lived on the outskirts of the village of Waterbury, Vermont. It was a fifteen-minute drive to the nearest grocery store. They were accustomed to the snow in Vermont, and their used suburban got them most of the places they needed to go in the wintertime. However, the dirt road often caused an issue. Since they were the only residents who lived on the road, the village had never paved it. Rick considered doing it himself, but it was on the list of things he hadn't gotten around to.

"No need to worry about unloading the truck. We can do it tomorrow," Rick told his boys, Eli and Toby. "Let's get inside, have a bite to eat, and call it a day."

"Can we sleep late in the morning, Dad?" questioned Eli. He was the youngest, only thirteen, and he didn't like having to get up early to do his chores.

"We're all sleeping late tomorrow, Dumbo," said Toby. "It's Christmas, as if you haven't heard." Toby was fifteen and enjoyed teasing his younger brother. They were close enough in age to get along well together. However, three weeks living together in a camper could cause tension to mount. Toby was looking forward to sleeping in his own bed without his brother or dad beside him. He loved selling the trees in the city. It was an exciting place. For the past three years, he helped his dad with the Christmas-tree business, and more than anything, he wanted to move to New York City. First, he had to finish high school. He knew his dad would flip out if he mentioned it to him so. It was his secret, a dream he shared with no one.

Rick Early worked at the local lumber company. He'd been there for nineteen years. It wasn't an exciting work, but it suited him. He started out on the floor cutting wood, and two years later, he was promoted to manager. For years the owner of the company, Teddy O'Neal, left most decisions up to Rick. Teddy stopped by occasionally to check out new equipment Rick ordered or to bring lunch to the staff. He was a jolly fellow who acquired the business from his father, who opened the lumber company in 1952. Teddy was eighty-one years old, a widower with no children. Rick was like a son to him. The lumber-company business was always slow the weeks leading up to Christmas, and Teddy had given Rick his blessing to shut it down for three weeks so he could sell the trees. He wasn't sure why Rick enjoyed all the work the Christmas-tree business required, but it was a tradition now. The store would close, and Rick would sell trees in the city. After the New Year, the lumber company opened its doors again, and life returned to normal and ordinary until the same time next year.

Mary Early met Rick in Stowe, Vermont, when she was on a ski vacation with her girlfriends. It was the cutest town she ever saw, and she fell in love with the place immediately. Rick was working as a desk clerk. He was handsome but edgy, and she was attracted to his California accent, which he was trying to lose. She wondered why a guy from sunny California was working at an inn in Vermont, so she asked him.

"I was tired of the constant sunshine," he huffed, barely looking up from the book he was reading. The constant flow of beautiful women in and out of the place didn't appeal to him. He barely noticed them. He lived in a small room the hotel provided, read books, hiked, and took piano lessons. Every day, he mourned the loss of his wife and was drawn to the piano because the sound erased his fear. The last thing he wanted in his life was a woman. No one could or would replace Nora.

A year later, Mary received a job offer from an elementary school in Stowe and bought a house on the outskirts of Waterbury. She hadn't forgotten the brooding inn clerk with his funky glasses and stack of books. Once she got settled into her home and career, she dropped by the inn, hoping to find Rick. She didn't even know his last name. She found the manager of the inn and was disappointed when they told her Rick no longer worked there. She dropped her head in regret, thanked them for their time, and turned to leave. It had taken her too long to get back there. Now, she'd never see him again.

"If you really need to see him, you can find him at the lumber store. He's there every day," said the inn manager.

Mary stopped in her tracks, wiping the tear from her cheek. "Thank you so much. I met him a year ago, and he was helpful to my girlfriends and I, and well, I wanted to thank him for his kindness."

"That doesn't really sound like Rick," said the innkeeper with a snort. "Are you sure you have the right name?"

"Oh yes, thank you again. I'll find him," she said, making her way to the door. She couldn't help but laugh on her way to her car. The manager was right. Rick wasn't what most folks would call helpful. Regardless, Mary was ecstatic; he was still in the area.

To her delight, a slight grin lit up his face when she walked through the door of the lumber company. She wanted a large porch added to the three-bedroom cottage she purchased. After a little negotiating, she convinced Rick to take a look at it and give her an estimate. Rick was a good carpenter. He had no formal training but took small jobs to supplement his pay. He wasn't convinced he was the right guy to build the porch but Mary was. She convinced him to build it on evenings and weekends, whenever he had free time. By the time the porch was completed, Rick Early moved in with her. He told her about losing his first wife and how the pain in his heart would never heal. Mary promised herself that she would never deny him his right to grieve, even if it was forever. Mary also knew about Penny. She wanted Rick to reconnect with her, but he refused. Rick felt Penny would never forgive him for leaving her, and he didn't want to put her through more pain by introducing himself into her life. Nora's brother and his wife had raised her. They were her parents now. He had no right interfering. Mary didn't try to change his mind. It was his decision. A sales representative at the lumber company offered the Christmas-tree gig to Rick and a light bulb went off in his head. He knew he could check up on Penny by being in her neighborhood. He never expected her to come to the corner and buy trees from him. He planned on spying on her, but the whole progression was easy. Every year she showed up with happiness in her eyes and Christmas joy in her heart. Her mother loved Christmas too, and it didn't surprise him. She looked just like Nora.

Her hair, her face, and even her awkwardness came straight from her mother. The first time she showed up looking for a tree, Rick had to steady himself. He disappeared quickly, darted into the camper, and stayed there a few minutes to get used to the idea. Finally, reappearing to walk her around the lot of trees. He helped her find exactly what she was looking for, and it was a proud moment for him. Most people in the city wanted a small, thin tree to fit into their small apartments. Penny wanted nothing small and nothing less than grand. When he delivered the tree to her home, he sighed with relief. It wasn't a room or a hobble but a comfortable, lovely home. He walked out feeling proud and then realized he had absolutely nothing to do with her stability. William and Carol had raised her well, and she seemed completely at ease. His guilt over deserting her was overwhelming. He considered himself a weak man, a coward. When she was born, he failed her. He wanted to love and protect her, but when he held her in his arms the first time, he knew it would never happen. He hated himself for not being strong enough. The pain in his heart from the loss of his wife was debilitating. He barely had the will to get up in the morning and knew he wouldn't be able to care for her. For a couple of years, he wandered around San Francisco, working a few odd jobs, but he was fired from each one. Rick sold his house down the street from Nora's brother. It held only memories of the happy times he and Nora shared. He lived off the money for a few years and became an avid reader. One day a suspense novel in the window of a bookstore pricked his interest. When he read the book, he fell in love with Vermont. The primary character in the book lived in a quaint town, and it sounded mysterious to him. He had a strong urge to be surrounded by nature. The fast pace of the urban environment no longer held any fascination for him. He landed in Vermont with one suitcase and a backpack and built a new life. Nora never left his mind, and even though he was happy with Mary and his new family, there was a constant dull pain, which never went away. Mary accepted him with the baggage. When she found him sitting on the porch with a distant look in his eyes, she knew he was someplace else and left him alone. She accepted his right to daydream or mourn and welcomed him back to the present when he was ready. Sometimes it frightened her, but Rick warned her before she took the challenge and married him. In her eyes, everyone mourned in their own way. She knew he loved her and his sons, but part of him never left the past. Mary pleaded with him to reach out to William, Carol, and his daughter and welcome them into his life, but he said it was unnecessary. She could tell he couldn't forgive himself for not raising his daughter. "It's never too late" was her motto, but he was adamantly opposed.

When Rick climbed into bed at four thirty, Christmas Eve morning, he pictured Penny's face glowing with enthusiasm and smiled.

❧

"Yes!" Kate yelled. Phillip reached up to hug her and held her in an embrace for a full minute. She pulled away from him with tears in her eyes and looked at him with suspicion. "Are you sure? You've thought about this and you're sure?"

"Kate, I'm sure. I want to spend the rest of my absurdly lucky life with you. I know you love me. This is exactly where we belong."

"I know!" Kate yelled again. "I can't believe it, but it's true."

"I love you; now stop talking and kiss me," said Phillip, pulling her to him. He was the happiest man in Manhattan. Kate was the woman of his dreams, and in seven months, they'd have a baby. He wasn't scared of the responsibility or the commitment. As far as he was concerned, he met his mate, and nothing could take him away from her.

Kate looked at her hand with the ring on her finger. "It's beautiful, Phillip; you know me so well."

"I have to be honest. I picked three out and had to call Penny for the final choice. She was impressed with each one but said this one had your name written all over it." Phillip was nervous picking out the ring. How could you put all the beauty of Kate in one ring? He stood for hours examining the three rings and finally admitted to himself that he needed a second opinion. Penny was thrilled to help. Her excitement was contagious, and Phillip found himself giddy in the jewelry store. The worries he had vanished when Penny arrived. She was pleased with his three choices but told him without a doubt the one he gave to Kate today was the winner.

"I'm happy you involved Penny. She likes to give advice." Kate laughed and kissed Phillip again. "I'm so happy we found each other."

❧❧

When Penny got back to the city, she went to visit Ivan at the pawnshop in the East Village.

"Penny," said Ivan when she walked in. "I was just thinking about you."

"I wanted to speak to you in person, rather than texting you. You know, in case someone's on my phone as well."

"So blue-car guy is still messing with you?"

"Yeah, he showed up in Connecticut," said Penny, and she regurgitated the events of the weekend.

"Whoa, this guy sounds like nonprofessional. I'd say it's the only good news about the whole uncomfortable experience."

"Can I take you up on your offer? Do you think your guys can find out who is behind the charade?"

Ivan walked out from behind the counter. "I'm sorry this idiot is bothering you. I'd like to…"

"No, no violence. I only want to find out who hired him. Then I'll know what I'm dealing with. But I'd like to pay you."

"You're kidding, right? I don't want to remind you that I think it's the least I could do for a friend."

"All right; thanks, Ivan. I really appreciate it."

Ivan walked her to the front door and looked outside. "I dare him to show up here. I'll call you with the information, and if it's dangerous, I'll send you a message to come here. Stay solid."

⁂

Wes exited the subway station at Houston Street and walked briskly toward a coffee shop on Spring Street. He was meeting the detective today and could hardly wait to hear about Rick Early. A wave of guilt washed over him as he walked down Broadway. "Honestly," he thought to himself, "I had no idea he was Penny's birth dad." A part of him almost wished he never met the guy. It was too late to turn back now. The wheels were in motion. Wes spotted the detective when he walked in. The undercover guys always stuck out like sore thumbs.

"Nice to meet you, Wes," said the detective as he stood up to shake Wes's hand. "Great weather today."

"Pleasantries," thought Wes. "Great weather for a winter day. Thanks for meeting me here. Can I buy you lunch?"

"No, thanks; I ordered a couple of coffees, join me," he said, sitting back in his chair at the table. It was ten o'clock on a Tuesday morning, and the rush hour was done. The place was empty except for a few people in the back. "I've got all the information you requested."

Wes reviewed all the paperwork the detective gave him. He was surprised to find out Rick Early appeared to be an everyday guy, making a decent wage and living a normal life. There was nothing wrong with him. It took Wes by surprise. "Thanks for your help. I really appreciate it," said Wes as he slid a paperback book across the table for the detective. "It's a pretty interesting read. Don't forget to take out the bookmark."

"You're welcome," said the detective, flipping open the book and spotting an envelope on the inside. "Anytime."

Wes was elated when he left the coffee shop. He wouldn't have to tell Penny her birth dad was a loser or an alcoholic, because none of those things were true. But even with the good news, he still had no idea how he was going to explain it. Would she want to meet her dad? He started thinking he should drive to Vermont and talk to Rick himself and then he thought of Kate. Should he enlist her help? Penny hadn't shared the truth with anyone. It would be a betrayal to go behind her back. He had to face Penny with the news or drive to Vermont and talk to her father. Both of those choices left him speechless and weary.

∝⧟⧟∾

Regina was thrilled to see Valerie and Henry healthy and happy. Valerie was buried in her studies but took a few days off to join in the holiday festivities. The timing for Regina's visit was fortuitous. On Christmas Eve, Valerie suggested Regina invite Doug over to join them. A group of their friends were gathering for wine, beer, and appetizers. Then they were going out in the bitter cold to sing Christmas carols in the neighborhood.

"My phone says it's twenty-five degrees with a feel like temperature of twelve, and it's only six o'clock. Are you sure the caroling is a good idea?" asked Regina. She completed two of the stand-up shows on their seven-show schedule. She and Doug had three days off and then they would complete the other five nights. Even with a blizzard and frigid temperatures, the club had been packed each night. She was getting spoiled opening for Doug. The crowds were thick and solid, not a heckler in the house.

Apparently, they were in a relationship or at least the beginnings of one. When she discussed it with Valerie, she could feel her cheeks burning with embarrassment. Regina was ashamed to admit it, but she'd never had one before.

"What about that guy, the bartender?" questioned Valerie. "I thought you two were an item at one time when you worked at the ale house." She couldn't believe Regina had never been seriously involved with anyone. It was interesting to see her squirm when she talked about Doug. Regina was beautiful. How had she avoided getting involved with someone over the years?

"No, he and I weren't involved. I mean we slept together a few times, but it was nothing." Regina was focused on her career with little time to ponder men. She spent the first few years of her life in New York City just trying to keep a roof over her head. Then she discovered her talent and the stage, and there wasn't any man who could compete with that. She lived for the stage. It wasn't always pretty. There were times when she performed and the audience existed of three people and they were chatting with each other, completely ignoring her. Other times, she was wrought with stage fright and had to down a couple of shots of vodka to shake it off. But once she hit the stage, it felt like home. Regina had hopes of finding a partner, a man to share her life with, but her focus was always on herself and her career, giving her little time to daydream about a man. It made her blush when she talked about it. "I must sound like a sixteen-year-old girl. I have zero experience when it comes to dating. I don't even know the procedures. Are there certain rules to follow?"

"You're serious, aren't you? You're not trying out a new comedy bit on me, are you? I won't stand for it, Regina. I don't want to be in your act." Valerie wasn't kidding with her. She didn't want to be used for material. She knew all comics used their day-to-day life and their friend for laughs. "Remember four years ago, when you were talking about your roommate onstage and I almost slid under the table? It's a rule. No Valerie in your set!"

"No, I'm not using you. I can't believe you would think that. I really have no dating experience. Give me a little advice. I'd call Penny or Kate, but they're wrapped up in holiday celebrations with their boyfriends, family, and stuff."

Regina looked so innocent and needy, Valerie felt sorry for her. "I mean it's all pretty simple really. Has he kissed you yet?"

"Yes, several times," said Regina confidently.

"And you've been to dinner or out to a movie?"

"We've done both several times," said Regina.

"Then you're dating!" Valerie was relieved. At least she could help her friend out with a definition. "You don't have to have any rules. Listen to what he says and answer honestly. If you want to continue seeing him, then let him know with verbal and physical cues. Don't go and tell him you love him first; let it happen naturally. And, even though almost none of us do this, don't sleep with him until you know if you're ready for a relationship."

"Oops," said Regina.

Valerie gave her a hard look. "Oh no, you didn't?"

"No, I didn't. I was teasing with you."

"See, I knew this was part of some comedy routine." Valerie was exasperated.

"I love you, Val. I really should put this in my set, but trust me I'll leave you out of it. Thank you for the advice. I appreciate it. I think I understand how to handle it now."

"Really? It was helpful advice?"

"Yes, very helpful." Regina gave her a hug.

"So are you going to keep seeing him?" asked Valerie.

"Definitely," said Regina with a smile. "I'll invite him over for caroling, and if we all turn into frozen statues on the sidewalk, people can drape Christmas decorations on us to remember our dedication to their happiness."

"I can remember you and I out on the streets of New York City in two degrees and you never complained. You're getting soft from all this traveling. I bet you've been doing shows in San Diego and Los Angeles."

"Ha-ha, I'm not soft. I'm going caroling tonight; just you wait and see," said Regina as she opened her travel bag and pulled several packs of hand warmers out of it.

"Wimp! You're too funny. I'm looking forward to meeting Doug. He's pretty famous now. Henry watched his HBO special on Netflix a few nights ago. He laughed until he cried. He'll be so excited to hang out with him."

"Honestly, he's totally different offstage. It's cute that he's shy."

"That's hard to believe. I hear some celebrities talking about how different they are in real life, so I guess it's not so odd. Henry will probably be starstruck if Doug joins us."

Regina heard her phone signal text message. "I bet it's from Doug. Let's see if he has time for us tonight or more interesting plans." Regina cackled and ran to get her phone from the kitchen.

I have for the first time found what I can truly love—I have found you. You are my sympathy—my better self—my good angel—I am bound to you with a strong attachment. I think you good, gifted, lovely: a fervent, a solemn passion is conceived in my heart; it leans to you, draws you to my centre and spring of life, wrap my existence about you—and, kindling in pure, powerful flame, fuses you and me in one.
—CHARLOTTE BRONTE, *JANE EYRE*

Chapter 17

*W*es spent the entire day agonizing over his decision. One moment he was convinced he needed to discuss it with Penny, and two minutes later he was confident the drive to Vermont was a better idea. When he saw Penny, he was distracted, and she noticed.

"You're being weird," said Penny, grabbing another box of Chinese food and scooping it onto her plate.

"I know; I've got some things on my mind," said Wes, grimacing. He'd stopped by their favorite Chinese restaurant on his way over. Lately, he was in a routine of leaving his car parked at the firehouse and walking to Penny's house for dinner. It was a routine he was fond of. Tonight, he surprised her with sweet-and-sour chicken, one of her favorites, and pot stickers. To his delight, Penny had rewarded his kindness with a huge hug and kiss. The smile on her face was enough to send his heart soaring. He watched her dig into the little boxes of food with childlike enthusiasm.

"It's funny how much food fits into one of these takeout boxes, isn't it?" Wes tried to divert her attention away from his mood and back onto the food.

"You're changing the subject. Is something wrong at work?" Penny was concerned. Wes was always in a good mood. She contemplated it as she opened another container and poured some fried rice onto her plate. "I don't think I've ever seen you contemplative. You're avoiding eye contact with me."

Wes knew he was an open book. He'd never been able to hide his emotions. "Good thing I don't play poker, huh?" He joined Penny at the table and dug into the takeout bag for the chopsticks. "Can I have a pot sticker, please?"

"Of course! I'm sorry; was I hogging everything? I'm really hungry. Thank you for being so thoughtful." Penny got up from the table and grabbed some napkins. "Now spill the beans, or I'll have to torture you with my chopsticks." She laughed, trying to lighten the mood. Wes was clearly upset about something.

"Penny, you know how I feel about you," said Wes.

"Uh, yeah."

"All right, I'll go ahead and tell you, but before I do, promise me you won't be upset with me." His palms were sweating, and he felt a twinge of nausea.

"Now how can I make that promise, Wes? I have no idea where this is going." Penny stopped eating.

"OK, so you can't promise you won't get upset with me. But could you promise me that if I told you, my intentions were good?"

"Wes, I know you don't desire to harm me in any way. You've proven that. What could possibly have you this upset? Just tell me, and we can go from there."

"Remember when I asked you about Rick Early, the Christmas-tree guy?" Wes hadn't planned on talking to Penny about it tonight, but she had a way of getting him to fess up. All she had to do was flash her emerald eyes at him, and the words began to flow.

"Oh no, Wes; you didn't do anything to Rick! He's the nicest man, a simple man from Vermont. I see him every Christmas; he's part of the holiday tradition. Did something happen to him?"

"No, nothing happened to him. Rick Early is fine," said Wes with a sigh of relief, and then he started laughing and couldn't stop. The tension he'd been holding onto for days suddenly released through laughter. It was inappropriate, and he knew it, but he couldn't stop.

"Are you laughing at me? I'm confused; why are you laughing?"

"I'm sorry," said Wes, holding up his hand and trying to compose himself. "Nothing's funny. I can't stop laughing." Wes left the kitchen and went to the bathroom. He stared at himself in the mirror, hoping his reflection would sober him up. With a red face and tears in his eyes, he slowly regained control of his emotions. "I'm OK, Penny; sorry, it's been a stressful week," he yelled.

When he rejoined her in the kitchen, she was making tea. "If you're upset, I'll make you some tea."

"Tea would be great," said Wes. The first night Penny invited him to her apartment, she offered him tea. Since then, he drank tea every day and never turned it down when she offered. He knew it wasn't always a code word for sex, but it didn't hurt to roll the dice. Plus, he'd grown fond of it.

Penny placed a cup in front of her and then slid one to Wes across the table. "All right, so now back to Rick Early."

Wes took a sip of the tea. "Oh, that's delicious, Penny; thank you."

She nodded and looked at him with anticipation. It was odd seeing Wes upset. He was a rock of stability.

"I know you must remember how puzzled I was when he knew I was picking out a wreath for you. It bothered me. Even if he comes to your neighborhood once a year, there are a lot of people who live here. I thought it was odd, and I wanted to know more about him."

"Did you put Frank on him?" Penny was defensive. She immediately remembered how Frank was going to look into Phillip to make sure he wasn't a pervert or criminal. It wouldn't surprise her if he'd done the same thing with Mr. Early.

"Not exactly. I had a detective from the NYPD check him out." Wes didn't think it was pertinent to bring Frank into the picture. Frank was his best friend; he didn't want Penny to have negative opinions about him. The important fact was a detective had done the research.

"Good gosh, Wes, that's crazy! You thought he was interested in me?"

"No, I was shocked at how comfortable he was regarding you. I'm sorry, Penny, but it was weird. You have to put yourself in my shoes. I walk up to buy a wreath for a beautiful woman who loves Christmas, and he knew it was you. It's New York City, Penny, not a small town."

"The West Village is a small town," she said defensively. "There's nothing odd about it. I know him. We talk every year for the past nine years. I don't know exactly how many years but a lot. He knows everyone, not just me."

"Penny, you're right. He's a nice guy, or at least everything points to that." Wes knew she was going to freak out, but he continued, "Again, I want to emphasize I only looked into him because I was worried about your safety. I understand you find that completely idiotic. However, I found out something fascinating, and I'm not sure if you're going to be happy about it. Maybe you will be, not sure. I'm going to spit it out. He's your real dad." Wes looked Penny right in the eyes, searching her face for a sign.

Penny stood perfectly still. The words were hitting her in slow motion, or at least it felt that way. "The earth stood still." She'd heard that saying, or was it a quote? Now, she knew what it meant.

"Penny?" questioned Wes.

"Yeah," she muttered but didn't move from the spot she was standing in.

"Are you feeling all right? It's big news; I know it must be hard to believe. It was for me too."

"Your detective is mistaken." Penny went back to the table and picked up her chopsticks. "It's absurdity. Someone is messing with you, Wes. Maybe it's a prank from one of your buddies. Did you tell anyone about my birth dad or mom? That's what it is. One of your police buddies or something."

"Penny, I haven't told anyone. I would never betray you!"

Penny stared at him with a blank expression.

"I'm sorry. I didn't mean to find him. I know I told you we should look for him. I thought it would be cool. But I would never have gone behind your back and looked for your real dad." Wes's voice cracked when he said it, and he began to sob. He couldn't handle her face. She thought he betrayed her, and it was more than he could handle.

Penny ran to him. "I'm sorry. I know you wouldn't hurt me." She grabbed his hand and pulled him to the sofa. "You found out something by mistake. I get it. Really, I don't blame you."

Wes laid his head on her shoulder and cried. "I've been so conflicted. I wanted to hide the information from you once it was delivered to me, but how could I? Then I thought I would drive to Vermont and talk to him before I told you. That, too, seemed wrong. I didn't know what to do, so I told you the truth."

"We'll go to Vermont together, Wes," said Penny.

"I don't want you to go unless you want to," said Wes. "I mean the good news is you already know him and like him."

"My real dad's name is Jimmy O'Connor; it must be a mistake."

"He changed his name when he moved to Vermont. It appears he left California behind to heal his heart and start a new life."

"Oh," said Penny. She was convinced the detective had it wrong, since the names didn't match up. But Wes had an answer for that. Now she felt her heart beat faster. Could Rick Early really be her birth father? It was surreal.

"Penny, a penny for your thoughts?" Wes pulled himself together. He was relieved Penny didn't fault him for his find. Now he could tell it was finally beginning to make sense to her. He loved to make her laugh and tried his "penny for your thoughts" line, which typically made her chuckle. It received not even a glance in his direction. "Penny, babe, are you OK?"

"Uh, yeah, I'm fine," said Penny, distracted. Could it be possible Wesley had mistakenly found her real father?

"I know it's big stuff; let's think of the positives and let go of the negatives. He's a great guy from all I can find out, and I'm guessing he would be thrilled to have a relationship with you."

"OK, yeah, it's odd, but let's make a plan. We'll go to Vermont and meet him. Is it a coincidence he sells trees in my neighborhood?"

"I don't think so. I'm pretty sure he was keeping tabs on you. I'd do the same if you were my daughter."

"You wouldn't have deserted your daughter. It's an unforgiveable sin. Nice guy or not, he deserted me."

"I'd like to think I'd never do something so horrible, but a broken heart is a mighty sword. I've heard it can cause a man to lose touch with all reasonable thoughts. I'm pretty sure he's been living with the guilt. Maybe that's the reason he hasn't come forward. Probably thinks he doesn't deserve to be in your life."

"You're talking like a therapist. Who made you so smart and reasonable?"

"Honestly, I'm trying to think like a man. We react to emotional things much differently than women."

"I've never thought of it that way," said Penny. She pictured Rick Early in her mind. He seemed like such a nice simple man. Suddenly, she remembered the young boys who helped him with his business and recalled they were his sons. "He's got two sons! I met them. Gosh, could it be true? I have two half brothers? Wow, this is crazy."

"He married again after he moved to Vermont. They have two sons together. So, yeah, you've got two half brothers." Wes watched Penny closely. He was nervous the load of information was going to be hard for her to process. Considering the news, he felt she was handling it well.

"How about this weekend? Maybe we could find a cute cabin to rent?"

"I know you hate leaving the city."

"No way to avoid leaving. We have a mission to accomplish." Penny could hardly believe Rick Early was her dad. It seemed completely absurd. There was no way she could leave the information on the table; she'd have to confront it and see what happened.

"Should we give him a heads-up that we're coming?"

"Absolutely not. He deserted me. You think I want to make this reunion cozy for him?" Penny's mind was reeling. She wanted to confront with no warning. "He deserves to squirm."

"I guess we could find him at work on Friday. It'll be a surprise for sure." Wes didn't like the idea of visiting without a conversation before, but this was Penny's adventure, and he would let her decide how to handle it.

"Where does he work?"

"A lumber company. He's been there for years, pretty much runs it from what the detective told me."

"So my birth dad fled California, moved to Vermont, works at a lumber yard, and has two sons. Wife?"

"Yes, her name is—" Wes realized he couldn't remember the name. "Hold on, I've got it written down on a piece of paper." Wes gathered his coat from the chair and dug into the pocket for the notes he wrote down. "Mary, her name is Mary. I can't believe I couldn't remember that." Wes chuckled.

"Right, he's married to Mary." Penny laughed too. "Wow, this is a lot of information."

Wes walked over to the sofa where Penny was sitting. He put his arm around her and pulled her close to him. "What do you think your parents will say about this? Are you going to tell them?"

"Gosh, I haven't even stopped to think about that. I don't want to tell them until we get back from Vermont. I'll call them Monday."

"How do you think they'll feel about it? If you were to guess?"

"They'll be ecstatic, I'm sure of it. But they'll go into pro-tection mode. Good or bad guy, they'll be worried about me."

"I can understand that."

"Do you have the weekend off? Would you like to go with me?" asked Penny. "I'm sorry, I didn't ask you if you could do it."

"You bet I'm going with you. I got you into this mess. Also, Mom and Dad have a place in Stowe, Vermont. Years ago, they used to like to go up on weekends and ski. I think Wyatt uses it occasionally. It's a little fancier than a cabin. We could stay there if you want."

"Really? That's awesome. I'd love to stay there. How far is it to Rick's town from Stowe?"

"Not far at all, maybe thirty minutes, max. Do you have a plan? You think you want to confront him at work?"

"Yep, that's what I'm thinking. I guess he works Monday through Friday? I don't want to go to his house. I'm not sure I want to meet Mary right now."

"That makes sense. If we're driving the six hours, we should leave Thursday evening. I've got a better plan; why don't we fly? JetBlue has a flight from JFK to Stowe. I've taken it many times. We can rent a car and drive to the family compound, get settled in, and then head to Waterbury."

"Yeah, that sounds much easier. Last-minute flight will be expensive, though." Penny couldn't get used to the fact that Wes was wealthy. It still hadn't totally sunk in.

"I've got a ton of miles. We can use them. If not, they'll probably never get used. I haven't been skiing in four years."

"Great. It's a plan then." Penny laid her head on Wes's shoulder.

"All this talking and planning has made me thirsty. Would be great to have another cup of tea." Wes turned to Penny with a sly smile.

✤✥✤

Doug Cullman joined Regina and her friends on Christmas Eve. They managed to survive the Christmas caroling despite frigid temperatures. Henry and Doug hit it off and kept them all laughing.

Four days later, Doug and Regina were sitting at Starbucks in downtown Boston with their faces in their laptops, each writing some new comedy material. Regina's agent had booked her for a two-week vacation after the Boston gig, so her stage duo with Doug would be over for a while. Regina was overjoyed to have some time off to regroup. It was fun working with Doug; in fact, she'd never had so much fun, although she was beginning to feel like she was June Carter touring with Johnny. Doug's hotel suite was so comfortable, she'd moved in. Valerie had a lot of studying to do, and Regina felt it would be easier on her and Henry if she took Doug up on his offer to spend their last week in Boston with him. He ordered room service for them, and they watched *Walk the Line* with Reese Witherspoon on Netflix. Regina thought it was an awesome film and couldn't help but compare the lifestyle of the traveling musicians with the comedy circuit. Doug made being on the road fun again. He was so easygoing and considerate. She also discovered she laughed a lot when they were together. He wasn't cracking jokes all the time that would be obnoxious. It was subtle, and she loved it.

The Boston Westin was luxurious. The feather down comforters were so lovely, Regina slept an extra hour longer than normal. Doug was an early riser, and by the time she stumbled into the living room, he had breakfast ordered and coffee made. It felt like a home. Doug laughed at her when she told him she loved it so much she wanted to stay forever.

"We can't move into the Westin and stay forever," Doug teased her. "We have a world of people who need us to make them laugh."

"They'll find someone else. C'mon, let's stay." Regina was kidding, but a part of her had never felt so at home. She realized the home she'd grown up with, although filled with love, had been extremely short on spaciousness. Her beloved Lower East Side studio in Manhattan was her home, and she loved it. But it didn't have fluffy comforters and wide-open space. "I could do yoga in each of these rooms, including the kitchen," yelled Regina from the master bedroom. "In fact, I could teach a class of three in this room." She was used to living in tight quarters, so the suite felt like a mansion. She made a note to herself to buy a down comforter for her bed in the city once she got settled in.

"What are you planning to do on your vacation?" Doug was sitting at the dining-room table sipping his coffee.

Regina noticed how relaxed he looked. "I have two weeks off. I'm thinking of going back to the city and staying with Kate at her place in Chelsea. But I haven't asked her yet. Also,

I haven't been to visit my family in Tennessee for years. My mom has been begging me to visit. 'Show your face around here' were her exact words."

Doug laughed. "You've got to love the south. They've got a funny way with words." He attempted a Southern accent. "You ain't from around here, now are you?"

"I'm going to have to teach you a Southern accent," said Regina. "You sound like you're from India instead of Tennessee."

"I know! Every time I attempt any accent, it comes out Indian." Doug's phone on the table began to vibrate. "Ugh, who is calling me this early?" He glanced at the number. "Hey, it's my agent, got to take it."

Regina gave him a thumbs-up and left the room. She wanted to give him privacy. His agent had a great reputation in the comedy world for getting his clients work. She was a little envious. She spotted her nail polish sitting on the counter in the bathroom. Regina grabbed it and bounced onto the fluffy bed. While she painted her fingernails, she contemplated a trip to Tennessee. She did miss her mom and dad and made a point to call them once a week even if the conversation was short. There was a weekly reminder on her iPhone: call Mom and Dad. Her mother had long given up hope of convincing her daughter to return home. She knew entertainment was rooted deep in Regina's bones. It wasn't her style to whine and beg. It made Regina smile thinking of her family. Maybe it would be a good time to visit them.

"Regina, are you busy?" Doug called her from the dining room.

She opened the bedroom door and stuck her head out. "I'm painting my nails; what's up?"

"I've got some crazy exciting news!" Doug was pacing back and forth in the kitchen.

"Must be good; your face is aglow. Did your agent hook you up with something fabulous?" Regina felt a twinge of jealousy. She'd love to have a team of people as awesome as Doug had. Then she quickly scolded herself for the thought.

"Yep, they have me booked to fly to Los Angeles tomorrow. I'm going to be reading for the lead in a sitcom. It's insanity, crazy good news."

"Wow, that's wonderful. I'm so happy for you." Regina ran to him and gave him a huge hug and a kiss. "Are you nervous?"

"Not at all. I mean I might be when I'm in the audition, but right now, I'm psyched. Do you want to go with me? It would be a lot of fun. Think about it; we could leave the East Coast snow behind for the West Coast sunshine. We could find a Westin there too."

"I can't go to Los Angeles with you," said Regina flatly.

"Why not? You have vacation, and the flight is free."

"How is the flight free?"

"I asked my agent if I could bring a plus-one. They said sure. I have to e-mail them the information in a few minutes. No problem."

"Hmm, it's tempting. Would be fun to see you nail a sitcom!" Regina laughed. "I had kind of talked myself into visiting my family, though. I really need to drop in for a visit."

"How about this? I'll have them book us from Boston to Los Angeles, Los Angeles to Nashville for two or three nights, Nashville to New York, and we'll get to stay here tonight instead of checking out."

"You're completely insane. Aren't they going to bark at you for dropping by Nashville?"

"No, we'll stop in to see the booker for the Nashville Comedy Club—what's his name?"

"Don Mayes," said Regina quickly. "Good idea. That's a hot club; everyone wants to headline at that place."

"Exactly." Doug was proud of himself. He'd figured out a way to include Regina. Things were going so good between them. He didn't want her to run off to Tennessee by herself. It might be a month before he could catch up with her on the road. Doug made it clear to his representation that he preferred Regina as his opening act. He'd leave it up to them to figure out how to make it happen. He hadn't told Regina yet. She seemed happy being part of the team, but he felt a little guilty for not discussing it with her yet. It was on his mental to do list.

"OK, let's do it. I haven't been out there in a while. It'll be fun, and you'll have a cheerleader by your side. If you get a sitcom, I want a recurring role. Handshake on that, and we've got a deal?"

"Your lips to God's ears," said Doug, reaching out his hand. "I could totally see us on a show together. I think we make a good team."

"Great team," said Regina.

I thank You God for most this amazing day: for
the leaping greenly spirits of trees and a blue
true dream of sky; and for everything which
is natural which is infinite which is yes…

—E. E. Cummings

Chapter 18

The runway was covered with snow when the 727 touched down. Penny peered out the window as the plane rolled slowly to a stop. "Wow, looks like we've got a healthy amount of snow here. I love it."

"I know you do. Is there something lucky about landing at an airport covered in snow?" Wes laughed. He was proud of himself for remembering Penny's eccentric "good luck, bad luck" notions.

"I don't believe I've heard that one, but we can start the chain. Let's do it. I say it's a sign of good luck to land at airport which is covered in snow."

"I'll go along with it. Sounds good; we can always use some extra good luck. However, I'd like to go on record and say as long as you're by my side, I consider myself a lucky man." Wes could hardly believe the sappy boyfriend he'd become. Penny still refused to admit they were in a relationship. He figured it was better to avoid the issue. They were getting along well, and he didn't want to upset her by asking her to admit he was her boyfriend. Penny insisted labels were unnecessary, and it was easier for Wes to play it cool and enjoy their companionship. He didn't want to remind her they were spending almost every day and night together except for Tuesdays, which Kate and Penny had reserved each week for girls' night.

"Aww, that's sweet, Wes. Are you trying to romance it up for the weekend in the woods? I can't wait to see your family's cabin. I bet it's cozy." The whole real-father issue was continually playing in her head. Penny had no idea what she was going to say to Rick. She practiced several speeches ranging from angry to sympathetic and had no idea which emotion would show up when she stood face-to-face with her birth dad.

"The cabin, ha, it's more like a compound. It's a little extravagant, but Wyatt likes it. He's always been fonder of the lavish lifestyle. My parents puzzle me. They are simple people, and yet they always go overboard when it comes to their homes."

Penny laughed out loud. "The last thing I would say about your parents is they are simple people. You are in complete denial."

"You've only met them once, Penny. They're simple people surrounded by wealth."

"OK, you're right. I shouldn't make a judgment based on a single meeting. Don't get me wrong. I found them warm and interesting. You're lucky to have such a wonderful family." Wes, Wyatt, and Nick seemed to be well-rounded men. It was clear they grew up in a happy home.

"Let's get this party started," said Wes. He grabbed the roller-board suitcase from the overhead bin and offered Penny his hand out of the tight row of seats.

"Thank you, Wes." Penny shimmed out of the row. "I can't believe they make these seats so small. But we arrived on time, so I guess I shouldn't complain."

"No, you can complain; all airline seats are too small. C'mon, let's get a move on; we've got a car rental waiting."

❧

Wes pulled up to the airport fifteen minutes later in the huge sport utility vehicle he rented. Penny was waiting at the curb. "Could you have rented a larger car? This is like a small bus."

"Sorry, but you never know when a blizzard is going to hit, and this one is the best for traction. I did my research."

"Look at you, always thinking about our safety. It's very kind of you. I didn't mean to sound ungrateful." She smiled to herself. Wes was always thinking about their well-being. It was still odd being with a man who was thoughtful and kind. Beckett danced through her mind, and she blinked hard to keep the vision away. "How far is it to your place?"

"We'll be there in fifteen if the roads and traffic is good." He opened the door for her, tossed their shared suitcase into the back seat, and was at the wheel again in two seconds.

Penny stared into blank space.

"Something on your mind?" Wes was used to Penny drifting. She often seemed to be in a world of her own. He found it interesting. One minute she was in a conversation and moments later, far, far away.

"Nope, just happy you're in charge of this adventure. I'm not sure I could do it without you. I mean, I'm not sure I'm ready for the real-dad confrontation and yet here we are. I mean he left me, and thirty-one years later, I'm in Stowe, Vermont, with a man I spilled water on, seeking out my father." Tears welled up in her eyes, and she started to weep.

"Hey," said Wes. "We can turn this car in right now and go back to the city. We could go to the compound, forget about Waterbury, and drink spiced cider by the fireplace and never talk of Rick Early again. I don't want you to do anything you don't want to do, Penny. If I pressured you into this, I'm sorry. Don't cry, baby; it'll be all right." Wes put his hand under her chin and wiped the tears from her cheeks.

"No. I'm fine." Penny pulled a tissue from her handbag and dried her eyes. "I've thought a lot about it, and I want to talk to him. You didn't force me into this. I made the choice to confront it. I'm emotional, that's all. I never imagined I would find him. I didn't think I'd ever see him. The weird thing is, I've been speaking to him every Christmas for at least eight years. How could he do it? Why didn't he reach out to me instead of pretending?"

"That's a question you can ask him. I believe he feels he doesn't deserve to be in your life, and I can't blame him for it. He doesn't deserve you, but maybe you deserve to know him. I'll get us to the house; we'll grab some late breakfast and decide what to do next. How's that?"

"Perfect," said Penny. "I'm OK; don't worry." She snapped her seat belt on and gave Wes a broad smile. "It's a beautiful snowy weekend in Vermont. Let's enjoy it."

Penny gasped quietly when Wes pulled their vehicle into the long driveway toward what she had called "the cabin." It was a large beautiful home. She imagined she might have seen it before in a magazine. "Wow, you weren't kidding. It's fantastic and huge. It's a compound."

"Like I was saying, I'd prefer it to be smaller, but I suppose they were thinking all the kids could fit into something this big. We'll close the upstairs off and use the downstairs. There's a fireplace in the living room. The master bedroom is on the main floor, so we'll make it cozy." Wes flashed a wide grin her way.

"I love it. Your parents certainly have great taste. Can't wait to see the inside."

"Your wish is my command." Wes put the SUV in park and hurried around the car to catch Penny's car door. "After you." He grabbed the suitcase from the back seat and grabbed Penny's hand. "Let me show you around. I think you'll be more impressed with the interior. I've always been found of a rustic modern blend, and this house has it."

When Wes opened the front door, Penny was in love. The hardwood floors were breathtaking, large wide planks in a weathered light brown. The fireplace was the main focal point of the living room. A fire was already burning.

"Looks like the housekeeper was here a few minutes ago. Oh look, she left us breakfast in the kitchen." Wes glanced over the feast. They had a basket full of fresh croissants, with butter and jelly on the side. He noticed there were three omelets on the stove still warm to his touch. A stack of pancakes with maple syrup and a large bowl of oatmeal with honey and cinnamon sat nearby. "She got all my favorites. I've always been fond of Audrey."

"I'm guessing Audrey is the part-time housekeeper?" Penny rushed to join him in the kitchen. She was famished and felt she could eat a little of everything. Penny tried to focus on all the delicious food, but the dining room, kitchen, living-room combination was distracting. Her eyes danced around the room.

"Don't worry; you'll have time to check out the house. I know it's intriguing, but let's eat!" Wes was already setting the table with the china he pulled from the cabinets. "Oh, and yes, Audrey is the part-time housekeeper. I've known her since I was a child."

"She even made us coffee," said Penny, grabbing a large mug and pouring herself a cup. "You boys must have grown up spoiled, but I would never have guessed it."

"Spoiled, no; fortunate, yes. Our parents never failed to remind us." He smiled. "I'm glad they did. I mean, they tried to keep us grounded, and for the most part, I think they did a good job. We had our ups and downs through the years, but I always respected and appreciated their guidance. Like I told you before, Dad was often tough when it came to education and expectation, but he was reasonable."

"They have amazing taste," said Penny. She was still gazing over the wide-open space. Each piece of furniture had been carefully selected. The colors seemed to flow into each room, creating a warm space. There were pops of color, which blended perfectly into the earthy tones. "Kate would freak out. She'd love every bit of this house."

"Maybe we could all come up here for a long weekend sometime."

"Yes, let's do. This is wonderful." Penny sat down at the table and watched Wes pull everything together.

"What would you like?"

"How about everything?" Penny laughed. "I'm starving, or at least my stomach thinks I am."

"Wonderful. We'll have it all." He turned on the stove to warm the oatmeal up. "It's warm, but I like it hot enough to melt the honey. Honey?" Wes watched Penny closely for signs of grief and anxiety. She seemed perfectly content sitting at the table watching him put their breakfast together. He felt a twinge of guilt for getting her into this situation. He hoped when they looked back at the experience, it would be a positive thing in her life. Rick Early was possibly going to get the surprise of his life. That is, if Penny decided to go forward with the plan.

Penny laughed. "Honey, I'll take some honey too." Even though she was racked with stress over the forthcoming confrontation, it was nice to be in his family's home. It was cozy, and she looked forward to coming back for a happy weekend with Phillip and Kate. "I'm going to do it, Wes. I've come this far; I will meet him today."

"Perfect, if that's really what you want. There's no rush, you know. We could hang out here and relax and then come up for the meeting another weekend. It's all up to you, no pressure."

"No, I'm sure. I want us to go together to Waterbury. I'll speak with him. I can handle it. It's settled."

"Well, let's go on our adventure with a full stomach," said Wes, placing a large omelet stuffed with cheese and vegetables in front of her. "We'll start with the omelet." He leaned over and kissed her cheek. "You're one of a kind, Penny Robinson. I'm glad you're my friend."

"Whoa, did you say friend? I think it's a little more serious than that." Penny dug into her omelet without even waiting for Wes to sit down.

"Really?" Wes laughed out loud. "Well, I'm proud to hear it. I wanted to say girlfriend, but you get bent over labels." Wes turned the oatmeal on low and joined her at the table.

"Thanks for being here with me. I appreciate the support." Penny placed her hand on his on top of the table.

Wes picked her hand up and kissed it. "Let's eat!"

After they finished a four-course breakfast, Wes showed Penny the rest of the house. They both took a shower and changed their clothes.

Penny grabbed her purse off the counter in the kitchen. "I'm ready if you are." She shouted toward the master bedroom. She heard her phone chime, text message. It was from Ivan. Penny took a deep breath and clicked on the message:

Good news—it's not a professional. Bad news—it's Beckett.

Penny bit her lip hard to keep from screaming. *Thanks, Ivan. I can take it from here.* She had bigger things to deal with right now. "Has Beckett totally lost his mind?" Penny wondered.

Oh, I don't think you'll be seeing the guy in the blue car anymore. You're good. Later.

Penny smiled. "Thank you, Ivan," she whispered.

Wes yelled from the bedroom, "Give me a minute; just putting my boots on." Seconds later, he was at the door, keys in hand. "OK, here we go."

❧

Penny and Wes pulled into the lumberyard at a little before noon. The parking lot was empty except for a few cars.

"Looks like they aren't overwhelmed with business right now. I guess it's a good time to step inside and see him." Wes glanced at Penny. She showed no signs of anxiety.

Penny eyed the automobiles in the parking lot, trying to figure out which one might belong to her father. "All right, let's go shopping for some new hardwood floors or something of that nature. Time's a wasting."

When Penny and Wes walked into the store, a bell rang and Penny jumped. "Gosh, how loud is that? I guess they don't want anyone sneaking up on them. Surely, he's not the only person who works here. He must have an assistant, helper, or colleague; I mean surely he's not here alone." She realized she was babbling as the adrenaline rushed through her body. Her hands began to shake a little, so she tucked them inside the pockets of her goose down coat.

Rick Early was at the far end of the store on a ladder arranging some items on a shelf. When he heard the bell ring, he climbed down the ladder, dusted his jeans off with his hands, and headed toward the front. He felt his head spin when he spotted the redhead with the handsome fireman. His first thought was "She found me." His second thought was "Be cool, they're tourists browsing the area." He took a deep breath. "How can I help you?"

"Rick, is that you?" Penny had several ideas about what she was going to do and say. She gave up on planning and decided to be organic. The words were flowing out of her mouth without thought or regard.

"Wow, you're one of my customers from the village! Penny, right? What brings you to Waterbury? I hope you don't want to return your Christmas tree; we're completely sold out." He laughed out loud at his joke. It was a good attempt at casual, but his palms were sweating, and he could feel a sweat moustache forming. It never bothered him to see Penny in the village when she was shopping for a Christmas tree, but she was on his territory now, and it felt odd. He reminded himself it was only a coincidence. There was no way Penny knew his real identity.

Penny laughed at his joke. "No, my Christmas tree was wonderful. I enjoyed it very much." Penny glanced at Wes, who was standing quietly with his hands in his jean pockets. "We enjoyed it," said Penny. "I don't know if you know Wes. This is Wes Lane, one of New York City's bravest firemen."

Wes held out his hand to shake. "Nice to meet you. I hear your trees are the best in the city." Wes didn't want to bring up the fact that Rick had helped him with the wreath he bought for Penny. He hoped he'd forgotten about it.

"I'd like to hope so. What can I do for you two? Are you in town for some skiing? We got a big snowfall a few days ago; the slopes should be pretty enjoyable." It was casual conversation, small talk. He was used to chatting with the customers, but he felt uneasy. Penny was in Vermont, in his lumberyard.

"No, I don't think we'll have time to ski this time. Wes has a vacation home in Stowe, and we flew up this weekend for some relaxation. We're looking for a good restaurant for dinner, and we thought you could give us a recommendation, Jimmy." The words flew out of her mouth. She didn't stop to edit them. Her heart was beating so fast and yet she was focused on his eyes. His emerald eyes looked exactly like hers. She'd never noticed it before. Each year, he patiently helped her pick out her tree. She never once noticed how green his eyes were.

"You mean Rick; I think you said Jimmy. I'm Rick Early. I don't think I ever told you my full name. Most of the residents in the village call me Rick."

"Why did you leave me? I was only a baby?" Penny wiped her cheek, expecting to find tears flowing down them, but there were none. It was anger she was feeling. The lies were continuing. He pretended she made a mistake. It was he who made the mistake. "What gives you the right to peek in on my life once a year when it's convenient for you? How dare you?"

"I'm sorry. I don't know what you're talking about. I think I'm going to have to ask you to leave." Rick stood steadfast in his lie.

"I don't think so," said Wes. "She came here to have a conversation. You owe her a conversation." It took a lot to make Wes angry. He always prided himself in keeping his cool. "We found out who you were by accident, but the truth is on the table now. I'd encourage you to have your say." He started to walk away. "Penny, I'll be right here, but I'm going to give you and your dad a little space."

"Thank you," said Penny. She gave him an encouraging smile. "I can handle this." Penny directed her attention back to Rick. "How could you walk out on me?"

Rick stood perfectly still. He felt his life crashing in on him. The last thing he wanted was to hurt Penny. He knew it was too late for that. "Penny," he said and then stopped. He wanted to embrace her. He wanted to tell her how sorry he was and how much he hated himself for leaving her. But he couldn't find the words. "Penny, I don't know where to begin."

"That's a start," said Penny. "Please explain to me how you could leave a newborn on my mother's brother's doorstep."

"Not exactly on his doorstep," said Rick. "I was devastated. I loved your mother more than life itself. It was a normal pregnancy. She was young and healthy and so excited to be pregnant. Our love was the kind people dream of. It all happened so fast. She was in labor, and I drove her to the hospital. They took her into the delivery room. It was supposed to be routine. Two hours later, the doctor came out and told me I had a healthy baby girl, but my wife had passed away." Rick steadied himself on a shelf nearby. His tears began to flow. "You look just like her, your mom; she was beautiful like you. You have her spirit and her sense of adventure. I wanted to reach out to you, but I couldn't. When your mom passed away, it was like the world came to a halt. I wanted to die. Each day was a challenge. I couldn't eat, I barely slept, and when I finally did pass out from exhaustion, I'd sleep twenty hours straight. I tried to get help, but my mind was so messed up. I was unable to function. I've regretted it my entire life."

"What made you move to Vermont?" Penny wanted to reach for him. She felt sorry for him, but she remained cool.

"I wandered around San Francisco for a few years. I was a complete loser. I sold the house we were supposed to live in as a family. It was the only way I survived. I became an introvert, but to get through each day, I took up reading. I read novels, the kind you get lost in. The novels helped me escape to another land. One day, I picked one up and the setting was Vermont. It sounded beautiful. I didn't want to be around people, but my money was running out. I bought a ticket to Vermont and legally changed my name. I worked at an inn in Stowe for a while. Slowly, I began to live a little. I'm not making excuses for my mistake. I've regretted leaving you every minute of every day."

"But once you got it together, why didn't you find me? You could have told me everything."

"I knew I didn't deserve to be in your life. By that time, you had a mother and a father. I couldn't replace them. They saved you from me. I owe them everything for taking care of you, for raising you, for making you the strong, successful woman you are today. How could I intrude on your life? I'm not worthy to be your father. I messed up, and I know it can't be repaired. I'm sorry."

"Why not let me decide whether you were worthy? I'm the child. I have a say." Penny felt the anger leaving. She was replacing it with empathy. "Maybe I wanted you to be a part of my life. Maybe I am old enough to understand what love can make you feel and do." A tear rolled down her check, and she angrily pushed it away.

"By selling the trees in the city, I could see you once a year. I looked forward to it. The minute I leave New York City, I count the days down until I can see you again. I wanted to make sure you were safe in the city. I didn't know how I could be a part of your life. I don't deserve your forgiveness. I knew better than to ask." Rick stopped talking for a minute and looked lost in thought. "Your mother was the light and I was the dark. She was the good and I was the bad. Without her, nothing made sense. Each day, I ask her to forgive me for not being strong enough. I let her down, and after I left you, she stopped talking to me. I felt her presence occasionally, but she never uttered a word to me after I dropped you off. It's not only you I disappointed; I let her down as well. I'm unworthy of your love, Penny."

"You're unbelievable. You're unworthy. I hear you say it, and I wonder why you assume we wouldn't forgive you! Maybe mom forgave you and isn't talking to you because you're a coward for not approaching me. You knew where I was and you avoided having this conversation with me. She probably wonders how you could be so ignorant." Her words were harsh, and she knew it, but she couldn't let him off easy.

"Yes, I'm a coward, a coward unworthy of forgiveness. Why? Because there are no words that explain the state of disability your mother's death put me in. A grown man who chose to die because his heart was broken. I walked away from you, the greatest gift I'd ever been given. It's simply disgusting. I hate myself. I wish Nora had lived and I had died."

"But here you are and here I am. We're alive, and we're standing in a lumberyard in Waterbury, Vermont, talking about the past. What about the future? Maybe you can redeem yourself and win my mother's love back."

Rick started to sob. He grabbed Penny and held on to her.

Penny didn't push him away. It felt right to allow him to grieve again. It sounded as if he'd never stopped grieving. She hadn't planned on forgiving him. She only wanted to confront him and let him know she found him. While her father sobbed on her shoulder, she felt relieved. It was clear he wasn't exaggerating about the depth of his suffering. Penny suddenly realized she wanted, more than anything, to know her birth father. "I forgive you," she whispered.

Love recognizes no barriers. It jumps hurdles, leaps fences, penetrates walls to arrive at its destination full of hope.

—Maya Angelou

Chapter 19

Spring arrived in the West Village in its typical wondrous fashion. Kate, now almost seven months pregnant, was completely obsessed with getting her nursery in order. She and Phillip sat patiently in the OBGYN office. Kate could barely contain her excitement. The sonogram today would reveal the sex of the baby. They'd delayed the discovery until now for accuracy. The due date was drawing near, and Kate suddenly felt rushed. It was time to paint the nursery and buy the necessary items babies need. Phillip was actively researching baby products and finished reading three books on parenting. Kate kept up her frantic work schedule, and most days she needed to be reminded she was pregnant. Lately, the baby kicking at all hours of the day kept her on her toes.

Penny was itching to throw Kate a baby shower. "You could have found out months ago," Penny screeched into the phone last week. "Why in the world are you waiting so long?" Her best friend was handling pregnancy in the manner she did everything—perfectly. It amazed Penny how beautiful Kate was, glowing with radiance and joy. She was the envy of women everywhere. Kate had gained inches only in her belly, and the doctor told her she was on track for a perfect delivery.

Kate looked down at her phone. It was another text from Penny. "She's driving me a little crazy."

"Penny again?" questioned Phillip. He'd grown to love Penny almost as much as Kate did, but he had no problem telling her to back off. "Tell her not to text you again for three hours or until we reach out to her."

"Ugh, I don't want to hurt her feelings. She thinks she's having a baby. It's so touching and sweet I want to provide as much support to her as possible."

Phillip looked at her with disbelief. "Give me the phone." He reached for it and texted Penny. "Don't worry; I won't hurt her feelings. You're the one having a sonogram today, not her. We're the parents; she's only the godmother." He laughed out loud at Kate's burrowed brow. "Relax, she knows I love her."

The nurse opened the side door into the waiting room. "The doctor will see you now."

Phillip squeezed Kate's hand. "Here we go, sweetie. You ready?" He grabbed hold of her arm and led her lovingly toward the nurse.

"Phillip, I'm not sick, only pregnant. Don't be such a goof." He was the prefect fiancé. Phillip was an awesome cook and a great listener, and each time Kate looked at him, her heart fluttered.

The gel made Kate wince when they placed it on her belly even though it was heated. Moments later, she saw Phillip's eyes dance when he heard the baby's heartbeat. "Can you believe it? It's the most magical sound in the world. Our baby has a strong heartbeat." Kate looked up at Phillip with dreamy eyes. She wasn't sensitive regarding the baby, but the strong thumping sound made her emotional.

The doctor agreed. "Sounds like we've got a healthy baby. Are you ready to know the sex?"

"Yes, please," Phillip said eagerly.

"We're absolutely ready," said Kate.

"It's a boy," said the doctor. "You're going to have a boy."

"Yes!" Phillip yelled and clapped his hands together. "We're having a boy!" He gave Kate a hug. "I mean, a girl would have been great as well, but it's a boy!"

"I knew you wanted a boy. You thought I couldn't tell, but I saw it in your eyes. I'm happy too," said Kate. "Thank you, Doctor. I really appreciate all the support from your nurse and staff. Each time I call with a question, they get back to me quickly. We're so excited."

"I'm lucky to have a great team. Let me show you both on the screen so you'll be able to show your friends and family. We'll also give you a copy of the sonogram in case you want to share it on Facebook or keep it in your photo album." The doctor pointed to the sonogram screen. "He's rolled up in a ball, but here you can see his legs, that's his arm, and right there you'll notice the sex."

"Wow," said Phillip. "It's tremendous. I mean, seeing the baby is tremendous. It's amazing."

"It's certainly a miraculous event. Childbirth never fails to amaze me, and I've been delivering babies for fourteen years.

Now, let's get your belly cleaned up and complete your seventh-month exam. You're only a week away from it. It'll save you a trip to the office next week."

"Yes, that would be great. Thank you." Kate glanced up at Phillip, who seemed eager to start texting his friends with the news. "Phillip, why don't you wait in the lobby for me? I know you can't wait to call your parents and spread the news."

"You know me so well," said Phillip. He kissed Kate on the top of her head, thanked the doctor, and hurried out the door.

At seven months pregnant, Kate was used to being poked and prodded. It seemed there wasn't a part of her body someone hadn't looked at or examined.

The exam was standard, and the doctor was gentle and efficient. "You can sit up now. I want to do a quick breast exam, and you'll be ready to go."

"I'm glad you brought that up. I noticed a little bump on my left breast, which wasn't there before. I figure it's my glands getting ready to produce milk but would be nice to have an official explanation."

The doctor ran her hands gently over the tissue. "This worries me," she said. "It's probably nothing, but we'll need to order you a breast ultrasound immediately. I'd also like to have the nurse pull some blood. Other than that, are you having any other issues? Feeling extremely tired or overworked?"

"I'm always overworked." Kate laughed. "I'm very blessed but a bit of a workaholic. Yeah, I've been tired for months now, but I thought it was normal for pregnant women. Isn't it?"

"Some tiredness is normal." The doctor continued to exam Kate's breast. "Let me get one of the nurses in here, and we'll get your blood. She'll also give you all the information regarding the follow-up tests. Although the lump may be nothing, we need to be proactive."

The nurse entered the room, prepared to take Kate's blood.

"Wait, you think this might be breast cancer? Is that what you're saying?"

"Let's start with a few tests. It's better to be on the safe side. If it is cancer, we can start treatment immediately. Please, Kate, don't worry. Diane will schedule you for a breast ultrasound. Let's start there. Breast cancer can be hard to detect during pregnancy due to changes in the breast tissue. I'll be in touch with you soon. Congratulations on your baby boy. He looks and sounds terrific."

Kate stared at the nurse as she pulled her blood. She felt numb. The doctor was talking about breast cancer. She felt her head spin, reached for the nurse, and passed out.

꩜

Penny arrived at Beth Israel Hospital and found Phillip pacing in the emergency room. "What happened? Where is she? How is she? Is the baby all right?"

"She passed out in the doctor's office, and they brought her here in an ambulance. Honestly, Penny, I don't know what's going on. I tried to get information from them, but they keep telling me she's fine and they're doing routine tests. I don't understand. We had the ultrasound, and the baby looked healthy. I stepped out to call my family with the good news, and the EMT showed up and took her out on a gurney. I followed them, but they wouldn't let me in the ambulance. I grabbed a cab and followed; that's all I know."

"Did her doctor tell you anything?"

"I didn't ask. When I saw Kate leaving on the gurney, I followed and then grabbed the cab."

"I'll call the office now. They should be able to tell us something." Penny was dialing the doctor's office when Wes walked in.

"How is she? What's going on?" Wes was in the middle of a day shift, so he was dressed in full FDNY gear.

"No one will tell him anything. We don't know. She passed out in the doctor's office." Penny was frantic. She had her phone to her ear, but the call went to voice mail.

"Hold on, babe. I'll find out what's going on." Wes marched to the admitting desk and began to chat with the clerk.

Penny watched Wes work his magic. The admitting nurse was putty in his hands. His good looks along with his serene presence allowed for easy communication. Penny wondered if it was his uniform but quickly scolded herself for doubting the power of Wes. He didn't need a FDNY uniform to get information. The power of Wes was his purity. Moments later, he walked over to Penny and Phillip.

"Her doctor is admitting her for tests. Apparently"—he paused for a moment, knowing the words he was about to utter would send Penny into an outburst of emotion—"apparently, she has a suspicious lump on her breast. They want to do a breast sonogram and a biopsy."

"A what?" Penny yelped loud enough for heads to turn in their direction. "A lump on her breast? Are you talking breast cancer?"

"Penny, settle down. Perhaps it's nothing. Let's not get frantic until we have more information."

Phillip looked pale and uneasy.

"Let's have a seat, Phillip. We can discuss this sitting down." Wes led him to a row of chairs on the far end of the emergency room.

"I don't understand what just happened. We were in the doctor's office, listening to the baby's heartbeat. I left the room to text my family, and next thing I know, EMT is taking Kate out the door."

"The admitting nurse told me Kate passed out in the doctor's office when the nurse took her blood. I'm pretty sure the EMT was the doctor's call. She probably felt it was safer to bring Kate here." Wes paused for a second. "I'm going to call Carmella; she's a specialist. If they're concerned about a lump, Carmella needs to be the one doing the tests. She's the best in the city."

The admitting nurse walked over to Wes. "Kate has been admitted. She's in room three twelve. You're welcome to go up and visit with her."

"Thank goodness," said Penny. "We appreciate your help." She reached out for Phillip's hand. "Come, Phillip, let's go find out what's going on."

"Penny, I'm going to have to get back to work, but could you text me when you speak to Kate and let me know how she's doing? Also, confirm the issue so I can get Carmella over here as soon as possible."

"Yes, yes, you're right. Carmella would be awesome. Thank you, Wes. I'll let you know as soon as I can. We appreciate your help." She gave him a kiss on his cheek. "Speak soon." Penny and Phillip hurried out the door of the emergency room and toward the hospital entrance.

Kate was sitting up in her bed sipping a glass of cranberry juice when Phillip and Penny walked in. "Phillip, Penny, I'm so happy you found me. It was a complete mess. I passed out, and the office completely overreacted. I'm fine."

Phillip ran to her and grabbed her with both his arms and cuddled her into his chest. "Kate, I'm sorry I left you in the exam room alone. I'll never leave you again." He sat on the side of her bed and held her at arm's length. "Look at you, you're beautiful. This totally freaked me out. Please tell me again, you're feeling good?"

"I'm fine, really; it was all a misunderstanding." Kate wasn't the least bit nervous. She realized it looked bad, but she had it all figured out. She didn't eat breakfast, and when the nurse took her blood, she passed out. "I think I'm a little dehydrated, that's all."

"Wes was here, and the admitting nurse told him they want to do a sonogram to rule out breast cancer. Did the doctor talk about why they admitted you?" Penny was pleased Kate looked great. She seemed to be feeling good. She also knew the hospital rarely admitted anyone because they passed out. It was evident to her; there was something else going on.

"Yeah, I have a little bump on my breast. I think my doctor wants a breast sonogram or a biopsy to rule out breast cancer. Penny, you know I told you how weird breasts get during pregnancy. You have no idea." Kate laughed. "I think once they get the blood results and do the sonogram, I'll be out of here."

A nurse walked in with a rolling device. "We're going to get you set up on an IV. Apparently, your doctor thinks you could be a little dehydrated. This will make you feel better pretty quickly."

"See, I told you guys, nothing to worry about."

Penny stepped out into the hall and called Wes. He answered quickly. "Hey, could you text or call Carmella and get her over here as soon as possible? I think they're going to do a biopsy or a sonogram of her breast. She's in complete denial. I'd really love it if Carmella could step in. Does she practice at this hospital?"

"She does. I'll call her right now." Wes was already scroll-ing names in his contact list. "Don't worry, Penny. Carmella will know what to do." He hung up, and Penny felt a sense of dread wash over her.

⋅⋅⋅

Carmella arrived at the hospital two hours later. She called Kate's OBGYN, whom she was familiar with, and got all the pertinent information. When she walked into Kate's room, Penny was elated.

Carmella decided to keep Kate in the hospital until all the tests had been completed. It would speed up the process. Plus, Carmella wanted Kate to rest. She assured Penny, Kate, and Phillip that if the tests showed positive for breast cancer, it was treatable. She didn't want them getting worked up until she had all the information.

When Penny left the hospital and went home for the night, she unraveled. She felt her heart aching for her best friend. It was supposed to be a happy time for Kate, and now the dread of breast cancer hung in the air. She thought of her birth mom dying in childbirth, bringing her into the world. By the time Wes called, she was hysterical. He wanted to come over and spend the night, and she told him she wanted to be alone. Her best friend was in trouble, and no one could comfort her right now.

⋅⋅⋅

Two days later, Carmella delivered the news they'd all been dreading. It was Stage 2 breast cancer. Phillip and Kate discussed the options with Carmella. She wanted to schedule a lumpectomy immediately. Kate could avoid a mastectomy, but radiation would be necessary, and they'd have to wait till after the birth of the baby to begin it. She wanted to discuss the possibility of scheduling Kate for a C-section at thirty-nine weeks. They'd have to begin the radiation treatment as soon as possible.

Kate was handling the news with optimism. She was sitting in her hospital bed with her laptop, researching breast cancer during pregnancy. "It's astonishing to read the stories of women who conquered breast cancer while growing human beings in their tummy. Do you know one in three thousand women get breast cancer when they're pregnant?"

"Unbelievable," said Phillip. "I never thought about it until it happened to us." He gazed at Kate lovingly. Their tender moment was interrupted as Billy and Luke rushed into the room.

Luke carried a huge bouquet of yellow roses, while Billy toted a crystal vase, buttercups, and daffodils. "How about some beautiful flowers for my gorgeous sister? I know you love yellow, Kit-Kat. How are you, my love?" Luke leaned over to kiss his sister, and Billy got busy arranging the flowers.

"Let's brighten up this hospital room." Billy was on a mission to lighten things up. Hospital rooms could be so plain and depressing. The flowers would add some color and perhaps, happiness.

"Thank you, brother. Thank you, Billy. I'm feeling great. They bring me food and drinks, and my fiancé and friends are here to keep me company. Now family has arrived. It's actually very comfortable. I'm enjoying my stay. Can you believe it?"

"That's my girl. A good attitude is half the challenge. What's the latest?"

"I've chosen a lumpectomy instead of a mastectomy. I'll be receiving radiation after the baby is born. They are hoping to schedule a C-section a few weeks before my due date in order to speed up the process. Then I'll have radiation."

Penny sat on a chair in the corner of the room and watched the commotion. It was as if they were at Williams-Sonoma, selecting a new sofa for the living room. She wished she could be as optimistic. Luke and Billy were laughing and chatting as if nothing bad was taking place. Phillip was calm, and Kate was radiant with peacefulness. Their nonchalant attitudes angered her. Right as she was getting ready to excuse herself, Regina walked in, and the comedy show continued.

"Kate, I'm happy to see you looking so fantastic!" Regina also brought a bouquet of flowers and a magic eight ball. "A blast from the eighties. If you're bored, you can ask the eight ball for advice."

The entire room erupted in laughter.

"Oh, and I forgot." She pulled a baby-blue teddy bear from her backpack. "A little something for the baby. I'm so happy to be back in New York City. I've missed you girls so much. I moved back into my apartment last night, me and my suitcase; feels so good to be home." Regina walked over to Penny and gave her a big hug. "Hey, big sister, how are you?"

"Ugh, I'm all right." Penny was delighted Regina was back, but her mood was dark. "We missed you too," said Penny, returning the embrace. "I'm looking forward to catching up. I hear you've got a lot of news to share with us."

"You bet I do." Regina looked at Penny with a sly smile. She could hardly wait to have her friends and her lifestyle back.

"I'm going to head home for a while. I'm feeling totally washed out." She walked over to Kate to give her a hug and then turned to Regina. "I can't wait for us all to sit down like we used to for a bottle of wine and a lot of girl talk."

"Penny, don't be so gloom. I'm going to be fine, and we'll all look back on this and chuckle. Go home, and get some rest. I have a lot of people to take care of me!"

"When is the lumpectomy happening?" asked Luke. "I think I can take a few days off and give Phillip and Penny some relief."

"I'm not going anywhere," said Phillip. "The nurse is bringing me a cot every night. I'll go home when Kate is released from the hospital."

"OK," said Luke. "Well, maybe Billy and I can keep you company."

"The surgery is scheduled for tomorrow," said Kate casually. "I'm not even having full anesthesia, only a local. Carmella is a world-renowned doctor. I don't know why all of you are so uptight. They'll probably release me several hours after the procedure. I should send all of you home, including you, Phillip."

Phillip looked shocked and hurt.

"OK, Phillip, you can stay. The rest of you have to go home and go to work and carry on with your lives. I will need each of you more than you know when the baby is born. I'm sure radiation won't be a pretty experience, so let's save the drama until then."

"I hear you," said Luke. "Billy and I can hardly wait to babysit. Have you decided on names yet?"

"We're contemplating Alex, after Penny. I don't know if you know, but her full name is Penelope Alexis Robinson. I haven't asked you, Penny; would you mind if we named our baby boy after you?"

Penny started to weep and ran out the door.

Regina ran after her and found her in the bathroom. She spotted Penny's shoes in the stall. "Penny, I know it's stressful, but everything is going to be fine. I know you're probably a little overwhelmed. I'm here if you want to talk about it."

Penny blew her nose. "I don't know what's wrong with me. I can't shake it. I'm frightened, and nothing seems right anymore." She opened the door.

Regina stood with her arms open, and Penny fell into them.

"It's a scary couple of words, breast cancer. She has a great doctor, and they know what they're doing. Why don't you go home and get a good night's sleep tonight? Maybe tomorrow you and I can hang out, go to lunch, stay away from the hospital, and let Phillip keep us posted. I think you're exhausted."

"Yeah, I do want to go home. Please tell everyone I'll speak with them later. I'll text you," said Penny. She grabbed more toilet paper and gave her nose another blow. "I'll be fine. Speak soon."

When Penny walked out of the hospital and the warm May air hit her face, she felt panicked. Wes was calling and texting several times a day, but she ignored his attempts to talk. Penny felt like calling her dad. He would understand her nervousness about the pregnancy and the cancer. Wes was sitting on her stoop when she arrived at her apartment.

"Penny, what's going on? I miss you." Wes stood up and walked toward Penny.

"I can't see you right now. My best friend is in the hospital. Remember? I have to be there for her. She needs me." Penny walked past him and dug in her purse for her keys.

"Penny, everything is going to be OK," said Wes. He was panicked. Penny was so stubborn, and he knew she was putting up her armor again.

"Why does everyone keep saying that? How do all of you know everything is going to be OK? You can't fix everything, Wes. I know you're the hero. You save people; that's your thing. Horribly things happen. Don't you all get it? You can't save Kate, and you can't save me."

"You're talking like a crazy person. I'm Wes. Remember, I want to help you. I love you." He reached for her and wrapped his arms around her.

"I don't want your help, Wes." She pushed him away with force. It took him by surprise, and he stumbled backward. "I want you to leave me alone. You can't replace Kate. No one can!"

"I'm not trying to replace Kate! Let me be here for you." Wes positioned himself in front of her so she couldn't get past him.

"Good, because you can't!" Penny pushed her way past him and climbed the stairs to her door.

"You want me to leave you alone, is that it? So it's over; are you telling me it's over?"

"I'm telling you it never began." She opened her entry door with the key and stepped inside, leaving Wes standing alone on the sidewalk.

You have bewitched me, body and soul, and I love, I love, I love you. I never wish to be parted from you from this day on.

—JANE AUSTEN, *PRIDE AND PREJUDICE*

Chapter 20

The next morning Penny woke up and called Regina. She was certain she made the right decision about Wes. It wasn't a relationship; she made it clear to him from the start. He was a great guy, but he wasn't right for her. Besides, all her spare time had to be directed to Kate. She'd help her fight the cancer. She didn't have time for Wes, and it would only frustrate and confuse him. It was the right thing for both of them. Better not to drag it out; it wouldn't have ended eventually. Phillip and Kate would need her after the baby was born.

Kate asked Regina to keep Penny away from the hospital. Phillip would text her when they were back home, and they could both stop by later in the evening, if all went well. Regina's mission for the day was to keep Penny busy and sane. She had a list of things to do to distract her. The first stop was breakfast in the East Village; from there she planned on taking her to antique and thrift shops. She knew Penny couldn't refuse the adventures on her list.

By late afternoon, even Regina was tired. They stopped by Starbucks in Chelsea. Penny was at the counter, buying a latte when a text from Phillip arrived.

Everything is going well. She's settled at home and wondering when her friends will come and visit her. BTW, could you stop and get some cookies at Starbucks? You know the ones she loves. It's a direct order.

Regina texted back a thumbs-up, along with *See you in ten minutes.*

When Penny joined her at the table, Regina relayed the information. "Oh, great news! I'll get the cookies."

Ten minutes later, the doorman sounded, "Hey, Penny! Hey, Regina! They're expecting you," when they entered the building.

Kate was lying on the sofa, wearing a beautiful pale-pink silk-pajama set from Barney's. Phillip surprised her with the gift when they arrived home. "I'm so happy you brought me cookies!"

"I'm pretty sure it wasn't negotiable," said Regina. She opened the bag and placed the cookies on a plate. "How about a decaf soy latte?"

"You're the best," said Kate. "Please bring it all to me. Thank you."

Regina, Kate, and Penny settled in on the sofa around the television. Phillip retreated to the bedroom to let the girls have their time together. Within minutes, they were laughing with no thoughts of breast cancer or C-sections.

Regina was sharing a new bit she planned on adding to her comedy routine. Kate was howling with laughter, when an emergency bulletin posted on the television. They dropped their conversation and stared at the screen.

"A gas explosion in the East Village has leveled a building, and an adjacent building is on fire and in danger of collapsing," spouted the news reporter. The network was trying to gather the information quickly. They flashed an aerial shot from a helicopter.

"What? This is unheard of. It's East Eleventh Street and Second Avenue. Penny, we were there today. This is horrific."

Penny and Regina gathered closer to the screen.

Phillip heard the commotion and joined them in the living room.

The news reporter continued. "The fire department is on the scene. They have confirmed three dead and possibly twenty people injured. Several firefighters have been taken to the hospital. We're hearing reports that this horrific incident may have been caused by an illegal gas connection at a restaurant in the collapsed building, but that report is unconfirmed." They flashed back to a wide helicopter shot of the area.

"Oh my God," said Penny. "It's Wes's team. They're on the scene. He's fighting the fire."

"Was he on duty today? Maybe it's his day off," Phillip said. He admired Wes and enjoyed spending time with him. Phillip started to bite the nail on his thumb, his go-to stress-coping habit.

"Nope, pretty sure he's working, and if not, he'd be there anyway." Penny felt her heart ache. She replayed the scene from last night in her head. "I told him to leave me alone."

"What? When?" Kate couldn't believe what she was hearing. "Why would you do something so stupid?"

"I agree. He's possibly the coolest guy I've ever met," said Phillip. He was looking forward to hanging out with Wes when the girls were busy.

Penny looked blankly at the screen. "I don't know. But I definitely told him we were done. I was pretty harsh."

"Penny, I've known you a long time. I love you, but you made a huge mistake. This is what happens when I don't talk to you for a day?" Kate couldn't believe it. Penny could be extremely crazy when she fell into a depressed mood, but this was the worst action ever.

"I don't know what I'd do if something happened to him." She turned her face away, unable to look at the scene unfolding. "What if something happened to him?"

Penny's phone rang, and they all jumped. "It's my phone. Maybe it's him, but the number is unfamiliar." She stood frozen, looking at her phone. "I don't know the number; maybe I'll let it go to voice mail."

Regina picked up the phone. "Hello? Yes, this is Penny Robinson. Yes, I'm his emergency contact. Yes, thank you. I'll be there as soon as I can." She hung up and looked at Kate, Phillip, and Penny's faces staring back at her.

"What did you just do?" Penny was horrified. "Someone called about Wes? He's been hurt? He put me down as his emergency contact?" Penny began to wail. It wasn't a small whimper but a full-blown ear-piercing cry. "I'm his emergency contact. I love him so much."

"He's at Beth Israel. Grab your coat. Kate, you're not going, but we'll call you as soon as we know what's happening. Phillip, clearly you're to stay here with Kate. Hold down the fort." Regina was always good under pressure, and she took charge, assigning everyone tasks and hurrying Penny to the door.

Penny went to gather her belongings and then stopped in her tracks. "Did they tell you anything, Regina? Did you get a hint as to how serious it is?"

"Nothing. I have no idea. They weren't offering anything more—no explanation, only a call."

"What have I done to him? It's my fault. He never gets hurt. He was probably off his game due to his insane girlfriend."

"Penny, move forward, not backward. Get it together. Go to the hospital. It'll make him happy." Regina was leading her around and pushing her toward the door.

"Do you think he chose me as his contact rather than his mother? Should I call her to see if she's been contacted?" Penny's mind was hazy as she continued to put her coat on and gather her purse.

"We'll do that in the cab. C'mon, let's move," said Regina.

Penny and Regina hailed a cab. Penny scrolled contacts and realized she did have his mother's cell-phone number. He'd given it to Penny in Stowe. She tried to remember why. Penny clicked on her name.

She answered on the first ring. "Penny," she said. "We're on our way. We don't know any more than you do. I will see you in a few minutes, sunshine. Chin up." Emma hung up.

"Did you reach her?" Regina fumbled with the cash in her coat pocket. The cab driver was flying, and they were sure to be at the hospital in minutes.

"Yes, she's on her way. She said, 'Chin up.' You always say that to me. Gosh, I'm an idiot, a cruel witch. What have I done to Wes?"

"Chill, baby, chill; we'll be there soon. Maybe he had a scrape, that's all."

⁂

Penny and Regina rushed into the emergency room and immediately found Frank pacing.

"Frank," Penny screeched. "Where's Wes? Is he OK?"

"Penny," said Frank. "He fell. It wasn't pretty."

Emma and Thomas walked through the door and spotted Penny and Frank.

"Frank," said Thomas. "How is he?"

Emma grabbed Penny's hand.

"He fell," said Frank. He choked back tears. "He never gets hurt. I saw him go down. We were searching the building for residents, trying to get them evacuated, you know. The flames were pretty bad. The floor gave out, and he fell. We got him out quickly, but I don't know. It was a fifteen-foot fall." Frank was overcome with emotion.

"There's nothing we can do but wait for news from the doctor. Is that what you're telling us?" asked Emma. She was squeezing Penny's hand really hard.

"Was he talking when they brought him in?" Thomas asked.

"Yeah, he was alert. I don't know what kind of injuries he sustained. His uniform probably protected him from burns, but I don't know about anything else." Frank began to pace again.

A doctor walked out of the emergency room and into the waiting-room area. "Frank Dellosso, anyone here named Frank Dellosso?"

"Me, that's me," said Frank, stepping forward. "I'm with Wes Lane; he's with my department."

"He's asking for you." The doctor joined the group.

"How is he, Doctor? I'm his mother." Emma stepped forward with authority.

"He took a hard fall—scrapes, cuts, a broken arm, but no internal injuries. We need to keep him here for observation. Sometimes, a concussion is hard to diagnose. He'll need to spend the night, but he should be able to go home tomorrow or the next day, depending on the arm. Frank, you can follow me. If you folks will be patient, he'll be in a room within the next hour. He's a lucky guy. It could have been a lot worse."

Emma turned to Penny. "He's going to be all right, dear. He's going to be fine." She grabbed Penny and held her in an embrace. "I'm forever worried about him. I know he's a great firefighter but a little too brave for my blood."

"It's part of who he is." Penny held onto Emma for a few extra seconds. The guilt she felt for hurting Wes was overwhelming. Would he forgive her? It was the only thought on her mind right now.

"Thank you, Doctor," said Thomas. "We really appreciate all you do for the residents of this city." Thomas turned to Frank. "Could you let him know Penny and his parents are here? We want to see him as soon as we can."

"Will do, sir," said Frank as he followed the doctor. Before he entered the emergency-room doors, he turned to the group with a broad grin and held up two thumbs.

"We are thankful and blessed," said Thomas. "Penny, care to join us in the cafeteria for a bite to eat and a cup of decaf?"

"I'd love to," said Penny. In her excitement and relief, she almost forgot about Regina. "Oh, by the way, this is one of my best friends, Regina." Penny drew Regina to her side. "She was instrumental in getting me to the hospital. I was so upset with the news I was practically walking in circles. Regina, this is Mr. and Mrs. Lane, Wes's parents."

"It's so very nice to meet you," said Regina. "Your son is amazing."

"Please call me Emma," said Wes's mom. "Would you like to join us in the cafeteria?"

"I'd love to." Regina gave Penny a quick hug. "It's all good, sweetie." She leaned into Penny's ear. "You can now redeem yourself. There are no small miracles."

❧

The summer sun was blazing. It was mid-September, and another heat wave was upon them. The neighbors all said it was "summer's swan song." Penny didn't care what they called it. She couldn't stand the intense heat another minute. She talked Wes into driving to Stowe for a week of relaxation and cooler temperatures. They were making regular trips to the country house. Each time they were in Stowe, Penny deepened her relationship with her birth dad. They spoke on the phone almost every day. Her parents in San Francisco were elated to have him back in their lives. They noticed a change in Penny immediately. A prayer, she didn't know she had, was answered.

"August is always so painfully hot, and now it's September too," said Penny, carrying another plate of burgers to Wes. He bought a fancy outdoor grill and was busy putting it to good use. "If we were in the city today, I bet I could fry an egg on the sidewalk. Global warming is definitely real."

"It's always hot in September. You forget because you think September doesn't sound like a heat-wave month, but it is in New York City. Every year we say the same thing. 'It's too late in the summer for this kind of heat.' But, Penny, it happens each and every year. Summer doesn't go out with a whimper; it goes out with a wave." Wes chuckled at his own twist on words.

It made Penny smile to see Wes so happy. He loved it when she laughed at one of his jokes. "Sorry, I was a little late. I didn't get it for a couple of seconds."

"That's OK. You got it and that's what counts." Wes flipped the burgers with intention. He really loved the grill.

His right arm was back to full strength. It was broken in two places. The cast stayed on for eight weeks, and he spent six weeks in rehabilitation. Now it was perfect. "You can thank Mom and Dad for this house in Stowe. I think it's twenty degrees cooler here in the summer. We can escape the city heat whenever we want. They're so happy we're using it."

"They're the best." Penny adored Emma and Thomas. Since Wes's accident, they'd grown closer. Emma was addicted to Amazon Prime and sent Penny packages every week. Wes said she did it for all the kids. When she saw something online she liked, she bought it. A sweater with a Labrador retriever on it was the first gift to arrive. After that, it was a kitchen towel adorned with dachshunds. Later, it was a mug with a dog walker leading six dogs down the street. A pretty cashmere sweater, a sundress, and a pair of fancy flip-flops were among the items delivered. Everything she selected for sending was unique and thoughtful.

"Yeah, I told them about your dad living nearby, and guess what? They gave us the house!"

"What? You planned on telling me this when?" Penny almost dropped the tray of hamburgers. "They're giving us the house?"

"I'm telling you now, it's our house. Oh, don't mention it to Wyatt or Nick yet; they don't know."

"Not a peep," said Penny. She was still processing the information. Her apology in the hospital room the night of the incident was touching and genuine. When she thought she might lose him, she realized how much she loved him. Wes welcomed her explanation and regret with open arms. She knew he could have made her work harder, but a big ego wasn't part of his personality. His love was a gift, and together they were strong. Penny no longer feared abandonment. The relationships of her past were over and done with. She was free to love again.

Penny hauled more ice from the kitchen to huge silver containers outside. "How much beer did you buy?" asked Penny, exasperated.

"It's always important to have more beer than people can drink; nothing is worse than a cookout that runs out of beer. Why don't you let the caterers handle the ice, Penny? They're getting paid to do it."

"All right. By the way, there's no chance we're running out of beer. I think we'll have beer for the entire year." Penny was excited about their cookout. Everyone had been invited to stay the week if they wanted. Wes had gone overboard on the preparations. He hired a catering company to set up tables and decorate the outside backyard. He insisted on doing the beer and burgers himself.

The first guests to arrive were Kate, Phillip, and Alex. Kate was cancer-free. She'd just recently completed the radiation treatments. Penny admired how gracefully Kate had handled the sessions. Phillip was by her side every step of the way. The delivery had gone off without a hitch. Baby Alex was nine weeks old and the best baby ever. Penny thought he looked just like Kate. Phillip was a doting father, and they'd finally set a date for their wedding. It would be a Christmas wedding. They'd gotten married before the baby was born, but the real wedding was set for December 14.

Regina and Doug arrived shortly behind the others. Doug was on hold for the sitcom, and they were hopeful he'd get the contract. They were adamant they'd only take the show if it were filmed in New York City. They couldn't picture themselves moving to Los Angeles. It was a fine place to visit, but their heart belonged on the East Coast.

Wyatt arrived with Carmella, and Nick brought his wife but left the kids with Emma and Thomas.

Frank arrived an hour later. He took JetBlue and a rental car, since he planned on staying one night with Penny and Wes. "It's great to finally see Casa Penelope," said Frank when he got out of the car. He named the Stowe house after Penny.

"We love the name. I'm thinking of getting a sign made to hang on the door." Wes chuckled and handed Frank a cold beer. "C'mon, buddy, let's join the party."

"You don't have to ask me twice," said Frank. "I'm glad things are working out for you and Penny. Nobody deserves happiness more than you."

Wes gave him a manly hug and patted him on the back. "Thanks, man; I really appreciate it."

Rick Early arrived with Mary and the boys. Penny spoke with him on the phone every day. Eli and Toby were completely in awe of their half sister. "Penny!" yelled Eli when he got out of the car. "Mom said you added a volleyball court."

"We did," said Penny. "After lunch I'll challenge you to a game."

Toby walked up to her and gave her a high five. "Eli and you against me and Wes."

"You got it," said Penny.

Mary had fallen in love with Rick again. He was a different man since Penny embraced him.

Rick pulled Penny to his side after Mary and the boys were a safe distance away. "She's talking to me again, Penny," he said with a twinkle in his eye. "I know you're the only person I can tell this to. Anyone else would have me committed. Your mother is happy, and I hear her voice again."

"I believe you, Rick. I'm so happy," said Penny. "It'll be our secret." She gave him a firm squeeze. "I never knew her, but I miss her. Could you tell her that?"

"I will, but she already knows." Rick took Penny's hand. "She's very proud of you."

"Thank you for telling me that Rick. It means the world to me." Penny grabbed Rick's hand and led him toward the party. "Make sure you comment on Wes's new grill. He's very proud of it."

Luke and Billy were the last to arrive. Billy insisted on stopping along the drive at antique stores. Luke complained about it but was delighted to find an amazing light fixture for the brownstone. They were both so excited about the antique andirons they scored at an estate sale that they begged Kate to come out to the car and look at them.

After everyone had eaten, a local cover band showed up to play for a few hours. Penny was a closet country-western-music fan. Kate and Wes knew how passionate her love of country music was. They began to play "Check Yes or No" by George Strait, and Penny howled with delight.

At the end of the song, the lead singer handed Wes the microphone.

"Thank you all for coming today and for enjoying a weekend with Penny and me at our beautiful home in Stowe, which Frank has lovingly named Casa Penelope."

Everyone cheered.

"I kind of like the name too." Wes chuckled and then continued. "You're each a special part of our lives, and we love you so much. With gratitude, we celebrate Kate, who is cancer-free."

The crowd cheered again.

"Rick, Mary, Eli, and Toby, we welcome you into our tribe. It's always an adventure when Penny is part of the plan. I'd like to make a toast to Phillip, Kate, and Alex. You're an example for all of us, a witness that love can overcome any obstacle, to Kate and Phillip and Alex."

"Woo-hoo!" yelled Phillip. "I'll toast to that."

"One last thing." Wes cleared his throat. "Water girl, will you step forward? I'm pretty sure you all remember how Penny and I first met."

Penny had Alex cradled in her arms and handed him back to Kate. "I'm right here." Penny stepped shyly forward.

"Penny, I know I've asked you this numerous times since I've met you. In fact, I think I asked you the day after I met you, but today is the day." Wes handed the microphone back to the singer. He got down on his knee. "Penelope Alexis Robinson, will you marry me?"

Penny turned and looked at the group of people gathered and then back at him. "Without a doubt, Wesley Lane. Yes, I will marry you!"

"She said yes!" yelled Frank. "He finally did it!"

The band began to play "Penny Lane" by the Beatles.

"Can I have this dance?" asked Wes.

"This dance and every dance for the rest of my life," said Penny. She grabbed his hand and cuddled close to his body. "Everything is everything."

"Everything is everything," whispered Wes.

Thank you! A special thank-you to fur babies Carmie, Frankie, Phillip, Oscar, Lily, Sherman, Peluda, Ice, Sasha, Noa, Fritz, Wyatt, Lucy, Hemingway, Chloe, Henry, Grace, Zoë, Penny, Ella, Sawyer, Betty, Jagger, Indie, Neo, Ricco, Kingston, Charlie, Igor, Sandy, Bentley, Sawyer, Gigi, Poppy, Patches, Louis, Zora, Carl, Livy, Marcel, and Miles for your inspiration. Thank you to my mom, Doris, for her endless love; to my sister, Roxy, for her patience and support; and Virginia, for your wisdom and guidance. I love you all.

About the Author

$\mathcal{K}$im Carson is an actress, writer, yoga teacher, and dog walker. Her new novel, *Mad Beautiful Love*, shows all the possibilities her vibrant hometown of New York City has to offer.

Carson has been a member of the Screen Actors Guild for twenty years. Her rigorous study of characters for her performances helped her bring Penny, Kate, and all their friends to life!

Made in the USA
Middletown, DE
12 June 2017